# A DARK HOUSE and OTHER STORIES

## Ian Colford

Vagrant
PRESS

# ADVANCE PRAISE FOR
## A DARK HOUSE

"It's impossible to read *A Dark House & Other Stories* without feeling changed. In these nuanced, unsettling stories, existential unease and an inborn insouciance collide to shatter preconceptions of how things are or ought to be. Ian Colford's innocents navigate a world of duplicity to meet painful truths head on. With his exquisite observations and wry, exacting prose he leaves them, and us, disarmed, and all the wiser for it. Bravo!"

—Carol Bruneau
author of *A Circle on the Surface* and *A Bird on Every Tree*

"Ian Colford is a masterful writer whose short fiction moves with stylistic grace and emotional subtleties. *A Dark House & Other Stories* is an accomplished collection that demonstrates not only his tolerant and wise grasp of human nature, but also his range of sympathy and understanding for a variety of characters from all walks of life….Colford's narrative tact, knowledge, understated wit, and nuanced writing are evident in each and every story."

—Kenneth Radu
Governor General's shortlisted author of *The Cost of Living*

"Ian Colford has the uncanny knack of creating characters that are both odious and ordinary. The people in these stories are caught in the horrific act of being themselves. Whether men made miserable through divorce or parents struggling to provide, Colford's characters make dangerous and devastating choices that will shock you, move you, and force you to see parts of yourself that you didn't know existed—as only the best writing can do."

—Karen Smythe
author of *Stubborn Bones* and *This Side of Sad*

*"But that is another tale, and as I said in the beginning, this is just a story meant to be read in bed in an old house on a rainy night."*

—John Cheever, *Oh What a Paradise It Seems*

*For Bruce, Christy, Kaleigh, Sean*

Vagrant Press is an imprint of
Nimbus Publishing Limited
3660 Strawberry Hill St, Halifax, NS, B3K 5A9
(902) 455-4286 nimbus.ca

Printed and bound in Canada

NB1421
Design: John van der Woude, JVDW Designs
Editor: Kate Kennedy
Editor for the press: Whitney Moran

*These stories are works of fiction. Names characters, incidents, and places, including organizations and institutions, either are the product of the author's imagination or are used fictitiously.*

The following stories have been previously published: "The Ugly Girl" in *Grain* 24/3 (1996); "On the Beach" in *Grain* 26/3 (1998); "Stone Temple" in *Canadian Fiction Anthology* no. 96/97 (1999); "A Dark House" in *The Antigonish Review* #131 (2002); "The Comfort of Knowing" in *The Dalhousie Review* 81/2 (2002); "The Music Lover" in *Riddle Fence* no. 4 (2009); "The Dictator Considers His Regime" in *The Dalhousie Review* 92.1/2 (2012)

Nimbus Publishing acknowledges the financial support for its publishing activities from the Government of Canada, Canada Council for the Arts, and from the Province of Nova Scotia. We are pleased to work in partnership with the Province of Nova Scotia to develop and promote our creative industries for the benefit of all Nova Scotians.

# CONTENTS

# STONE TEMPLE

//

As day breaks a man appears holding the hand of a small boy, leading him across the frozen waste of an empty field. The two figures are backlit by the rising sun. The horizon is streaked pink and mauve. Behind the stand of pine they've just passed through is an old house. It's the house where, until a few minutes ago, the boy lived with his mother.

The boy's name is Luke and the man, his father, is Bobby Flint. He's tall and gaunt and unsure that what he's doing is right, but he's doing it anyway because what else can a man do when he's denied his son through a perversion of justice? Mary Beth lied to the judge. When she said that he'd beaten her and threatened Luke, Bobby could hardly believe he'd heard correctly. He understood at once that her mother had put her up to it. On her own, Mary Beth would never dream of lying. But it was too late for him to invent his own story. Everyone was staring at him. Nothing he said was going to convince them Mary Beth's story wasn't true. So he didn't say anything.

Excited at first, Luke is tired now and when he stumbles Bobby lifts his son gently into his arms. Luke is still wearing his pajamas and has only running shoes on his feet and nothing on his head because Bobby had to move quickly and quietly to get him out of the house. It's February. They breathe thick fog into the air. Bobby has a blanket and some food in the truck, which, once they get across the field and over the fence, will be visible just where the Old Mill Road veers into the Hatcher property. The truck will be warm too because Bobby left the engine running. Nobody will be out there to notice a truck with its engine running, not at this hour.

The moon sits placid behind slivers of drifting cloud. It grazes the top branches of the tallest trees.

"Daddy, look!"

Luke, who is three going on four, has spotted a huge bird gliding in silhouette against the brightening sky. He points, his small hand bare, and Bobby realizes he's forgotten mittens as well as boots and a cap.

For a moment he stops walking and lifts Luke higher, seating him on his shoulder. He adjusts the wool cap that covers his own head. It turned cold this morning, very cold.

The bird could be a hawk, or an owl, or maybe it's only a crow. He can't see well enough in this dusky light to be sure. But there are eagles in these woods too. Bobby's seen them at Colby's, fifteen of them perched in a willow tree, waiting to be fed chicken entrails.

"It's beautiful," Bobby murmurs and glances around at Luke. Luke watches as the bird lowers itself into the trees, which shudder for just a second. Then he turns and smiles at his father.

"Neat, huh?"

"Neat, huh?" Luke echoes. His breath stirs the air.

Bobby starts walking again. When they reach the fence he lifts Luke from his shoulder and places him on the ground on the other side. As he's climbing over the fence he realizes his mistake. The snow will hold his footprints. He should have worn rubber boots and taken a wider route, crossed the stream behind Hatcher's and approached the house through the forest. Then he could have gone back and waded upstream, away from the truck, before retracing his steps.

"Daddy, I'm cold!"

Luke is about to wail.

"Sorry, bud."

Bobby's over the fence. His heart thudding, he hoists Luke high into the air and sets off at a trot, his son's delighted squeals echoing like the tolling of bells off the trees and across the snow-smooth field back toward the house.

"You like that?"

Luke is examining a plastic package containing a small foamy chocolate cake. He can't open it himself so Bobby takes it and, one hand on the wheel, splits the plastic with his teeth.

"There you go," he says, and, returning it to his son's hands, forces a smile.

Luke seems happy now. The truck bounces over ruts and through potholes. This is a game for the boy. But Bobby has realized that his plan ended the second he opened the door and put Luke into the cab of the truck.

He wanted to get on the highway and just keep driving. Once they were safely out of the province they'd stop for gas and something to eat; a real breakfast with coffee, not the sweets he's brought for Luke. Then he'd put his foot to the floor and keep driving—New Brunswick, Quebec, Ontario.

But two RCMP cruisers silently passing the truck at high speed were enough to convince him that Mary Beth had already been on the phone to her mother, who had called the police. Bobby has been turning over in his mind the idea of being hunted. He does not want to go to jail. He does not want to lose his son.

So he left the highway at Windsor Junction and found the trail out to Barrel Lake. He remembers that the trail follows the edge of the lake and that if you stay on this trail it will take you all the way to Highway 6. He's driven the route before, but only in summer, only in daylight, and only on an ATV. Taking the truck through there will be a new experience. But then, as Mary Beth used to say, if we don't keep up the search for new experiences we might as well be dead.

When he looks over he sees that Luke has chocolate icing all over his face and fingers. But at least he's smiling.

With a grunt, Bobby raises the log to a standing position and lets it topple over backward. It's no problem. He feels good, like he could do this forever. But this is already the third time he's had to stop the truck in order to clear debris and fallen branches from the path he's been following. He's pushing himself through snow up to his knees. His feet are wet inside his workboots, and he knows that's not a good thing. He had hoped to be long gone from here by now—it's nearly noon—but a while ago the trail fooled him by swerving away from the lake and has narrowed to the point that he doubts he can drive much further. Luke grins at him from behind the windshield and Bobby stops what he's doing to wave.

He's going to have to leave and scout ahead to find out where they are. It's too cold to take Luke. The panic that stilled his blood the first time he struck rock and spun the tires has subsided to a languid, almost contented state of anxiety. He's confident he can find a way through, but until he catches sight of the highway he won't be able to conceal his doubts, at least not from himself.

He returns to the truck and climbs inside. It's warm. The droning engine and the whirring fan mask the forest's silence. He removes his wet gloves, folds his hands together over his mouth, and blows. He deliberately does not look at the gas gauge.

Luke is eating a jam-filled pastry. The sweet sticky smell of raspberries nearly turns Bobby's empty stomach. New problems arise by the minute. He'd brought food but nothing to drink. A few miles back when he realized this he retrieved a crushed Tim Horton's cup from under the seat, blew it up like a balloon, and went outside to fill it with snow. He takes a sip from the cup now.

"Luke, Daddy's going to go on ahead for a bit to see if the road's over there." He gestures expansively as if indicating distance, vastness. But they are surrounded by trees. He can see no more than ten metres in any direction. "When I come back we'll hit the road and make good time."

Luke raises his fist. "Hit the road!" he shrieks. "Hit the road!"

Pastry crumbs fall from his mouth to his lap. One of the reasons Bobby lost his temper was because Luke screamed and screamed for no reason. He just let loose, hitting those high notes and shattering the quiet that Bobby wanted preserved after working another ten-hour shift at Colby's meat-packing plant. The cushioned rasp of saws ripping through flesh and bone still rang in his ears hours after he got home.

Luke whoops and hollers, but Bobby doesn't say anything, just sips water and stares through the windshield at these trees that have him utterly confounded. They couldn't be that far from the highway, not after going all this distance. He knows these woods. He grew up here. But the forest in winter.... His father had told him once when they were out rabbit hunting, the forest is a wild animal with a bloody leg. Make one mistake and it turns on you.

He was only going to be gone fifteen minutes. He rolled Luke up in the red blanket and told him to go to sleep. Then he turned off the engine and slammed the door quickly to preserve the warmth inside. He knew it would get cold in the cab very fast. But he wanted to save gas in case he was able to get the truck out of here.

But now it's more than twenty minutes since he left. There's nothing but trees in every direction. He came upon a clearing where the remains of a collapsed hunting shack were visible: a mound of twisted slats and boards, like bones beneath the snow. He found the lake and stood at its edge, gazing out over its undisturbed surface. He shielded his eyes against the glare and, after urinating against a tree, turned to go back to the truck. His heart is throbbing now with the effort of dragging himself through snow that's two feet deep in places. He knows the highway is close, but he'll never get the truck through. He'll have to back out, or else just leave it there and walk to the highway with Luke in his arms.

As he nears the truck he hears crying. He runs.

The window on Luke's side is down three inches and the inside of the cab is freezing; Luke is sobbing. Bobby jumps in and rolls the window up and inserts the key into the ignition. To his relief the engine immediately turns over.

"What in the...?"

"I opened the window to say hi."

Hardly comprehending the words, Bobby looks at his son. It's at least minus twenty outside, probably colder. He hadn't said anything about not rolling the window down. It hadn't occurred to him that he'd have to.

"There was a deer...."

He rubs his hands together and then takes the trembling boy into his lap and holds him. He doesn't want to get angry. Anger is pointless. He'll get them out of here first. The lecture can come later.

He closes his eyes.

"I'm sorry, Daddy."

"Shhhh," Bobby whispers, rocking his son in his arms. "It's all right now. I'm here."

In a few minutes Luke has calmed down and their shivering limbs are warmed and Bobby is able to think. It's one o'clock. They have four hours of daylight left; a quarter of a tank of gas. He switches on the radio. He doesn't remember any snowstorms in the forecast, but then he wasn't listening closely because he'd assumed that by now he'd be in another province.

They sit quietly listening to Garth Brooks on the country music station. Bobby tries to concentrate on the music, tries to ignore the tensing of muscles in his abdomen. When he looks down he notices that Luke has fallen asleep, his thumb in his mouth. No wonder. Poor kid's been up since five A.M.

Finally there's a weather forecast. Clear today, flurries overnight, and clear again tomorrow. Very cold. He switches the radio off and carefully moves Luke from his lap back to the passenger's seat. He grips the steering wheel. The sun has descended to a point just below the tops of the trees and it blinks at him through the branches. The truck flinches as he shifts into reverse. He twists around to get a view through the rear window and presses the accelerator. A grinding noise comes from below, but the truck doesn't move. He tries not to swear as he opens the door and gets out. The back tires are wedged against a fallen tree that was buried by snow and not visible earlier. He tries shifting into neutral and pushing from the front. But it's no good. He can't budge it.

Now he swears.

They have to abandon the truck.

Luke is wrapped tightly inside the red blanket. Bobby cradles the bundle in his arms as he strides quickly over the uneven forest floor. The only sounds are his steps and his laboured breathing.

Luke asked once where Mommy was. Bobby could not prevent his lips from curling into a sneer. Luke has not asked again.

Bobby's ears throb with the cold. His toes are numb, as are his fingers. He cannot feel his face and his eyes are as dry as cinders.

Overall, however, he's in good shape and proud of it. He never abuses his body, doesn't smoke, seldom drinks. He knows he can walk for a long time. But with each lungful of air he feels more like a slab of meat than a living creature, a carcass stripped of skin and hanging from a hook in a freezer. He's beginning to hate what he's done. But he can't see how he could have done anything else. His son is still his son. Nothing will change that no matter how many lies Mary Beth tells.

Suddenly he sinks into snow to his hips, and as he struggles to pull himself free he realizes that he's wondering if he can get them out of here. The thought of failure empties his mind of everything else. All he can see are the trees that surround them on all sides. He doesn't have any idea where they are. He's been following the sun, but now he's confused. If he was heading in the right direction he would have reached the highway long ago. Every few minutes he stops to listen for the swish of car tires on asphalt, the moaning whine of trucks gearing down.

It occurs to him, as he kicks free of the snow and starts walking again, that it's all Mary Beth's fault. If she hadn't stood there and lied he would have been allowed to see Luke every week. He wouldn't have had to take him from her. He didn't want to do this, but she left him no choice. Their life together was over, he could understand that. But it didn't mean she had to lie about him. All he'd ever done was frighten her. He'd frightened himself too. Whenever he got angry it was like a fire in his head, lights flashing in his eyes. He yelled and threw things. He broke furniture. But he never hit anyone. He'd seen enough of that growing up. Anger was his father's only legacy. He didn't want to complete the circle.

He got himself into therapy and talked about it. But it was already too late. Even though he controlled his outbursts from that day forward, Mary Beth was afraid of him. He could see the fear in her eyes and it reminded him of being small and in bed huddling under the covers listening to his parents fight. He moved into his own place and visited whenever he found the time. But one Saturday he went over and Mary Beth's mother was there and she wouldn't let him in. She called him names and said he was dirt—said that his whole family was dirt—and told him he'd get inside over her dead body. So he went and grabbed the rifle from the truck and emptied a couple of rounds into the front door. And he knew, even before the explosions faded, that he'd done exactly what she wanted him to.

So before forcing the window this morning and creeping upstairs to Luke's room, he hadn't seen his son in more than two months. He knows he's lucky they didn't send him to jail. But he also knows it isn't fair what they did to him. He isn't a criminal. He didn't do anything wrong.

A branch strikes his face. He stumbles but keeps his balance. There is desperation in his actions. He feels it, a tightness in his bowels. He's never been this cold or this alone in his life. Nothing has gone right and he senses the futility of each step he takes. When he slows his pace for a moment and listens, all he hears is the sighing of the trees as a breeze passes through their limbs. He wonders how many miles he's strayed from the path he wanted, and at this thought his burden seems to lighten because maybe the house he shared with Mary Beth for almost four years is just over the next rise. Preposterous. But to his exhausted mind even this appears as a possibility.

As he enters a clearing a sob emerges from within the blanket and when he separates the folds a biting stench follows. Reeking steam. He flinches, averts his head. Luke howls, kicks against the restraint of the blanket. His pajamas are a mess of piss and shit.

"Goddammit! Goddammit!" Bobby growls, but he can't even hear himself above Luke's wild bellowing.

He drops the blanket on the snow and sets Luke on it. He pulls the wet running shoes from Luke's feet and uses the pajamas to wipe the boy off as best he can. Everything stinks. He feels tears in his eyes when he sees Luke's bare skin redden as the freezing air assaults it. The tiny genitals shrink from the cold.

"Hold still!" he shouts and grips Luke tightly by the arm.

But there's no need to yell. Luke is suddenly quiet. Bobby can almost see the heat being drained like blood from the boy's slumping body. He tosses the pajamas away and hoists Luke into his arms. It's happened faster than he would have thought possible. Luke's eyes are glazed; he seems to be sleeping. Bobby lowers the zipper of his coat and squeezes Luke inside. But the coat is too small; Bobby can't get the zipper up again, even with Luke pressed firmly against his ribs. Cold air pours in and grips him in a painful embrace.

He takes Luke out and pulls the zipper up. Luke, nearly naked, flops limply in his arms like a freshly cut side of ribs. Bobby seizes the blanket and pulls, but it rips where frozen urine has cemented it to the ground. He drops it and searches the clearing with his eyes, as if the forest is hiding a secret fountain of warmth. But there are only trees, snow, bare domes of exposed stone. He rests Luke on the blanket and starts removing his coat. But the cold air singes his throat and for a moment he struggles to breathe. He stops what he's doing as a sound of muffled whimpering reaches him—the kind of mewling groan a trapped animal might make as it chews off its captured limb. He holds himself motionless to listen, hoping that it's Luke making the noise. But it isn't. Tears burn his eyes. He's so tired—he sways, almost falling.

Slowly he pulls the coat back on. Gently, solemnly, he folds the corners of the blanket over the small body until it's hidden. He wipes his eyes and watches the blanket for signs of movement.

He stands before the shrouded remains of his son and scours his mind for words that will excuse, or explain, what has happened. His breath steams the air.

"I'm sorry, bud," he says and focuses his eyes on the blanket, still watching for movement.

Behind the trees the sun is almost level with the horizon. Its rays peek through and catch Bobby's eyes, making him squint. The blue of the sky has deepened and taken on hints of green, yellow, red. He feels he should stay but a clenching in his stomach tells him to get moving. He adjusts his wool cap and backs off, his eyes on the blanket. At the edge of the clearing he steadies himself against a tree, then lowers his head and turns away.

# THE COMFORT
# OF KNOWING

//

think my disappointment at the sight of my youngest sister holding hands in public with a man who is not her husband can be forgiven. Not that I am asking anyone to forgive me. Morals are morals and, when it comes down to nuts and bolts, who is going to protect our children? Who is going to take a stand and say, "No more"? You're probably thinking I'm a product of a bygone era, dead and departed and good riddance, but I realize as well as the next person that times change and that we're living in a more tolerant culture. Everyone is being called upon to compromise and adapt. I know some people find it hard to accept, but I think it's a good thing! I'm all for social progress. Attitudes evolve. It's not about lowering standards or turning a blind eye; it's about compassion and letting people live the life they were meant to live, in peace and free of judgment. Listen to those TV evangelists and you'd think we're all on the fast track to eternal damnation. But in the twenty-first century it turns out that our children don't need our protection. By the age of ten they've seen it all. They head out into the world ready for anything. I'm the first to admit that I've had to unlearn a lot. But I'm a far better person for it.

Valerie, though…. From time to time, Valerie has presented a special challenge. Believe me, I've never enjoyed tromping the high moral ground, especially where she's concerned, but who else is going to do it? I'm not the holier-than-thou type, but my siblings have lives of their own and my parents are old and oblivious and, anyway, Valerie is their darling and can do no wrong in their eyes. It's not that I despise her, or even dislike her. She's my sister and I wouldn't have it any other way. I only wish I could understand why she does these things.

At times of crisis one naturally turns to one's spouse, but Gloria was in a forgiving mood and didn't seem inclined to support my view.

"It's probably nothing," she advised placidly, "but if it upsets you, try not to think about it."

She sat in front of the television knitting a sweater for one of our grandchildren. A few years ago our son Todd moved his family to Seattle so he could take a job with a computer firm. We've been meaning to travel out west for a visit, but haven't managed it yet.

"So it doesn't bother you," I remarked a bit testily, "that she's having an affair."

"Warren, do you know for sure that's what's going on?"

"Of course not. What do you expect me to do? Confront her without any proof?"

"I don't expect you to do anything. Why you feel you have to confront her at all is beyond me when it's clearly none of your business."

"My sister's behaviour is none of my business." Even though we've discussed Valerie's improprieties before, I stated this evenly, as if it were an unfamiliar phrase I was reading off a stone tablet. "I'll have to remember that. My sister's behaviour is none of my business."

Gloria shook her head and bunched her eyebrows together.

"Why don't you pick up the phone and talk to her instead of sitting there stewing? You're working yourself into a state. It's not healthy. Better yet, stay out of it. It doesn't concern you."

Then something happened on the screen and she laughed.

I noticed that my fists were clenched and that the muscles in my neck were like iron. In an effort to calm myself I let out a long breath. She was right about one thing: I'm no good to anyone when emotion gets the better of me.

"I need a drink."

I left her with the television for company and went upstairs to cool off. I took my glass of scotch outside. The evening air was fresh and still. August was nearly gone but the warmth of a sweltering summer day continued to radiate upward from the soft turf. We live in a modest neighbourhood and our clapboard house is nothing special. The backyard is bounded on three sides by other backyards and gardens. My lifetime's attainments are nothing special either. I teach civics and social studies at a junior high school and I've been doing this for the last thirty years. It's a kind of work I enjoy, and I know that enjoying the task that is the source of one's daily bread is a rare blessing not everyone can claim. I'm also a practicing Christian and as I grow older I find my faith is such a great comfort to me on a daily basis that I simply cannot imagine existing without it. I realize that fervent belief in a being higher and more sophisticated than one's self is unfashionable and generally frowned upon in this secular age, and that declaring it as baldly as I have done makes some people uncomfortable. Absurdly enough, there are even those who consider this way of thinking socially unacceptable, and after an unpleasant episode some years ago I am careful to omit all references to the scriptures from the lessons I deliver in the classroom. It's natural to want to spread the saving grace of God far and wide, but I'm wasting my breath when I mention it to my family. My parents, old as they are, have never embraced Jesus and are indifferent to His Word. My siblings don't even pretend to listen anymore. Gloria accompanies me to church and tolerates my habits, but is spiritually lax. Todd's move out west was in part motivated by his wife's indignation at my efforts to bring them into the fold. And I've learned through bitter experience that Valerie listens to no one but herself.

Valerie is so much younger than me that I can hardly communicate with her—words form an inadequate bridge across a span of almost seventeen years. I was in my final semester at school when she was born, and in fact I shared household space with her for only a few months. We have nothing in common but the blood in our veins and the good name of the Connor family, which, it seems to me, she has set out once again to tarnish.

I should mention that we have been close as a family for as long as I can remember. We all live within a fifty-mile radius of Springhaven, and though career and other commitments make it difficult to get together as often as we'd like, when we do manage it, every couple of years or so, it is invariably an occasion that lives pleasurably in the memory. At fifty-seven I am the oldest of ten. I will list my nine siblings in order of birth: Reginald, Katherine, Donna, Cameron, Matthew, Andrew, Virginia, Bridget, Valerie.

The house where I grew up is gone now and in its place is an apartment and shopping complex. A few years ago, the neighbourhood was rezoned and bought up, and on a grey afternoon in October the houses were ploughed under one by one. By then my parents were ready for the move. After working for forty years in a stuffy office at the department of health, my father was collecting a pension which he richly deserved, and so the sale of the house and property gave them the cushion they needed to obtain a spot in an upscale retirement home. Though in his eighties, my father plays eighteen holes at the nearby Briarwood Country Club a few times a week, and my mother has lots of people her age close by who share her interest in bridge and reading and swimming. I was glad when the opportunity came along for them to free themselves of the responsibilities of maintaining a house, and though I lamented the destruction of the old neighbourhood I could see they would be better off. Valerie, however, was opposed not only to the sale of the house but to the rezoning of the neighbourhood and the development project that followed. She helped organize a group that took out ads in newspapers and held vigils and demonstrations. She was interviewed on a morning radio talk show along with one of the developers, and the discussion turned shrill and ugly. I found her attitude impossible to fathom because she was battling forces she couldn't hope to conquer and speaking out against interests that had won over the entire municipal zoning board and a bevy of city councillors and aldermen. As a last resort she tried to convince our parents to renege on the sale of the house and to sue the city. I had put up with her antics to this point, but when she sought to enlist our parents into her futile campaign, I had to put my foot down. Squandering her own energy on a lost cause was one thing, but she was not going to ruin the last years of two fine people who had raised all of us to follow our hearts but also to be reasonable when reason was called for.

I took the morning off work and went over to her house, I'll admit, without phoning first. I didn't want to give her a chance to prepare a rebuttal to what I was going to tell her, and for this I was willing to risk that she might not be there. But she was there, along with some of her cronies in the cause. The street was lined with vehicles, and as I pulled into the last remaining spot I wondered if Valerie's husband, Tristan, who is Swiss and a bit of an innocent if you ask me, knew that their home had become headquarters for a bunch of ragtag radicals who had nothing better to do than disrupt a legally drafted business proposition that hundreds of well-meaning folk had bought into, including his own in-laws. I also wondered, since he was an architect who made a good living designing, among other things, shopping malls, what he thought of his wife's activities.

I was born even as the conflict raged in Europe, but Valerie is a child of the sixties. She protested the War Measures Act and cel-ebrated the American withdrawal from Vietnam, bared her backside at pop concerts, mourned Joplin, Hendrix, and Morrison, sampled every drug available, and (I suspect) had a hundred lovers by the time she was sixteen. I've never asked for a chronicle of her exploits, and since I wasn't living at home I'd be in no position to appreciate them anyway. But from my brothers and sisters I've learned of the night she spent in jail, the appearances in juvenile court, the secret abor-tion, the drunken car accident that nearly claimed the life of a mother of three, the shoplifting, the embarrassing letters to the editor, the attempts to run away from home, the time she had her head shaved and her nose pierced, the tattoos, and all the other indignities she put my parents through. All in all, I suppose she's turned out rather well, married to a man practicing a time-honoured profession and living in a huge house in Rockingham with a brace of poodles and three surprisingly well-adjusted children. But just the same, that gave her no excuse to carry on with a senseless crusade under the banner of historic preservation or environmentalism or whatever, and to draw my parents into the fray.

I parked and walked up to the house. I recall that it was a fine June morning, near the end of the school year. As I was about to ring the bell, a young man with a beard and long frizzy hair opened the door and came out. He smiled as he held the door open for me.

The house was full of people, young and old; it fairly hummed with the echo of a hundred voices and seemed vibrant and alive with a camaraderie borne of resistance to an injustice. It was evident these people had a mission. Their faces shone with it, as if they were evangelists bringing the Word to the ignorant masses. Nobody took the least notice of me as I threaded a path down the long entryway, and when I asked a young woman where Valerie was, she instantly directed me toward the kitchen.

The kitchen was plainly the seat of power. I don't mean to say that Valerie was in charge, but there seemed to be a decision-making mechanism at work around the table. Valerie was seated along with four others, two men and two women. Again, the virtue of their cause and the importance of their actions were manifest: in the upright posture of their uniformly slim bodies, in the profoundly serious expression shared by all their faces, in the weighty tone of voice with which they addressed one another. I was almost prepared to grant that their motives were only of the highest order: altruistic and unselfish and altogether humane and decent. It suddenly seemed very mean of me to oppose them, and I realized that I didn't necessarily oppose them at all, or at least not their ultimate aims; my problem with their campaign began and ended with what my parents stood to lose. As far as principles were concerned, I suppose I would have liked to see Valerie and her friends succeed, even if they made complete and utter asses of themselves in a public forum. But my priorities were different. I wanted my parents safely out of harm's way with enough money in the bank to come and go as they pleased.

And then, as I recall, I found myself swayed by another less charitable perspective on what these people were doing. What changed my mind was the jewelry. One woman raised her arm, revealing a diamond-studded bracelet, and when I looked further I counted enough rings and watches and necklaces to feed a developing nation for a year. I saw then that they were all impeccably dressed, that each and every one was well fed and well-to-do, and my mind returned outside to the street, which was clogged with the expensive minivans and Jaguars and BMWs favoured by our fine city's leisure class: the elite ranks of lawyers, doctors, university professors, and the loudmouth publicity seekers and professional yahoos who can easily afford the time that an organized crusade like this demands. Here in this house at this moment was the cream of the crop. There was not a hair out of place or a pimple among them, not a trace of smeared mascara, and not a single household income below two hundred thousand. They would gladly serve the cause, but they had to get away at some point for their massages and mud-treatments and electrolysis and pet-grooming sessions, and to drive Junior from his scuba lesson to his part-time summer job shining the Premier's shoes.

The people who had gathered in Valerie's kitchen may have been admirable in other ways, but in this one respect they turned my stomach: they opposed the development project not because of a conviction that the neighbourhood they wanted to save was especially noteworthy or unique but because life at the top of the heap was boring and here was something they could sink their capped teeth into without fear of reprisal. It was a lark, a fancy way to pass the time and have a little fun and meet some nice folks and maybe even get on TV.

"Warren?" I remember she seemed flustered by the sight of me, embarrassed perhaps. The others seated around the table fell silent and watched us. "What are you doing here? Is something the matter?"

"Can I have a word?"

She stared at me, concern levelling her features and erasing the smile that momentarily played across her lips.

"Yes, of course." She nodded stiffly. "This is my brother, Warren," she said to the others. "Warren, this is…." She dutifully went through the introductions, but I hardly listened. Thirty seconds later I couldn't recall any of the names.

"What's wrong?" she whispered. I led her down the hall toward the front door. The house was too noisy for a private conversation. She followed me outside.

"You're not using our parents in your cause. That's the end of it."

"What do you mean? They want to be involved. I asked Mom and she said I could help them."

"Mom doesn't know what you're doing. She doesn't understand what's at stake. She asked me to explain it to her since Dad didn't seem to be able to."

"Damn it, Warren, we're going to save their home. We're going to save all kinds of homes, and the park too. Those trees are a hundred years old."

"They're not going to cut down the trees. They said on the news that they don't have to. They'll build around them."

"And you believe that?"

I looked at her.

"If this deal doesn't go through, Mom and Dad will never get what that house is worth on the open market. Right now, they stand to make fifty thousand over and above market value. Your shenanigans will cost them."

She folded her arms and regarded me with disgust.

"That's all it ever is with you, isn't it? Money. It always comes down to one thing."

"Just listen to me," I said. "I don't want to see the old house go any more than you do. But sentiment isn't going to pay the bills and if they're stuck in that house for another ten years it'll drain every last cent of their savings. Did you even think of that?"

"We can help them take care of it—"

"And how far do you think that will go? Are you going to mow their lawn and fix the leaky roof and caulk the windows and shovel the sidewalk and then go home and do your own? Do you expect Reggie to drive in from Truro to take a turn? We've all got our own families and our own responsibilities, Val, and I wish you'd consider that for a moment before you put an end to something that will ensure they're comfortable for the rest of their lives."

I had spoken sharply. She turned away from me and I remember how her cropped blond hair glittered in the sun.

"Okay," she said. "Maybe you're right. I'll back off."

"I'm not asking," I said. "I'm telling you that our parents will not be playing any role in this."

"Warren, I said I'd back off." She glared at me. "Okay? Is that good enough?"

She rolled her eyes and shook her head as if I were a child whose demands were just too preposterous to be believed. This gesture has stayed with me. It made me furious with her and I walked away before she could notice how mad I was and turn it to her advantage. On the way to my car I passed a van marked with the logo of a local TV station, but I was fuming and barely gave it a glance. I had received what I came for, Valerie's assurance that she would leave our parents out of it, and I was fully prepared to take her at her word and let it end there. But I was still upset when I returned to school after lunch. It took a good hour of teaching and joking around with my students before I could put the episode behind me. And I thought I had done just that. What I didn't realize until much later was that our conversation had been captured on video and was being played and replayed on the local news.

The sequence they chose to air had been modified to emphasize Valerie's capitulation. She was shown in close-up looking pale and stricken, saying, "I'll back off," but exactly what she was backing off from was left ambiguous because they had somehow expunged my every word from the recording. In fact, they seemed to have deliberately manipulated, or somehow even altered, the video to exclude me from the shot. The back of my bald head bobbed into view once or twice, but other than this the impression one had upon viewing the edited footage was of Valerie standing on her front steps speaking to reporters about the activities of her protest group and admitting to softening the rhetoric and backing away from their declared intention to stop the development project. The effect of this was predictable and immediate. Half the members quit, those who remained fell to bickering among themselves, and in the meantime the project marched forward unimpeded. On the day the site was to be cleared, many former residents of the old neighbourhood came out despite the chance of rain to watch as their houses were reduced to rubble by machinery so immense and earsplitting it seemed to threaten the well-being of the entire planet. A few were crying while others stood about as if in a daze, like survivors of a natural disaster. The cameras were there again, whirring away. But Valerie was nowhere to be seen.

It turned out she was right about the trees. They took down every last one of them. Not even the puniest seedling was spared.

I only mention this to illustrate the kind of relationship we have. Valerie and I seem to approach apparently cut-and-dried issues from opposing directions and to expose the flaws in each other's argument. One's point of greatest clarity is the other's blind spot. It's just as well we never shared living quarters because each day would have seen new battle lines drawn and more blood on the floor. As it was, she grew up coddled and pampered, to the detriment of her character. She was permitted to do and say whatever she pleased. I suspect that by the time Valerie came along my parents had grown weary of the rigors of childrearing and were not as prepared as they might have been ten years earlier to clamp down on the wayward tendencies of an unruly child. The rest of us seemed to toe the line without being asked. But Valerie became the proverbial handful, by turns disrespectful and mischievous, beastly to her siblings, wasteful, and willfully destructive. For instance, she cried to take piano lessons, and once the fees for the whole year were paid she refused to go back. She wandered through the house as though it were a department store, helping herself to whatever she found, as if the very fact of its existence within arm's reach was proof enough that it belonged to her. Everyone learned to lock their things away and carry the key with them. She once carted off a small antique mantle clock that had belonged to our grandparents and tossed it into the bog, all because my mother had run out of grape jelly and she had to eat unadorned peanut butter on white bread. Her adolescence was fraught with difficulties and it's only by the grace of God that she didn't somehow kill herself and take a busload of other people with her. By the time she was fifteen she was hooked on cigarettes and amphetamines and was staying out all night long more often than not. When she was seventeen she left home for good, or so she claimed, and my parents despaired that they had seen the last of her. Then one Christmas she turned up on the doorstep accompanied by her husband, a lanky young man with a European accent and the doting ways of the truly besotted. Under his tutelage she had cleaned herself up, finished her grade twelve, and gained admittance to university. Tristan obviously had money, and it seems it was this and not just my prayers that had turned things around. Her transformation from a sullen delinquent to a beautiful young woman full of hope and promise seemed to me ample evidence of God's hand at work. But when I mentioned this possibility to her during a private moment, with the holiday festivities in full swing, she laughed and said affectionately, "Oh Warren, you're so full of shit." Within the week they had taken off, bound for Geneva to spend New Year's with his family.

I used to peddle God's Word door to door, much to the horror of my wife and neighbours. I wanted to be of value to the church and to ease somewhat the burden people carry with them by helping them discover the inner strength that genuine belief provides. I failed miserably. I didn't deliver any souls from the fires of hell or save anyone from the dark chasm of iniquity. One day I carried all the pamphlets to school and tossed them into the recycling barrel. I packed it in because I know a losing battle when I see one, and you can only watch the door slam in your face so often without wanting to put a bullet through your brain. Maybe I planted a seed that took root later on, but I'll never know for sure. In any event, I follow a more subtle model now—the soft sell—offering edification by example. I do this in the classroom, where I never raise my voice, never humiliate a student, and never let them see that I've lost my temper. The impression I'm aiming for is that I'm being guided by forces mightier than all of us put together, but it's every bit as likely they think I'm on Prozac. Just the same, I've managed to get a few kids to sign up for after-hours Bible classes, and without so much as uttering a single word that could be directly linked to the Good Book. So my efforts have not been entirely in vain.

Kids are one thing but adults are something else, and my faith has never made much of an impression on my family. So when Gloria suggested I phone Valerie to talk over what I'd witnessed, I instantly dismissed the notion as naïve, not to mention utterly pointless. Valerie would laugh in my face, deny everything, and then ask who the hell gave me the right, and on and on. I could see it happening in exactly this way, and when it was over I would be the villain and she would take every opportunity to inform family and friends about the silly accusations her Bible-thumping brother was throwing at her. Before I said anything, I wanted to be sure, and as I drained my scotch, got ready for bed, and then tried to sleep, I went over in my mind the events that had so unsettled me.

I had driven over to the mall to buy a trellis or some wooden lattice for the garden because there's always a need to expand the setting so the grape vines and Virginia creepers can continue their progress along the back wall. I wandered into the Christian bookshop while I was there and had idled away a few minutes glancing through a new volume on spiritual guidance when I looked up and saw Valerie walking in the direction of Walmart, which was where I was going, to see what they had in their garden centre. I left the bookshop, meaning to catch up with her and say hello. I had thought she was alone, but when I spotted her again through the meandering crowds, I could see she was with someone, a man, and that their hands were linked in the manner of teenage lovers. Instantly I began denying to myself every aspect of what I was looking at, at first questioning if it was Valerie at all, and when I had established that it was, conjecturing that the angle of my view made it impossible for me to tell if they were holding hands or just walking closely beside one another. Of course, I was able to verify quite easily that my married sister was holding hands with a man I had never seen before, and the effect of this on my disposition was crushing and left me peevish and indignant. I try, oh I do try, not to get worked up about things, but in this case I could not help it. I crept along behind them, with no particular purpose in mind. I followed them into Walmart and observed them as they wandered past the aisles of produce and kitchen items and into the jewelry department. They spent a few minutes in happy discussion next to a display case full of necklaces and bracelets and the like. I don't claim to know what they were up to or why their quest for jewelry had taken them to Walmart of all places, but once I had seen them I could not let them alone. From the jewelry counter, where they made no purchase, I followed them out of the store and back down the full length of the gleaming white marble mall, through swarms of shoppers and past all the showy lights to the food court, where they seated themselves and conferred for a moment before he stood and went over to the coffee and donut stand. I took this brief moment of separation as an opportunity to observe her. Valerie sat sidelong to me, her hands folded innocently on the table. She was wearing a pink top and black knee-length skirt and high-heeled pumps and looked like she had just stepped out from behind a desk in an office, though she has no job that I know of. Her hair was swept back in a stylish fashion from her face, which she appeared to have decorated with all manner of cosmetics, no doubt in an attempt to conceal, or at least play down, her forty years. She had no purse, a fact that struck me as very odd once I'd noticed, for it seemed to indicate that whatever was going on here had been embarked upon rashly and in haste, without forethought or planning. When her friend returned with two coffees and a donut for himself, I could see that he was much younger than her, perhaps still in his twenties. He was muscular, possibly a day labourer or weightlifter. His biceps bulged beneath the sleeves of his red checked shirt and his denim trousers were taut with a full load of buttock and thigh. When they joined hands again across the table, I decided I'd seen enough and left them to their sordid longings. My next stop was a bank of pay phones, where I looked up the number of Tristan's architecture firm. When I asked for Tristan Eckland I was informed that he was out of town for the week. Did I wish to leave a message? No, I said, and hung up.

It wasn't until I was pulling into the driveway without trellis or lattice that I realized I'd forgotten why I'd gone to the mall in the first place.

One regret of mine is that I don't know Tristan well enough to be able to claim him as anything more than a passing acquaintance, even though he's been married to my sister for going on twenty years. I like their children, but hardly ever see them. So why did I feel this driving urge to expose my sister's blatant infidelity for what it was? Why did I want to see her on the block, chastened and miserable and in tears, with all fingers aimed in her direction and a chorus of voices demanding the flogging she had earned for herself? I think I understand this much at least. Valerie has accused me of strait-laced and heartless self-righteousness on numerous occasions. It's true that I have recently tended to be more judgmental in my thinking than in the past, and maybe it's beginning to show in ways I'm blind to. But, generally speaking, I think she's dead wrong about me. And though I often find her permissive attitudes repugnant, especially where they pertain to herself, I've kept my mouth shut. However, I have never heard her utter a single word of apology for her youthful transgressions or for treating her entire family like a doormat, for causing her parents untold anxiety and for burdening them with expenses they should never have had to bear—like bail, lawyer fees, and exorbitant fines for vandalism, speeding, and reckless driving. She's lived her life as though it were a party at which she is the guest of honour and never once has she been called upon to answer for anything she's said or done. When I saw her in the mall and understood that she had strayed further than I ever dreamed she could, I knew it was my duty to bring her to account.

I did not mention Valerie's behaviour to Gloria again and let the whole matter appear to drop. What I was going to do had to be done in secret. I knew Gloria would only try to talk me out of it. I had never hired a private investigator before and I suppose, like any ordinary citizen who has never felt the need to consort with members of this profession, I had no idea where to start. But it was much easier than I thought it would be. When I looked in the phone book I found a whole range of services listed under the broad heading of "Investigators." Some had paid for ostentatious advertisements, promoting themselves as the answer to "all your security needs." Others were listed as "So-and-so, Investigator Services Limited." But the one that caught my eye was the economical and straightforward listing for D. Turk, Investigator. This was late August, and my mornings were taken up with in-service meetings in preparation for the regular fall session, which would begin within three weeks. I used a pay phone at the school to make the call. I spoke to a man who asked, business-like, what kind of work I wanted him to do. I could tell he was writing everything down.

"I want you to follow my sister," I said, keeping my voice low though I was deep in the shadows at the end of the hall and nobody was in sight.

I expected him to ask why, but what he said next was, "What am I looking for?"

I told him I suspected she was having an affair and that I wanted to confirm my suspicions before revealing anything to her husband. I expect this was all very mundane to D. Turk, who, during a lengthy silence, seemed to yawn at the other end of the line. I pictured him in a grimy smoke-filled office with the shades drawn, wearing a fedora and dark glasses, sitting back with his feet propped on the desk. Why he would have drawn the shades when he already had on dark glasses, I couldn't imagine.

"Do you require documentary evidence of this affair?" he asked.

"Yes," I said. "If possible. That would be very useful."

I thought he snorted, but I may have imagined it.

"I'll tell you what I need," he said, and went on to enumerate the items that would help him complete the job: two unobstructed photographs of the "target," a photograph of her husband, and any addresses where he could expect to "make initial contact." I was to mail these to the post office box number he gave me. Upon payment of his bill, he would mail the photographs he had taken, along with the negatives, to me at any address that was convenient for my purposes. He would also return the materials I had sent to him. I could phone him at any time if I had questions or if I simply wanted to check on his progress. He charged two hundred dollars a day and he said that in his experience a job like this took between three and five days and yielded about twenty to thirty good-quality photographs. Did I want to think about it?

"No," I said, hoping to sound decisive. "I'll send you the envelope this afternoon."

I hung up, feeling like I had made a pact with the devil. The fact that there were men and, presumably, women out there willing to engage in this type of work left a rancid taste in my mouth and it almost seemed like God was asking me to fraternize with one kind of evil in order to expose and eliminate another. Would it be worth it? I wondered, as I headed back down the hall to the meeting room. The money was a small matter; I would skim a bit off the top of our savings and send him the cash. It was the ethical price I was paying that troubled me. I believed I had lowered myself. I could almost feel my downhill progress quickened by a layer of slime on the bottom of my shoes. However, I drew a small measure of comfort from the knowledge that I was in full control of this transaction and that whatever intelligence D. Turk uncovered would remain with me until such time that I chose to make use of it.

I had no problem locating suitable photographs of Valerie and Tristan. The family album that Gloria maintained was full of cheery shots taken at recent gatherings. I sealed a few of these up in an envelope together with her home address and mailed it that afternoon. He had not asked for names, and so I provided none, not even my own, though I had written my return address on the envelope I mailed. Anonymity seemed to be the best policy.

If I suffered any doubts they stayed well below the surface of my conscious life. I hardly imagined myself a one-man crusade to elevate the moral sensibilities of a nation. My efforts were entirely local, and to some extent selfish, and over the following ten days I occupied myself with other matters and gave very little thought to D. Turk and what he was up to. I understood that Tristan would be home soon after the surveillance began, and that Valerie and her lover might cool things for a bit. But I also knew enough about human nature to expect that in very short order they would grow impatient for each other and that D. Turk would be there to track their movements.

I went to the bank to get the cash, but otherwise the intervening days passed without incident.

The following Tuesday a plain brown envelope appeared in the mail. It looked like a solicitation, and so Gloria paid it no heed and left it with the bills and other junk that I would eventually get to. I waited until after supper and took the day's mail and a glass of scotch into the study. Gloria was watching television. Inside the envelope was a single folded sheet of white paper with the figure $1,200 written on the crease in black pen. This had to be the ultimate in discretion. The amount was slightly more than I'd planned to pay, which meant I would have to return to the bank to make another withdrawal, but I did not foresee a problem. Of course, I couldn't help but wonder about the manner in which D. Turk conducted his business: no face-to-face contact, no names, unmarked envelopes travelling back and forth in the mail, numbers scrawled on paper, photographs held hostage until the money had changed hands—all the secrecy and intrigue seemed laughable, but I was saddened too to think there was so little trust in the world. I sat there for a moment, as if mourning my lost innocence, thinking of Valerie and Tristan and what a mess she'd been and how she'd turned herself around. In many ways she'd lived an exemplary life since then; the very fact that she was still with us today was a testimony to the power of the human spirit over a multitude of temptations. All the more reason, a voice within me argued, why at this late stage she should not be permitted to squander everything she'd built for herself. But who was

I to set myself up as her saviour? Maybe I had common decency on my side, but shouldn't she be permitted to follow the dictates of her heart? If she wanted to destroy her marriage, wasn't it up to her? My thoughts seemed all in a knot, tangled in a dozen lines of reasoning, none of which seemed unerring or from which I could easily free myself. I couldn't even figure out who was right and who was wrong. I went into the kitchen and poured myself another scotch and drank it down rather more quickly than I should have. I pleaded with God for guidance and instruction, but my conflicting emotions had stirred up such a storm in my vitals that all at once an involuntary chuckle escaped from my throat. The guttural reverberation that emerged seemed coarse and obscene to my ears. I felt my stomach lurch, and before I could question what it was I'd become involved in, I drained the glass and staggered off to bed.

I don't like keeping secrets. I'm no good at it because it usually comes down to telling lies, and I never lie, to my wife or anyone else. So I was hoping against all logic that when the package containing the photographs arrived I would be alone in the house and could safely retrieve it without Gloria ever having to learn of its existence. Of course, as luck would have it, on the day it came she happened to be arranging some flowers on the table in the porch, and when the postman strolled up the walk he delivered the mail directly into her hand. She brought it into the study, flipping the envelope over and examining it.

"What do you suppose this is?" she said, giving it a shake.

There was nothing scheduled at the school that morning so I'd spent my time in the study with my lesson plans and the textbook I'd been assigned. Up until a moment ago I'd been reading, but now I was only pretending to read. Gloria dropped the rest of the mail on the desk.

"Shall I open it?"

She seemed eager.

"Let me see," I said.

She handed it over and I felt the stiffness and heft of it. It felt exactly like a stack of twenty or so eight-by-ten photographs.

"It's probably that seed catalogue I ordered." I let it fall to the desk.

"Oh," she said, sounding disappointed. "I thought it might be something interesting."

"Well, who's to say the seed catalogue won't be interesting?"

She seemed reluctant to leave the matter be and took it up again into her hands. In answer to this, I started going through the other mail. Here were a credit card offer, a magazine renewal notice, and one of those envelopes of coupons that everyone throws away. I tossed it all back on the desk.

"I'll be at the hospital this afternoon," Gloria said, fingering the envelope as if trying to blindly ascertain its contents. I could hear whatever was inside sliding around. "Julia's mother's had her hip replaced and Abby wants to see her. She's coming by at one to pick me up. I shouldn't be more than a few hours."

I nodded. I was trying to avert my ogling stare away from the envelope.

"When do you want lunch?"

I remembered then that I was supposed to attend a meeting at St. Thomas's today. Father Ramley was planning a retreat and I was on the committee making the arrangements with the monastery in Ingonish.

"Oh, soon, I guess." I looked at my watch. It was already eleven-thirty.

We struggled through lunch, our conversation insipid and strained. Gloria seemed to have something on her mind, but I was in no state to ask her what it was. At one o'clock Abby came to get her, and once they'd left I returned to the study. The envelope seemed to jump out at me but I approached it warily, as if it might explode if carelessly jostled. It occurred to me that I had no idea what I was going to do with it. I hadn't given any thought to the fact that in order to determine the nature of Valerie's sin, I would have to look at photographs of her in compromising situations, quite probably naked and aroused and engaged in sexual intercourse, and I began to wonder which was worse: her sin or mine. Could I really carry through with a scheme to embarrass or humiliate her into admitting her guilt? Did I want her to do this publicly, or was I prepared to let her suffer behind closed doors and retain some fragments of dignity? I couldn't help but wonder why God had placed me in such an impossible position, and though His ways are mysterious it seemed to me that inflicting this sort of pain on someone I loved was not what the mystery was all about.

I decided I would destroy the envelope without opening it, or maybe hide it somewhere safely out of the way. Or was this just weakness on my part? Was I backing down from a position of moral authority that nobody else seemed willing to assume?

I slipped the envelope into the top drawer of the desk and went off to my meeting. Afterward, when the discussions were over and the others had left, and I was helping Father Ramley clean up and put the tea things away, I posed a question.

"Father," I said, "if you know someone has been sinning and keeping it a secret, is it your duty to expose the sinner and see that they suffer the consequences of what they've done?"

He didn't even pause to take a breath.

"Warren, it's not your duty to see the sinner is punished. Only God can do this. But you can let the sinner know that God is there to hear his confession." With these words, he calmly handed me a wet saucer, which I began to dry. Then he asked, "What is the purpose of confession?"

"Uh, to cleanse the soul and bring you nearer to a holy state."

He nodded. "Close enough. And what do you do after you've confessed?"

"Me? Well, personally, I say my Hail Marys and go home and try not to sin anymore. It's not easy."

He nodded again and handed me another saucer.

"Would God want it to be different for someone else just because their sin might be more...." During a lengthy pause he regarded me solemnly from beneath bushy eyebrows. "...or less grievous than yours?"

I nodded as he handed me the last saucer. It was his business to answer tricky questions and iron out moral dilemmas, and he had made his point and made it well. But even though wisdom seeped from his pores, I still wasn't sure what to do with the photographs.

Indecision takes many forms and in my case it looked very much like the brown envelope in the top drawer of my desk. I knew its contents would cause me no end of distress, but neither was I willing to throw it away. From one perspective it seemed I'd acted imprudently by commissioning D. Turk to take these pictures, but when I thought of the money I'd spent, it almost appeared like an investment or an insurance policy. If Valerie stepped out of line, I had in my possession the means to ensure her quick return to a normal, decent way of life.

What I needed was an opportunity to let her know the secret was out, that I (or someone) had the goods on her, so to speak.

In a family as large as ours there is always a birthday coming up, but the one we would celebrate in November was a true milestone: my mother's eightieth. The plan was to throw an elaborate party with every available member of the family and to give her a present that she wasn't likely to forget. We'd done this for my father's eightieth, rented space in a hall and given him a set of golf clubs that cost close to two thousand dollars and a lifetime membership at Briarwood.

Planning an event this large was going to take some doing. A group was going to have to meet at intervals throughout the autumn to check on progress and make sure all the details were covered by the middle of November. Gloria made some phone calls and came up with a list of five people who were willing to take charge of organizing the party. When I found out that Valerie was on this list I made sure to join up myself.

Autumn is my favourite time of year. When I can smell the crisp pungency of backyard bonfires, hear dogs barking at twilight, and listen to the distant thunder of a hundred lawnmowers as if it were music, I am happy to be alive. Late in the day the fading light takes on a bittersweet quality and there's something in the air other than the change of season. An autumn night is the perfect time for taking risks, for driving too fast, for falling in love. There seems to be an increase in social activity too, as neighbours return from cottages and emerge from their summer lethargy as if awakening after a period of hibernation. I was still wondering what to do about the photographs, but each day brought with it the distraction of teaching while trying to learn the names of a new crop of students and, after I got home, of meeting people I hadn't seen for months who came to visit or were out walking along the street. I had no leisure to think, and one evening I took the car and set out for nowhere in particular. I drove over the bridge and got on the highway for the airport. But I passed the airport and kept going. The sky was clear. As I passed the Elmsdale exit the glowing sapphire blue began deepening toward dusk. A short while later, stars appeared. Sometimes I look at the night sky and all I can see is the presence of the heavenly host, but other times it presents a disturbing enigma with nothing behind it but the random and haphazard forces of nature. I'm seized by doubt and begin to wonder if the path I've followed is an illusion and if one day I'll find myself at the edge of the abyss with no option but to step into a vast and terrible unknown. It's appalling to have your faith shaken by something as ordinary as the stars in the sky, and though it doesn't happen often, when it does the ordeal leaves me jittery and depressed.

I turned off the highway and after driving some distance along the secondary road came across a diner. I wasn't exactly sure where I was, but I was getting hungry and thought a piece of pie might do the trick. I pulled into the gravel lot, found a place to park, and got out. My legs wobbled beneath me, and when I looked up I thought I might actually topple over. But the stars were still in their place, nothing had changed, and seeing this was almost like a confirmation of something. I gathered my strength and went inside, where the air smelled of home cooking and a noisy community of the young and the old seemed to have gathered for no other purpose than to mingle and talk and listen to country music. The sentiments of country music always seem to function on a primeval or subconscious level, and as I took a seat and listened to a girl singing about finding herself "safe in the arms of love," I too seemed swept to safety by an unseen hand.

Presently a young woman with long hair and wearing a tag that said "Hi I'm Cheryl" came over and wiped down the table and asked, "What can I get for you, mister?"

But when I looked up she drew back in alarm.

"Whoa, you look like you've see a ghost! Are you all right? Do you want some water?"

"Water would be good," I said in a voice I hardly recognized as my own.

She brought a glass of water and I ordered some coffee and a slice of apple pie. There was something elemental about the place, and about her concern, that was comforting and which aroused in me an urge to curl up and go to sleep, as if I'd found my way back home after a long and perilous journey. The glowing clock above the jukebox told me it was nine-thirty, but I didn't care. The pie came and it was just fine, and the other people in the diner—the couples, the groups of older men and women—continued with their conversations and seemed to welcome me as if I were one of their own. Someone fed the jukebox and the music went on and on, and after a while I reluctantly stood up to leave. Cheryl was at my side in an instant and I was able to place the money into her hand and say, "Thanks."

"You're mighty welcome," she said as she began clearing the table. "You'll come again, won't you?"

"I will," I said, somehow feeling that I might.

Outside, night had advanced, but the sky was still vividly clear. Away from the city and its harsh oppressive lighting, I was able to see the stars with unaccustomed lucidity and even pick out a few constellations. For a long time I stood absolutely still and watched the sky, thinking that the diner was like a sacred and inviolate realm, a shrine to everything virtuous and honorable in human nature. Even the music and conversation seemed to have a cleansing effect as they drifted across the parking lot and wrapped themselves around me. On the road a man was walking a dog, and their trust in one another seemed profound and inexhaustible. All around the world, it seemed to me, people were finding the strength to carry on and the courage to face the unpleasant facts of life, and it was clear I was not to be spared. Without even knowing I'd reached a decision, I got back in the car and drove home.

The group organizing the party met a few nights later at Valerie's house. Present were Gloria and myself, Valerie, my brother Andrew and his wife, Margaret, and a peculiar little woman named Enid Sirk who played cards with my mother at the retirement home. Valerie's three children—Tommy, Elizabeth, and Tamara—all three of them well-spoken and polite though the eldest, Tommy, was only twelve—came and said good night before heading upstairs to watch TV or go to bed. Talk was general and people tossed ideas around until we settled on a plan of renting the hall at St. Thomas's and hiring a caterer. Gloria and I were to be in charge of the hall and the invitations,

Andrew and Margaret would take on the job of collecting the money and coming up with a list of possible presents. Valerie would handle the food. Mrs. Sirk smiled and seemed to think that everything was taking place exactly as God had ordained. Though I was curious I kept quiet, but eventually someone else asked after Tristan, and Valerie explained that he was in London consulting with a contractor on a job that was to begin sometime in the new year. After that he was off to Minneapolis. Mrs. Sirk asked innocently if Valerie did not find it difficult, having a husband who travelled so often and so far away.

"Oh no," she said without pausing. "I have plenty to keep me busy and Tristan likes to travel. It's never been a problem." She bestowed on Mrs. Sirk a lavish smile. "More tea?"

The evening ended pleasantly and we said our goodbyes and left.

Valerie had been welcoming and charming and everything she served us was wonderful, but she'd also exhibited a trace of smugness in her manner that left a tingling sensation at the back of my throat. She didn't seem like a woman whose beloved was six thousand miles away conducting business with strangers. She was altogether too content and sure of herself for my liking, as if she'd been given the secret of eternal youth and was keeping it to herself. Tristan was away and she was unashamedly happy, and I was the only one who knew why.

That night after Gloria had gone to bed I returned to the study with a glass of scotch. I opened the desk drawer and withdrew the envelope, took a pair of scissors and made a cut along the edge. Inside, I found the photographs I had mailed, which I would return to Gloria's album at the first opportunity, and the photographs D. Turk had taken, wrapped in plain brown paper fastened at the seams with plastic tape. I didn't want to look at any of them, so I switched off the desk lamp and worked in darkness. I unwrapped the photos. Then I opened another drawer and, feeling my way along, took a new envelope from the sheaf I'd purchased just that day. I slid two photos out of the stack, shuffled them into the new envelope, licked it shut and sealed it, slipped the stack of photos back into their original envelope, and returned this to the drawer. Then I switched the light on. Before me on the desk were Gloria's family shots, a single brown envelope containing two photos, and the paper in which D. Turk had wrapped his parcel. I placed the paper in my briefcase so I could dispose of it later. Then, using my left hand, I carefully wrote Valerie's name and address on the new envelope and affixed two stamps to it. The writing looked as if a child had done it. I put this in my briefcase, closed and locked it, drained my glass, and went off to bed.

The next morning on the way to school I dropped the envelope into a mailbox far from my home.

I wasn't expecting to hear anything, and I didn't. The next meeting of our party committee was to take place late the following week at Andrew and Margaret's home in Spryfield. Gloria and I picked up Mrs. Sirk on the way and arrived a few minutes late, but it wasn't until after we'd been discussing our progress for at least ten minutes that Valerie arrived. The change was shocking and everyone remarked upon it. Valerie appeared dishevelled and exhausted, as if only minutes before she'd raised herself from her sickbed. Her clothes were wrinkled, her skin was pasty white, she wore no makeup, and her hair was plastered to one side of her head and stood up on the other. After apologizing for her tardiness and brusquely deflecting the remarks of concern that came her way, she sat back in her chair and said almost nothing, only opening her mouth when asked about the catering firm she had approached. Her mind was clearly elsewhere, and I remember thinking that if this was what it felt like to hold the power of life and death in one's hands, then I wanted no part of it.

Valerie ate nothing and excused herself early. On the way home Gloria commented that she thought "the poor girl" looked ill.

"Maybe one of her children is sick," I ventured. Then I added, "Do we know if Tristan is back yet?"

Gloria didn't know, but she said she would make some inquiries the next day and try to find out what was going on.

That night I waited until Gloria was asleep before returning to the study to repeat the procedure of placing a photograph in a blank envelope and writing Valerie's name and address on the outside. In order to do this I had to fortify myself with a liberal dose of scotch. I knew I was doing the right thing, but I had also reached the conclusion that I was a weak individual, and I suspected that without the bracing effects of alcohol I would cave in to a compassionate impulse and let my sister off the hook. I knew she had to suffer to be saved and that I would be doing her a disservice if I destroyed the photographs or sent her the entire batch, including the negatives, in one delivery.

The next Sunday at church I prayed for Valerie's deliverance from temptation and, for myself, the strength of character to move onward with a painful task. I had hoped for a sign that I was indeed God's emissary in this matter, but Father Ramley's sermon was long-winded and filled with coarse sentiment, the woman in front of me kept sneezing into her hand, and near the end of the mass one of the acolytes tripped on a twisted edge of carpet and took a headlong tumble into the seating reserved for the choir. I drove home feeling lucky to have made it out of the building alive and shivering with the chill in my bones of someone who's been left out in the cold.

Nevertheless, I continue to mail the photographs one at a time, carefully avoiding any pattern of activity that would make it possible to trace them back to me. I also blinded myself to Valerie's suffering. When we sat across from each other at our meetings, I remained impervious to her skin bleached of colour and the trembling of her hands, and saw instead the pink glow of illicit gaiety she'd exuded that day at the mall. In this way I was able to maintain an elevated level of moral indignation long enough to get the next photograph into the mail.

Gloria came to me one evening while I was reading the newspaper and, assuming an air of great solemnity, said, "Warren, you're drinking a lot more these days. Is anything the matter?"

It hadn't occurred to me that I was drinking much more than usual, certainly not enough to be noticed. But because she was an observant, good-hearted human being, she had noticed. I'd never intended my burden to become her burden, but now I could see there was no way around it. And though I would soon be able to lay her concerns to rest, that day would not arrive for a few weeks yet, and so I told her I enjoyed a good stiff drink from time to time and was there anything wrong with that?

"No, nothing." She went away. I may have spoken more harshly than I'd intended because the sound of weeping was soon drifting downstairs from behind the bedroom door. But we were all beginning to show the strain of the ceaseless anxiety brought on by Valerie's troubles, which touched the entire family.

Inevitably there was talk. I heard Gloria speculating on the phone to one of my sisters-in-law that Valerie had been diagnosed with cancer and was braving it out in silence. My mother was naturally concerned, but went no further than to admonish Valerie for allowing herself to get so thin. The last time I saw my youngest sister was that November at my mother's eightieth birthday party, which was held on a Friday evening in the hall behind the Catholic Church of St. Thomas Aquinas. As planned, it was an elaborate affair with more than one hundred family members in attendance, ranging in age from less than one year to over ninety. I was chosen to unveil the present, an immense digital television with a forty-inch screen and stereo speakers and an endless list of advanced features my parents would never make use of, and two tickets for a three-week Caribbean cruise. I'd had nothing to drink all day and I felt fine, but I swayed on my feet, my speech was garbled, and my voice was gravelly and indistinct, like someone who has suffered a stroke. It worried me that in such a very short time I had developed the tottering gait, mumbled locution, and pugnacious mannerisms of the incorrigible alcoholic, and I resolved to make a visit to my doctor very soon. After this, while a DJ played swing and soft jazz, I watched Valerie from my position at the table with my parents, who both dozed intermittently and awoke with irrelevant comments on their lips. Valerie seemed to flit from one cluster of people to the next in quick succession, like a visiting dignitary, shaking hands and tilting her head inquiringly and making earnest small talk. She had pulled herself together for today's event, and looked radiant if fatigued in a black gown and high-heeled pumps, and I had to admit that the food was magnificent. Gloria was barely speaking to me by this time, and at one point I noticed her engaged in a lengthy discussion with Valerie and Tristan. They nodded a great deal, evidently in agreement with what she was saying. I noticed also that Valerie and Tristan held each other's hand tightly, like lovers who have made up after a quarrel.

The next day was Saturday, and I was deliberating what to do with the last two photographs and the negatives when I overheard Gloria on the phone and in this way learned that Tristan and Valerie had sold their house and were moving to Switzerland. Everyone else seemed to know already, but I had been kept in the dark. When I asked Gloria why this was the case, she said quite simply, "You're so disagreeable and you're drunk all the time, why would anyone tell you anything?"

She seemed unable to look at me after saying this, but eventually she raised her tear-filled eyes from her knitting and confronted me with a defiant expression. It was this moment that made my decision for me. I withdrew to the kitchen and emptied the bottles of scotch I had accumulated into the sink. Then I went to the study and removed the remaining photographs and the negatives from the drawer. Without looking at them I tore the photographs into quarters, trusting this would convey a clear message, stuffed the pieces and the negatives into an envelope, wrote out Valerie's name and address on the front, pasted on two stamps, and took it down the street and let it drop into the mailbox. At this stage I didn't care if Valerie had redeemed herself in the eyes of the Lord because I suspected she had redeemed herself in the eyes of her husband, and that was good enough for me. And at the very least I owed her the comfort of knowing she'd seen the last of the incriminating material. When I got back to the house Gloria was at the front door and I truly believe that if she had asked what I'd just been doing, I would have told her. But all she did was hold the door open for me as I went inside.

I begged off the farewell party for Valerie and her family that was held at the home of one of Tristan's colleagues a couple of weeks later, claiming a headache and stomach cramps. All the arrangements for their departure had been made. Their belongings were packed in boxes and waiting to be shipped out. Gloria reported that Valerie had asked after me and seemed saddened by my absence, but I didn't bother to tell Gloria that Valerie had called that evening and insisted, in a piteously beseeching manner most unlike her, that I call her back, which of course I never did.

I know the ways of God are mysterious and I don't claim to understand any of what He does, but we have to look for meaning somewhere and the world we're living in is as good a place as any. I was not about to stop attending church, but I was certainly not as rigorous in my devotions as I'd been in the past. So one warm Sunday morning in early December I told Gloria we were going for a drive, and I took her over the bridge and headed out the highway toward the airport.

The trees still held a few of their leaves, burnished brown and gold, and my spirits were buoyed by the knowledge that at the age of fifty-seven I could act on impulse and not call my sanity into question. We passed the Elmsdale exit and when I glanced over at Gloria she seemed relaxed by the rhythm of the moving car and content to simply watch the landscape slip by. Her trust in me was implicit; she didn't ask where we were going and said nothing when I left the highway at the next exit. The road looked familiar and I found the diner without a problem. However, I hadn't come prepared for the possibility that it might be closed, and from the look of things it had been closed for some time. The windows were dark and a wooden plank was nailed across the door. A strip of brown siding had slipped from its moorings and sagged to the ground. The large front window bore the starburst imprint where a stone had struck it. The building looked sad and neglected and nothing like the social hub of a community that had welcomed me warmly into its midst only a few months before. I sat there as close to tears as I've ever been and wondered what had become of Cheryl. Without a place to meet, where would all those men and women and young people spend their evenings? How would the community keep in touch with itself, now that its soul had given up the ghost?

"A trip down memory lane?"

"What?"

Gloria was smiling at me.

"Is this where you used to meet your old girlfriends?"

"I came out here once," I said, but I didn't know how to continue because no explanation I could devise made any sense. If I told her I'd stopped here because I was lost and needed directions, or because I couldn't come to terms with the stars in the sky, or because I wanted to spend some time with a bunch of strangers, or because I'd had a craving for apple pie and country music, she'd think I was mad after all. As I looked at the crumbling building I felt that heaviness of heart that comes when we see the old giving way to the new, and I was moved as if by the desecration of a monument. And I realized that in a short time many valuable things had passed out of my life.

"Or I guess it was here," I said as I put the car into gear and turned back toward the road. "But I could be wrong."

# THE DICTATOR
# CONSIDERS
# HIS REGIME

//

## THE DICTATOR

For the third day in succession it was raining. He stood at the tall window and surveyed the empty square far below. Rain streaked the glass. It glistened on the paving stones. The sky was a dull grey and every now and then a distant rumble of thunder disturbed the unnatural quiet of his office. He hated this time of the year, when the rains came and soaked the entire country and brought with them the chill air off the mountains. He'd always hated it, ever since he was a boy and his mother would take him by the hand and lead him squirming to school, water creeping into his boots with every step because they were full of holes and the winding roads that linked the towns in the hills were nothing but muddy trails. His father sent him out to work in the fields, and he could never get dry. He feared he would drown. They were very poor and the bad weather washed away what little they had. Oh yes, he hated the rain and the wind and all that they signified.

Today despite the rain his new driver, Paulo, had been ready at seven. He always tried to get to the office early and over the years this habit had become part of the way people regarded him. This morning the rain woke him at five and he tossed in his bed trying to get back to sleep. Finally he got up and made his way in the dark into the parlour room of his apartment, where he switched on a lamp and lit a cigarette and tried to read the latest report on agricultural subsidies. But the figures on the page seemed like random scratchings and after a moment he had to put it down and rub his eyes. It was depressing for him to think that none of the things in the apartment were his own. They all belonged to the state. When Irene had been alive they shared a few rooms in the presidential palace and filled them with their own antiques and heirlooms. For forty years they had lived together quite happily in the palace, even though he was often at the office for days at a time and sometimes out of the country on diplomatic missions. But no matter where he was, whether sweating under a brutal sun in one of the former colonies, or down at the State House giving a speech, or attending regular sessions of the Advisory Council, it was always at the back of his mind that he could soon return home and Irene would be waiting for him, that he could go into the private grounds and toss a ball with the dog or tend his flower garden. But then last year Irene had had a stroke. It came as a shock because she was younger than he was and her mother had lived a vigorous life into her nineties. He stayed with her until the end, though his presence had done no good and only intimidated the doctors. He'd heard rumours of high officials elsewhere who took movie stars for lovers or kept a cache of gold bullion in the basement in case they were deposed. But he was a man of simple needs who had never questioned the sanctity of holy matrimony, and on the day of Irene's funeral he found he could hardly hold himself upright at the graveside. For the first time in his forty years as president his people saw him as an old old man, standing with the aid of another's hand on his elbow. He knew it was vanity, but after all this time in power he'd grown unduly sensitive to the manner in which the press portrayed him, and on the day after the funeral the tottering image of himself in an editorial cartoon had left him with a chill in his heart. He did not like to appear weak.

So now, at his suggestion, the palace was empty. The antiques had been distributed among some nieces and nephews and he was living with a couple of servants a few blocks from the State House in a government-owned apartment that was full of functional but anonymous things. Some of these things were quite beautiful, but they had no connection with who he was.

He had not looked at his schedule for today, but soon his personal attaché would arrive with the transcript of yesterday's proceedings and papers for him to sign, and he was content to wait. Down below, in the square, a woman pushed a perambulator through the driving rain, and he wondered where she could be going with a baby at such an hour. And it reminded him that the world had changed in ways he did not understand. Parents left their children with strangers because both mother and father had to work. Young people drove their cars too fast and ravaged their bodies with drugs and alcohol. Nobody went to church anymore. It was all very mysterious to him because over the course of many years, through example as well as proclamation, he had done his best to weave a thread of moral responsibility into the fabric of society. Decades ago he had adopted education as a personal cause, and these days the universities had more money than ever and a higher education was available to anyone who wanted it. But according to the latest figures enrolment was falling and illiteracy had spread to every corner of the realm like some pernicious contagion. He shook his head. He did not understand.

Then he remembered something that had been troubling him. That woman was coming today, the mother of that boy who had gone missing. He would have to speak to her and assure her that everything possible was being done to locate her son, who was a journalist and who had written unflattering things about him and his regime. But the truth was that he knew nothing of what was being done and had in fact blinded himself to the entire issue.

## THE COLONEL

The Colonel looked through the window and regarded the young lieutenant narrowly in the weak light outside the barracks. The lieutenant stood apart from the other men beneath the shelter of the overhanging roof, smoking a cigarette. It was still raining, but not so heavily as before. Daylight had come, but you could hardly tell with the clouds thick and churning like the sea. The ground was muddy and water puddled and glistened on the tarmac. Their orders had come swiftly and without warning in the middle of the night, to get the prisoner out of the city. The generals were nervous, made nervous by events they themselves had set into motion, and now it fell to him to make it right. He focused on the scene outside his window. His young lieutenant was exchanging remarks with the men and a smile flickered across his thin lips. Only he and the lieutenant knew what their orders really entailed, and he could not smile about it. The Colonel had recently come to the conclusion that his lieutenant was a brute. How else could he smile on the day they were about to commit murder?

The Colonel had not seen the prisoner for a few days but had left orders that he be treated with decency and accorded respect. Only a few people knew that Roberto Branco was being held in the barracks prison and the men who had been engaged to transport him this morning had been selected for their stupidity and would likely not even know who he was. For them it was an adventure, something they would use to entice their girlfriends to raise their skirts and lower their britches. Only he and the lieutenant understood the full import of their mission, but even that was enough to make what they were doing dangerous.

The story had been in the papers and defied every effort to suppress it. Posters calling for Branco's release had appeared mysteriously all over town. Still, the government clung to its denials. The president had not addressed the issue, but the Colonel had been told he would do so soon. Branco was attractive and very popular and the Colonel felt that abducting him had been foolhardy, but he was not the one giving orders at that level. Branco's articles calling for elections and openness and mocking the president's recent lapses of memory could have been ignored. Or, if the generals had felt compelled to take action, it would have been simpler and wiser to discredit him, to leak a story about homosexual prostitutes or try him on trumped-up corruption charges. The propaganda office had carried out similar campaigns against other targets with great success. But because of his handsome profile and air of virtuous authority Branco made the generals nervous.

On the day the last article appeared they ordered some thugs to raid his flat and take him prisoner, but now they didn't know what to do with him. They wanted him out of the way. That's all they knew. And so the Colonel had been told to take care of the problem.

At last Branco was brought out wrapped in a dark poncho and put into the back of the covered transport vehicle. His wrists and legs were bound together with shackles and the leg-irons caused him to stumble like a drunkard. The Colonel left his office and approached the truck, which was dark green but bore no official insignia. He had decided he would ride in back with Branco.

The men stood at attention and the Colonel waved at them to relax.

He addressed the lieutenant: "Let's get this over with."

The young man nodded. "I would be honoured, Sir, if you would let me do this myself."

The Colonel paused and then said simply, "I'm coming."

"Yes, Sir."

He started to get in the back.

"Sir?"

"What? Don't you know it's raining?"

The lieutenant looked at him in momentary confusion. He shook his head. "It's nothing, Sir." He left the Colonel and could be heard giving instructions to the driver and to the men who were staying behind.

The Colonel got in back. He removed his hat and shook the water from his coat.

"How are you this morning, then?" For the prisoner's benefit he tried to sound jaunty.

Branco sat stooped over, looking downward. He didn't move. The Colonel thought the white faces of the two young soldiers on either side of him showed the strain of anxiety.

"Mr. Branco?"

He touched the man on the shoulder. Branco raised his head. The light in the truck was poor but even so the Colonel could easily see the pattern of welts and bruises covering Branco's face, the fat lip, the scar that split his eyebrow. He staggered. Confusion and anger almost brought him to his knees. He grabbed Branco's hand and found himself examining knuckles scraped raw, covered with scabs.

"Who did this to you?"

Branco said nothing. His lips appeared parched and his eyes were filmy.

The Colonel addressed the younger of the two soldiers. "Get him some water. Now." The man jumped from the truck and the Colonel turned to the other. "Take these chains off immediately." The man stared at him. His mouth dangled open stupidly. "Do it, or you'll be the one wearing chains."

The soldier jangled some keys and dropped them, then picked them up and with trembling hands began unlocking the shackles binding Branco's legs and wrists. The Colonel sat down and rubbed his hand over his face.

Just then the lieutenant pulled back the flap and climbed into the rear of the truck. He didn't seem surprised to see the soldier removing Branco's chains.

"Someone's been taking liberties with our prisoner," the Colonel remarked, his eyes on the lieutenant.

"He tried to escape. I was going to tell you."

The other soldier returned with a tall bottle of water. They all watched as he unscrewed the cap and handed the bottle to Branco, who lifted it to his lips and took a long drink.

"He's not been fed or given water either."

The lieutenant stared back at the Colonel, his manner full of a strange haughty defiance that hadn't been there a minute ago. As a smile spread across his lips, the Colonel felt a cold shudder descend his spine.

"Prisoners who attempt to escape are treated differently than those who cooperate. We all know this."

Branco returned the bottle to the soldier.

"Thank you," he said in a cracked voice.

The engine turned over and the truck trembled into motion. Rain battered the roof and for the moment made further conversation impossible.

## THE PRISONER

He had more or less resigned himself to his fate, to death. He would become a martyr for freedom and nothing would make him regret that. He would miss Christina's laughter and the soft light in her eyes, and he was sorry the plans they had made would come to nothing. Already their nights together were more like a dream than memory. And he would miss the first cool breezes of autumn, and the light slanting off the lake where he often went to swim, but it was all worth it if people were made aware of what was happening, and especially if they decided to do something about it.

But he hadn't counted on the pain. He had heard the Colonel deliver the order that he be treated like a guest rather than a prisoner and taken comfort from this, but as soon as the Colonel was gone, the lieutenant had entered his cell and stood gazing down at him, his youthful eyes full of contempt, and Branco knew immediately that he'd come face to face with his true enemy.

He was ordered to disrobe, and once he was naked he was chained to the wall of his cell. They turned out all the lights and shut the door and left him alone. There were no other prisoners and the only source of daylight was a narrow window high in the wall at the far end of the row of cells, and as he struggled to maintain a lucid stream of thought he watched for the transition of night into day and back into night. But inevitably he lost consciousness and in the end had no idea how many days had passed when someone finally came in and turned on him a painful spray of water, which washed his excretions and the insects who'd kept him company down the drain hole of the cell. They gave him something to eat then, but nothing to wear, nothing with which to dry himself. He sat on the cold stone floor of the cell and waited, trying to calm himself with thoughts of the outside world, but it was as if he'd come into existence in the cell and his other life was nothing but a dream or an idle wish. He could not remember the words he had written that had been the cause of his captivity, could not even remember the night he had been bound and gagged and taken by men wearing black masks and thrown into the back of an unmarked van. It was as if these things had happened to someone else. Then something changed and he was given food and water. His clothes were returned to him and he could tell they had been washed and pressed. When the Colonel visited again Branco was seated at a folding table that had been put in his cell, and using formal cutlery to eat a dinner of roasted cod and boiled potatoes. They'd even poured him a glass of wine. Then the Colonel left and he was stripped and the young lieutenant beat and kicked him until he was unconscious. He vomited up the dinner. That was the last thing he remembered before being roused and dressed this morning.

So now they were taking him out to shoot him and he was not at all sorry, though he was not glad either.

"You worry too much," the lieutenant was saying.

The Colonel's eyes darkened. "You don't think. You do things and you don't look ahead. They'll find his body and see how he was treated and it will be cause for more unrest."

The lieutenant sniffed and, turning sullen, averted his gaze.

"You don't think it will happen? Just watch. I'm sorry," the Colonel said, addressing Branco now, "that it has come to this."

Branco shook his head to indicate it was of no concern. The truck turned a corner and they all swayed in their seats.

"These are our orders and we have to carry them out." The Colonel seemed wistful about this point. He drew a long breath deeply into his lungs.

"Do you want a cigarette?"

"Yes, please."

The Colonel motioned for the lieutenant to give the prisoner a cigarette and to light it for him. For a moment the match light illuminated his gaunt but still dignified features. Branco drew on the cigarette and eased his torn and fragile body backward, resting himself against the wall of the rattling truck.

"You were educated here?" the Colonel asked.

"Yes," Branco said. "At the university in Coimbra."

The Colonel nodded. "My daughter goes there."

"Really?" Branco tried to appear interested as he wrestled to contain a fugitive hope for salvation.

"She's going to be a doctor."

The lieutenant snorted.

"And what's wrong with you?"

"You coddle him," the lieutenant said scornfully. "We should be interrogating him about his colleagues who want to introduce reforms. We should be making him scream for mercy."

"I leave that sort of thing to animals like you."

Branco lowered his eyes. "I take it the president knows nothing of this."

"I don't know what His Excellency has been told," the Colonel answered.

"What's going to be the official explanation for my disappearance and death?"

The Colonel shrugged. "Extremists? I don't know."

"It's going to be obvious to a lot of people that the military is behind it," Branco said.

"That's true," the Colonel admitted. "But they'll have no proof."

"In their minds they won't need any."

"Now he's threatening you," the lieutenant scoffed, "and you sit there and take it."

The Colonel remained calm. "I'll know a threat when I hear one."

Branco felt the truck lurch from pavement onto a rough dirt road. He guessed they were taking him to a pine forest up in the hills or to one of the boggy swamps that were an unappealing feature of the local landscape. In summer the flies and mosquitoes could be over-bearing even in the city if the winds were blowing the wrong way. He felt something descend heavily into the bottom of his stomach at the thought of summer, and the certainty that he had seen his last one swept over him like a sickness.

"Are you all right?" the Colonel asked.

"I'm not sorry about what I wrote," he said, regaining himself. "Every word of it was true."

"You were right about one thing," the lieutenant said. "The president is like a toothless old lion who doesn't know that his time is up."

The back of the truck became very quiet.

"I heard that about him," the lieutenant went on, "that he doesn't have a tooth of his own left in his head and someone has to feed him with a spoon."

One of the soldiers snickered and the Colonel shot him a look, quieting him instantly.

"He's just old," Branco said. "It's not a crime to be old. He used to be brilliant. But he hasn't even chosen a successor. When he dies there's going to be anarchy. We need elections to clear the air."

"You and your elections," the lieutenant sneered.

"So you think this is better?" Branco raised his voice. "How long can you go on eliminating people whose opinions are different from yours? I'll be gone but someone else will take my place. Killing me isn't going to solve your problems. Pretty soon there won't be any room left in your swamps and your hillsides and your abandoned quarries for more bodies. Someday you might even run out of bullets."

"I want you to know that if it was up to me, this wouldn't be happening," the Colonel said evenly. He met the sulky glance of his lieutenant.

"If it was up to me," the lieutenant said slowly, "it would have happened a long time ago."

Branco watched the two men glare without emotion at one another across the width of the truck. The intensity of their mutual loathing was almost palpable, like an invisible or ghostly presence. The two young soldiers shifted uneasily in their seats. And much to his surprise Branco found that he was searching his mind for the words of a prayer he had known, a prayer he hadn't recited since he was a small boy bathed in lamplight, balanced on tender knees on the floor beside his bed. He watched the two men, and as his lips began reverently to move he held his breath.

## THE DICTATOR

He was not a military man and he often reflected upon his rise to power, which had taken place in spite of this. He had never entertained political ambitions, never, truth be known, run for office of any kind. His early years were undistinguished, but he had attended the university in Coimbra and studied economics and social history. Working with an elderly professor who had died before the results of their inquiries were completed, he had published these as his own work and was promoted directly from graduate school into the chair vacated by his late mentor. He was the youngest professor in the history of a university that had been in existence for five hundred years, and he understood that it was this callous fact, rather than any conspicuous powers of insight he may have possessed, that had so quickly solidified his reputation. Still, he was not lacking in shrewd-ness and after the passage of a few years stories began spreading of a rationally deductive method he had devised for finding solutions to economic quandaries that had long baffled the best minds in the government. It was at a time when the economy was threatening to collapse and people were barricading the streets that he was called to the capital and granted singular access to the national treasury. His assignment was to solve the foreign-exchange crisis and get production moving again. Immediately he devalued the currency. Prices shot up, but then the factories that had closed down began to open again. He was drafted into the government and given the post of finance minister. His tactics were not popular, but they were effective, and even his most vociferous opponents could not argue for long against them without in the end sounding silly. When the government ousted its aging leader, he was the only member of the inner circle not burdened with the weight of political debt, and so, not yet forty, he was made president. Then fascism came and he was forced to declare a state of emergency, which gave the military the sweeping powers they needed to clear the countryside of rebel forces and defend the border against foreign insurgents. Forty years later, the state of emergency still pertained, and he sometimes wondered if maybe the people hadn't had enough.

His day was chopped into tiny pieces to make room for meetings and consultations. The deputy minister for external relations was coming at eleven, and he remembered him as a clumsy man with an awkward gait and recalled with distaste the abundant hairs on the back of his hands. In the afternoon he would see a delegate visit-ing from the Netherlands, and this would require a translator and probably call for official photographs. When his secretary entered the room to remove the tray of tea things, he adjusted his glasses and focused his attention on the paper he'd been reading. Had he dozed off for a minute?

"Mrs. Branco is in the assembly room," Isabel announced. She stood and gazed at him expectantly, waiting for him to acknowledge this piece of information.

He glanced up at her. She was an ungainly woman with thick glasses perched on the end of a long nose. "Yes. In a minute."

He returned to the report. They had kept this information from him, that in university Branco was known as a communist and a rabble-rouser. He had also travelled widely and had written a book about totalitarianism that was available everywhere except in his own country. As a journalist he'd kept his nose clean until recently. More often than not, his criticisms were dressed in the guise of human interest: stories of people whose loved ones had mysteriously disappeared, editorials on street crime, and profiles of twelve-year-old drug addicts. He had read the series of articles that had caused the recent fuss and winced at the charges of ineptitude levelled at himself, but overall he had thought them to be informative and solidly researched, if biased. After the last of these he'd toyed with the idea of asking Branco to head a commission of inquiry into political and social reform, but had been discouraged from pursuing this initiative by his military advisors. Then Branco had disappeared. After a few days it became clear that the local police were floundering, beyond their depth with this, and so he told his security minister to call in the military to aid in the search.

Outside, the rain continued to fall. He went and stood by the window and wished that this day could be over. He didn't want to talk with the mother of the young journalist but, overcome by a seizure of compassion, had foolishly yielded to her insistence. He gazed down at the square, which was empty now except for a few huddled figures splashing through the torrent. It was mid-morning but the sky was so dark with clouds it could have been midnight. The lamps on their high poles were lit and the bright conical beams shimmered across the wet paving stones like the flash of fire after an explosion.

Isabel held the door for him and he thanked her. Inside the huge assembly room a single woman sat at the long table. The table was in the centre, in the pit, and theatre seats looked down on it from three sides. The podium stood on a raised platform behind the head of the table, and behind the podium the presidential crest hung from the wall. A row of windows high up near the ceiling was their only link to the outside world, and all he could see there were dark clouds. It occurred to him to wonder why they were using this auditorium space when a small meeting room would have served just as well, but in the end he didn't trouble himself to ask the question.

The woman stood when he entered. He found the steps hard to negotiate. Isabel took his arm as he slowly made his way down. His back had been sore for a week, and he had slept poorly because of the rain. He didn't want to spend any longer than ten minutes here.

"I'm so grateful to Your Excellency for agreeing to meet with me," she said. She spoke loudly and with overstated clarity, and he guessed that someone had told her he was going deaf.

He lowered himself into the padded chair at the head of the table. Isabel placed the papers before him and then pulled out the chair next to his. He motioned for Mrs. Branco to be seated.

He briefly surveyed the papers, which had nothing to do with this matter and were only brought along for effect. He raised his eyes and fixed the woman with an unflinching stare. This would unsettle her and give him the advantage. Too often people came and because their cause was noble imagined they had the upper hand. If she was thinking this way, he wanted her to know that she was wrong.

"Your son is missing," he said needlessly. "I'm so sorry."

"Thank you." She lowered her eyes.

"I hope you realize, Mrs. Branco, that everything is being done to locate him. I've called in the military and they are scouring the countryside looking for the perpetrators of this heinous—" Here he paused, unsure of the word he needed to complete the sentence. After a few seconds Isabel poked him under the table.

"This heinous act of cowardice," he said. He raised both hands in a gesture of helplessness. "We are doing our best."

Mrs. Branco nodded.

"My dear lady, why did you want to see me today?"

She looked up once again. He could see she was struggling to hold back her tears. Her chin trembled. But then all at once she seemed to be in control. She lifted her chin slightly and suddenly appeared very dignified. Her features were dark and her hair held a rich colour full of depth and highlights that reminded him of the night sky when there is no moon.

"Your Excellency," she began. "Your Excellency, I hope I can speak frankly."

"Of course."

"Your Excellency, I have reason to believe that my Roberto is already in the hands of the military."

He allowed a smile to cross his lips, though he meant no disrespect. The woman was distraught, grasping at straws.

"I can assure you that our military personnel are highly skilled and very patriotic. They would not take part in something like this."

"Your Excellency, I have something to show you. I was the first one in Roberto's flat after he disappeared." She opened her purse and drew out a small white envelope. "At first I didn't know what had happened, but then I found something, and it began to make sense."

At his side, Isabel pulled herself upright in her chair, suddenly alert. She reached across the table and snatched the envelope out of Mrs. Branco's hand. Her entire manner had altered unaccountably. She seemed guarded and suspicious, as if she'd received warning and knew what was coming. He had to reach over and forcibly disengage the envelope from her stiff fingers.

"That is only a copy of what I found. I put away the original before the police came. It's in a safe place."

He opened the envelope. Inside was a single piece of paper, a photocopy of something. He squinted and raised the paper until it was very close to his face. Looking over his shoulder, Isabel gasped.

"You can see that it is a copy of a military identification card belonging to one Georgio Parma. He is twenty-three years old and was born in Evora. I made some inquiries and found that Georgio Parma was recently assigned to the Special Services division of the military police, the ones who have been watching my son. I found that card on the floor under Roberto's bed, which is where he was when they came to take him away."

Isabel was on her feet. He looked from the paper to Mrs. Branco, who was now also standing.

"The president is not well," Isabel stated with the uncompromising authority of one who knows what she is talking about. "We will conclude this meeting at another time."

"I—"

Then he heard a door open and there were steps. A man in a dark suit was holding Mrs. Branco's arms behind her and leading her away. Another man was going through her purse. The paper was gone. Then there was a great commotion and suddenly the room was crowded with officials in uniform. Isabel helped him to his feet.

"Come, we'll get you to a doctor."

"But I'm fine."

"You've had one of your spells."

He didn't argue. She led him up the steps. He felt a strange stiffness in his limbs and the blood pounding in his brain.

## THE COLONEL

An expectant pall hung over the occupants of the truck. The Colonel maintained a morose silence as they neared their destination and the smell of wet boot leather stuck in his throat. Branco asked for another drink, and without looking at him the soldier passed the bottle. The lieutenant sat with his legs wide apart, crowding the others, taking up more space than he was entitled to. If not for the prisoner, the Colonel would have used the butt of his pistol to wipe that smile off his face. He had never witnessed such insolence. The man would have to be disciplined before his attitude infected the entire unit. Such people were not to be tolerated, and he wondered how such an arrogant specimen had qualified for the rank of an officer.

This was, of course, one of the most distasteful tasks he had ever been called upon to perform. In his years of service he had seen people eliminated and had presided over the disposal of bodies. This was nothing new. Lawlessness was always just around the corner. In these days of universal discontent the integrity of the realm hung by a thread. He was only doing his duty. But this was the first time in his experience that the condemned man was simply a nuisance, a writer whose words made the generals pull their moustaches and glance warily at each other. It is always better to ignore those whose weapon of choice is the pen, he thought, because sooner or later people grow weary of hearing their voices and their words fly into the air unheeded. But he knew that as soon as Branco's blood began mingling with the earth, he would become a man for all time and would never die. His face would repeat itself on banners and posters, and it was a face that you could not easily forget once you'd seen it, with its dark brows and eyes that always looked slightly startled, its finely moulded nose and chin, its air of boyish innocence, all beneath a tangle of black hair. Already he'd had to instruct some men to go to the main square and erase a spray-painted image of Branco off the concrete wall of the State House. Once he was dead this would become a daily occurrence.

The truck rounded a series of turns and with an abrupt jerk pulled to a stop. He noticed that Branco was looking at him, but in the murky dimness in which they sat he could not read his expression.

The lieutenant jumped out and the Colonel motioned for the prisoner to follow.

"If you please," he said.

It was not raining but the sky was still obscured by a brooding cluster of clouds. They were in a clearing at the edge of a dense forest. The place was familiar and was known to superstitious locals as Devil's Homeland because of a group of massive evergreen oaks that had been hit by lightning and now looked like gnarled pitchforks. To keep people away, the military occasionally fed stories to the press of wanderers disemboweled by unknown and unseen beings, and then used the area as a dumping ground for the bodies of undesirables. The Colonel guessed that several hundred people were buried across the fifty or so acres that were readily accessible. He hadn't been out here for years.

"What is this place?" Branco asked, gazing about in what seemed to be genuine amazement.

"It's hallowed ground," the lieutenant snapped. "You're lucky we're not feeding your carcass to the wolves."

"I'm warning you," the Colonel said, and the lieutenant turned away.

"We're twenty minutes or so from Ponte de Sor. It's all scrubland and forest. Very sparsely populated."

"You get rid of a lot of your problems here?"

The Colonel nodded. "If you cared to look," he said as if making simple conversation about the weather, "I'm sure you would find a great many casualties of our struggle to keep the peace."

"Now you're giving away classified information," the lieutenant said with annoyance. He approached the Colonel and Branco where they stood near the truck. "I could have you arrested for that."

"He's going to die. What does it matter?" The Colonel observed the twitching face of his subordinate and decided that when they got back to the base he would have the man transferred out of his unit. "Get these men moving or I'll have you arrested."

With a grunt the lieutenant assembled the two young soldiers and the driver and distributed a pickaxe and two shovels among them. They trudged across the soggy terrain in a mismatched group, the lieutenant a head taller than the other three.

"He's getting to you and he knows it," Branco ventured and regarded the Colonel with an earnest expression.

"I'm too old for this," the Colonel admitted, avoiding the topic as well as the doomed man's eyes. "I'll retire soon. I've put aside some money. After my daughter graduates she's getting married, and then we will all go to America."

Branco nodded. "And how will this drama turn out, I wonder? Unlike some, I care about my country. I care about the people."

"The people are ignorant and not worthy of your efforts to enlighten them. Don't deceive yourself. They will forget you. It's too bad you are so young," the Colonel said as he took a few steps away from the truck and allowed his gaze to drift among the trees. "I wish you weren't so young."

"And what will happen when the president dies? What if that happens before you make your escape? What if you end up in prison for the murders you have committed? How will your daughter feel?"

The Colonel turned and was momentarily stunned by the prisoner's handsome profile and the dignity of his bearing in the shadowy forest light, and he found himself wishing Branco could be spared. But he fought against this feeling, which he perceived as a betrayal of his military oath and a violation of the trust that had been placed in him. "Don't imagine you are going to use my daughter against me."

But Branco appeared to be listening to something else, and when the Colonel strained, he too could hear in the distance the imperious voice of the lieutenant barking orders and the rhythmic hammer-stroke of shovels moving earth. For a few minutes neither of them spoke.

"I don't want to die," Branco said finally, looking in the direction of the sounds. Then he smiled. "My father wanted me to stay in the army, even after I had served my time and was free to leave. He told me I would make a fine officer and said that writing was a waste of time. But I'd seen enough to know that military life wasn't for me. I don't like guns." He turned to face the Colonel. "Give me a clean sheet of paper and something to write with and I will make you a wiser man."

The Colonel kicked a stone out of his path and watched it roll down a gentle incline and disappear beneath some bushes. He could not look at his prisoner. "This will be over soon. I will see to it that you do not suffer."

They waited ten more minutes without exchanging a word. The Colonel turned his back but remained alert to the prisoner's movements. Then he heard the lieutenant returning up the slope with his exhausted troops.

## THE PRISONER

The lieutenant had brought back two of his men, the driver and the soldier who had given him the water. The other, Branco guessed, had drawn the short straw and was waiting for the execution to be carried out so he could fill in the grave. Now that the time was near he could scarcely believe it was happening. He looked toward the Colonel, who refused to meet his eye and whose face expressed nothing but a wish to be done with this business. He felt drops of rain on his head and heard the hollow impact of rain battering the hood of the truck. The trees rustled with the rain and shuddered as a soft breeze passed through carrying with it a fragrance of wet hay. The rain was not falling hard, but it fell steadily.

"Get the truck started and wait for us," the lieutenant said brusquely. His brows were knitted together. He scowled as the two men climbed into the front of the truck.

"They are idiots," he said and spat. Displeasure seemed to inhabit his soul. He reached beneath his tunic and drew out his pistol. "Idiots."

He motioned toward Branco with the weapon and Branco turned to the Colonel, who nodded.

They set out. The rain increased subtly and he grew conscious of its soft rhythmic patter against the earth and the dead leaves and twigs that littered the forest floor. He was limping because of the beatings and his sore ribs throbbed whenever he tried to breathe deeply. The lieutenant maintained a brisk pace in front; the Colonel, who had also drawn his pistol, followed closely behind. He recognized the utter futility of his position now. He had allowed himself to imagine that he had gained the Colonel's sympathy and that this meant his fate was still somewhat in question, that the man had not entirely relinquished his humanity and could still be reached. But in the last minutes he had watched the compassion drain out of the Colonel's eyes; they had turned black and stony, like figs left for too long on the tree. Still, he could not help engaging in foolishness, permitting himself a glimpse of the future, a future in which he sat at his desk describing his encounter with death and writing of these appalling times. Now, at this moment, his worst enemy was hope, because hope would lead him into despair. He had never paused to consider how he would face death. Lying naked and bleeding in his cell, it had not occurred to him that he would fail to make it out of this predicament alive. He was young and had much to offer, and death was many years away. Even now, at the thought of his own death, he saw himself in a hospital bed, wasted by disease and advanced age, breathing his last with the help of a machine. What was happening here, today, was not real. It could not be real.

The worst of it was dying at the hands of criminals who would then dispose of his body as if it were something shameful. How many times had they been to this place for no other reason than to kill someone whose transgression was to entertain ideas unsanctioned by the state? So many times that they now performed their odious tasks unthinkingly, like marauding animals inured to the smell of death, which without knowing they carried with them everywhere they went.

He was lagging behind and grimaced with each step. He had glimpsed his legs this morning as the soldiers struggled to dress him, even though he could hardly move and his limbs felt like wood. He saw the bruises covering his legs and had turned away from the sight. There were bones in his body that were shattered, he was sure of this. As the pain surged through him an involuntary complaint issued from between his lips.

"Silence," the lieutenant commanded. He turned around and Branco had to stop. He was stooped over from the pain, but as he struggled to breathe he stared up into the lieutenant's face and regarded the stern features without fear.

Slowly the lieutenant raised his arm and pointed the gun at him. He was smiling.

"It all comes down to this, doesn't it? Your elections won't help you now."

Branco heard a sound behind him, the click of a gun being made ready for firing.

"You will give me your weapon and return to the truck. I will decide on disciplinary measures when we get back to the base."

The lieutenant didn't move. Branco felt the pulse of his heart like the beating of drums in his ears.

"Old man, you don't know anything. These are the new ways of doing things. You take the enemy by surprise."

"But we must behave like human beings or else we are lost."

"Sentimental foolishness. We don't throw away our advantage."

He heard the Colonel sigh. "I will repeat my order. You will give me your weapon and return to the truck—"

Branco saw the lieutenant raise his arm. The thunderous detonation of gunfire startled him and he instinctively dropped to the ground. In the utter silence that followed, his ears were filled with a reverberant whoosh, a sound like propeller blades slicing the air. When he raised his head he saw the lieutenant lying face down on the ground, a trickle of blood staining the soil in the region of his neck. He turned and went to the Colonel, who was lying on his back.

"You're hurt," he said and knelt beside the wounded man, but he knew there was nothing he could do.

The Colonel's breathing was laboured. He grimaced as he spoke through clenched teeth.

"This is my contribution," he said. "I urge you to go now."

In the distance Branco could hear footsteps rushing along the forest path. He stood.

"Take his gun," the Colonel said, "and go. Hurry."

Branco followed his instructions. The pistol was a dead weight in his hand. He thrust it into the pocket of his jacket and slipped between two trees and into the forest.

## THE DICTATOR

He watched the doctor raise the syringe and press on the plunger. A trickle of clear liquid oozed from the end of the needle.

"This will calm you, Your Excellency," the doctor said, "and help you to relax. I'm concerned your blood pressure will soon become a danger if we do not treat it immediately."

"I suppose I was dizzy," he said. "But it only lasted for a minute."

The doctor nodded. "That is to be expected."

The doctor inserted the needle and instantly he felt himself being swept along in a rush of euphoria. The meeting had ended badly, he knew, but they would find Mrs. Branco's son. The certainty of this seemed a cause for celebration, but right now he was too tired to celebrate anything. Isabel hovered by his side and, sensing her hand bearing down on his shoulder, he allowed himself to sink backward into the soft mattress. He felt safe and warm. The bedroom had been added to his office suite a few years ago after he had stumbled and gashed his head on the corner of his desk. A doctor was available at all times. A sensible precaution, he'd thought, never dreaming he'd have to take advantage of it. But today he had been aware of an oppressive mantle cloaking his thoughts, some cloudy intrusion between himself and his efforts to make sense of even the simplest utterances. Words on the page danced before his eyes. The lack of sleep was surely to blame, but part of it was likely the rain and the pervasive damp that clung to everything.

He knew there was talk. He knew people grumbled that he was nothing but an old man whose old notions had not worn well. Perhaps after forty years it was time for him to hand over the reins of power. But he had not seen anyone coming up through the ranks who could be trusted or who possessed intellect and compassion in equal measure. All his underlings and advisors were either stupid or devious or both. Branco's call for elections had touched him deeply because he could remember the days when elections had been held, the music and the commotion and the excitement of hearing your candidate speak, the solemn thrill of casting your ballot. But the world seemed so much more complex now and he had long feared that elections would simply open the door for the fascists and the communists to advance their hateful programs and plunge the country into a long dark night of tyranny from which it might never emerge.

The room where he lay was small and cramped. Some paintings that had been gifts from presidents and prime ministers adorned the walls, but their images were lost in the gloom. The shades were drawn and Isabel sat in the corner near the door reading a magazine by the light of a single lamp. What time was it? he wondered. He could hear the rain drumming against the window. It seemed a shame for him to have taken this turn, and today of all days. The deputy minister of external relations he could see at any time, but he felt sorry for the Dutch representative who had travelled all this way and who would now have to leave without meeting the president of the realm. It seemed like a small token, to appear briefly with the man and shake his hand for the benefit of a few bored reporters. But he was unable to do even that much. He was about to signal Isabel to bring him a glass of water when she stood to answer a knock at the door. With the magazine still in her hand she left the room. He stared after her for a moment and felt her absence like a breach in his consciousness. He didn't know what to make of her sometimes and was often uneasy about asking her for help. But she was efficient and stubbornly loyal. Once, in a childish fit of anger, he had told her she was like an old mule, and all she did was laugh. He welcomed her pale green eyes that didn't miss a thing, and even on his worst days her bustling manner gave him great confidence.

He would wait for a few minutes and if nobody came he would call out. It occurred to him that what he really should do is ask if they'd found any trace of that young journalist and then he would tell them to bring the mother to him so he could pass along the news. He hoped they would find him because he had a good mind, and in combination with common sense a good mind was as precious as gold. He'd seen a photograph and the young man looked like the son he'd never had. He would want to meet him after all of this business was cleared up. They would sit and talk and have a cup of tea. Maybe they could do a series of interviews for the paper. He would tell him about his presidency, going all the way back to the beginning. He would talk about the time he met the Queen of England and how he had blushed at her youthful beauty. He would describe how he kept the Nazis out of the country through sheer political artifice and sham diplomacy. He would tell him about the Turkish ambassador who stole the table silver. There were so many stories he could tell. The young man would be impressed.

Finally the door opened, but it was not Isabel. A man in a light suit entered, followed by a stiffly ceremonial general wearing combat fatigues. This man was not his favourite among the army's representatives on the Advisory Council, but he was by no means the worst. The doctor was there as well, and following closely behind the doctor, his personal attaché appeared bearing documents. Isabel remained at the back looking from one to the other.

They stood in a nervous cluster, whispering and regarding him from the doorway. Perhaps they thought he was sleeping and did not wish to disturb him. Perhaps they had news to share of the missing journalist.

"General," he said, making an effort to sound robust and in excellent spirits. "How good of you to come." But his throat was dry and his attempt so speak produced only a hoarse whisper.

As more people crowded the doorway and the room was filled with the murmur of many conversations, he grew worried that his condition was more serious than he'd been led to believe. He opened his eyes without remembering having closed them. How was it they had allowed all these people in here when he was trying to rest? He was suddenly peevish, out of sorts. Something lumpy was digging into his spine and he flexed the muscles of his back trying to find a more comfortable position.

When he looked up again his personal attaché was standing over him holding a pen and a piece of paper.

"Your Excellency, you must sign." He sounded as if he were repeating something he'd already said many times. "Please."

He grasped hold of the pen.

"This is?"

"Excellency, it's the Transfer of Power you requested. I'm sorry it took so long to prepare."

He looked the young man in the eye, but saw in his slender features only the vexation of a bureaucrat under pressure and not the slightest suggestion of hypocrisy. He cast his eyes over the paper, but the words were unintelligible. The attaché directed his attention toward a clear spot near the bottom of the page, and he focused his mind on this.

Think, he told himself. You must think.

## THE COLONEL

Branco had been gone for only a few seconds when the soldier emerged through a gap in the trees, glancing from side to side, his pistol drawn and raised in the air, in classic combat position. But his hat had slipped down over his eyes and he looked frightened, like a boy playing at a game that had turned deadly serious. He paused over the body of the lieutenant.

The Colonel pulled himself up.

"The prisoner overpowered him and got away," he gasped and supported himself on his elbow. "He took his gun. We will have to organize a search party. Help me back to the truck."

"Which way did he go?"

"I didn't see. Here." He stretched out his hand.

With one arm draped across the young man's sturdy shoulders he limped along the crude path, in the direction of the truck. There was no breeze and the rain fell straight down. The pain converged somewhere in his lower abdomen and he felt the sticky warmth of blood soaking his leg and collecting in his boot. He hoped that by the time they got back to the truck and radioed for help, Branco would have vanished into the terrifying forest depths, though his progress would certainly be slowed by the severity of the beating he had endured. Under his breath he cursed the lieutenant.

When they drew within sight of the clearing he told the soldier to run ahead and alert the others. He took a few steps on his own and then slouched against a tree, but immediately he gathered his strength and drove himself forward. The bastard got him good. The pain was searing, as if a red-hot poker were being thrust into his crotch, and his legs trembled with exhaustion. He would keep silent and wait and see what happened. In all likelihood there would be no inquiry into the failure of an illegal mission, though certainly suspicions would be raised. But he didn't care about himself. Maybe he would be encouraged to resign his command, and if this occurred he would probably choose to retire and begin collecting his pension early. He could go to America and wait for his daughter to follow, or perhaps she would be able to gain admittance to an American university and study there. Her English was good. With Branco on the loose there was no telling where it would end. It would be best if he completely severed his ties with the army and slipped out of sight before they started digging up Devil's Homeland and unearthing the victims of forty years of martial law.

The soldier reappeared and helped him cover the last short distance to the truck and then lifted him up into the back. He was grateful to be out of the rain, and when he sat down the pain seemed not so severe.

"Thank you," he said with a groan.

The soldier assumed a formal posture. "Sir, we have radioed for help. There are other units in the area. They will be arriving shortly."

He nodded. "I think I will require medical attention. There is a field hospital in Ponte de Sor. Take me there."

"We will leave momentarily, Sir."

"What's the delay?" He studied the young soldier for signs of impertinence but detected none.

"The others, Sir, they've returned to the forest." He paused and with a quick glance downward added, "To retrieve the lieutenant, Sir."

"Ah, yes," he said. He nodded stiffly. He could not argue with this.

He directed the soldier to sit and they waited in a silence that was broken only by the drumming of the rain and the raspy sound of his breathing, which seemed to fill the entire space. Gradually his discomfort worsened. He closed his eyes but could see an odd pulsing light that appeared to come at him from a great distance. Fearing unconsciousness, he opened his eyes again. There was a pool of blood at his feet.

When they arrived with the body he felt himself hovering, teetering on the margin of awareness. His legs were numb. They loaded the body of the lieutenant into the truck and in a minute they were in motion, lurching over the rough terrain. The body was stretched out face up, lying on the floor between him and the soldier, crowding their feet like extra baggage. The lieutenant's tunic was rain-soaked and stained with mud. There were bits of earth in his mouth and twigs in his hair. His eyes were open and seemed to be staring upward. The body jiggled in response to the truck's movements, the head bouncing up and down. He noticed that the soldier kept staring straight out in front of him. It was as if his eyes were glazed over. Not once did he look at the dead lieutenant.

He thought of this thing he had done, of the sacrifice he had made. He wanted to believe that the survival of the country depended upon Branco being kept alive. But this was just his opinion. Had he made a mistake? Who was he to declare in this way that one life was worth more than another? Maybe the lieutenant's life was hardly worth considering, but he had been someone's son, somebody else's lover. Tears would be shed, even for a man whose reputation was founded upon cruelty. He sighed. He could not imagine what would happen now. But if it were revealed that he had allowed Branco to escape, then he would accept whatever punishment came his way. He would not complain. Never in his life had he contravened an order; his service record was impeccable. So perhaps they would be lenient. In the border skirmishes that had taken place twenty years ago he had distinguished himself. He had a letter from the president and a medal to prove it.

They hit a bump and he almost toppled off his seat. The soldier reached across to steady him.

"Thank you," he said.

They were driving on a paved surface now and it was a great relief, though he felt himself growing giddy with the loss of blood. He was soaked with it. It had flowed over the floor of the truck; it stained the lieutenant's tunic. It formed a pool that spilled out the rear, leaving a trail on the wet tarmac. In a few minutes he would lose consciousness. He wrapped himself round with his arms, suddenly cold, gripped by a creeping panic. He did not look down but was aware of the eyes of the lieutenant, empty and staring upward.

## THE PRISONER

He did not stop, even though he had no idea where he was or in which direction he was going. The region was strange to him; the forest guarded its secrets closely; the sensation that enveloped him was of shadows and airlessness. He was afraid in ways he hadn't been before, afraid of being discovered, afraid of further injury that would make it impossible for him to go on. He hurried but stepped carefully, avoiding hollows and stones that could twist his ankle. The forest smelled of decay. Everything was wet, but he knew that the rain covered the sound of his footsteps and he was grateful for each drop.

At last he slowed and, gasping noisily, gulping down the dank forest air, stopped and leaned against a tree. He was not in good condition and his lungs shuddered and throbbed. The air was cold and musky with the odour of rot. To reassure himself, he wrapped his hand around the gun. If they cornered him he would not hesitate to shoot, but it had been years since he'd held a weapon of any kind and the recoil would probably knock him over backwards. He looked around and noticed that the forest appeared to thin out about a hundred yards away. As he approached he could see more of the sky through the upper branches. The rain had eased off. He peered through the trees at the edge of the wood and saw he had come to a road, and he wondered if this was the same road they had followed on the way here.

The government had eyes everywhere so he stayed among the trees as he followed the road. The sky was grey. The exertion had loosened his limbs but the pain held on, a continuous ache deep within his bones. Now that his initial terror had passed he began to think. The Colonel had deliberately let him escape, but he would have to conceal this fact and alert his colleagues so they could begin a search. They would swoop down on the area with every instrument and vehicle at their disposal. They knew the forest well; he did not. His only chance for survival was to find someplace to conceal himself where they would not think of looking. But how was he to find such a place when he was not even certain where he was? Were these really the interior hills of the Alentejo, twenty minutes from Ponte de Sor? What if it was all lies?

He would have to find a village, or a farm. If he stayed with the road, would he not eventually encounter the local inhabitants? They could not all be agents of the government. But his survival also depended upon his ability to keep moving, and he was beginning now to feel a hollow pit of hunger in his stomach. His last food had been the elaborate meal of fish and potatoes that had not stayed where he'd put it. And at the thought of that meal he was touched by the keenness of a profound despair, a crushing agony of loss. He leaned over, his stomach knotted. He knew nothing of wilderness survival and suspected that any berries or roots he ingested would flood his veins with poison and stop his heart as effectively as a bullet. He would have to keep moving.

He continued to follow the road. He didn't try to count the hours. He noticed it was raining again, and then he noticed it wasn't raining. At the sound of vehicles he halted his progress and stood upright behind a tree. A couple of jeeps and an army truck rumbled past, heading up into Devil's Homeland. They didn't appear to be in a hurry. He resumed walking and tried to move quickly. He came to a shallow river and splashed through. Soon after this he heard the voices of children and, when he looked past the bushes at the edge of the road, saw a small, whitewashed schoolhouse constructed of stone and mortar.

Leaving behind the safety of the forest, he stepped out of the bushes and walked along the road, toward the town. His leather shoes were ruined and inside them his feet were wet. He was aware of the figure he presented, knew that his jacket was torn, that his black pants were blotched with mud, that his face was marked with scars. Using his fingers as a comb he tried to straighten his hair. The people here, what would they think? He had no money, no identification. Everything had been taken from him. All he had was the gun.

He passed a small white church with its doors closed. A black bird perched in the recess of a window seemed to follow his movements. Up ahead was a grocery market and when he came to this he heard more voices. A group of about forty men had gathered in the stony field behind the market. He watched them from the corner of the building. Some were smoking and he fought a craving for a cigarette. They were all ages, teenagers to men in their middle years. He didn't hear a woman come up behind him.

"If you're looking for work you should join them." Beneath the black kerchief that covered her head she was neither young nor old. He stared dully at her until her smile faded and she began to back away.

"I'm sorry," he said. He eased the muscles of his jaw and softened his expression. "I'm not from here. My car broke down and I'm trying to get home. What is this place?"

She named a town with which he was not familiar.

"Are we far from Ponte de Sor?"

She shook her head. "A long way, I'm afraid." She gestured in the direction of the hills.

He stood back from her and, gazing around, released a sigh.

"There is a bus," she said and consulted her watch. "It will come in an hour."

"I have no money," he said, and when she appeared surprised he explained. "Thieves beat me and took my money. They dragged me into the forest. I've been wandering for hours."

He laughed uneasily and looked for a sign that she believed him. She told him she was sorry.

"These men?" he asked.

"A work detail. They are going to the capital."

"What will they do there?"

"You haven't heard?"

At that moment a boy emerged from the door of the market clutching a paper bag. He came to her and, regarding Branco solemnly, took her by the hand.

"Heard what?"

"Ernesto," she said, "tell the man what you heard. Go on."

When the boy remained as if mute Branco said gently, "It's all right, Ernesto. The police can't hear us."

"My friend has a radio," the boy said as if making a confession. He studied the earth between his feet. "He told me that the president is dying and there are riots."

"These men will help the police build their barricades. They will keep the rabble under control." The woman said this with some bitterness. Then she sighed and appeared wistful. "We will miss him."

She met his eyes briefly before turning to leave, dragging the boy behind her.

Branco watched them go. Then he heard the groan of an engine and turned to see a large open truck with high sides, a cattle truck, which pulled into the clearing behind the market. Adjusting the collar of his jacket to hide his face, he clutched the gun and strode into the midst of the waiting men. A brash young cadet wearing a beret and fatigues herded them into the back of the truck, which lumbered into motion before they had settled themselves into their seats. He sat at the end of the row and avoided looking at the others. The conversation was boisterous and full of expletives. They spoke with sympathy of the president, and one boasted of what he would do with the journalist who had caused all the trouble with his articles.

"Crack his neck," he said and made a twisting motion with his immense hands.

The others laughed.

Branco stared at the floor and fought a sensation worse than any dread he had ever imagined.

# MCGOWAN ON
# THE MOUNT

//

ife was good. Oh, life was very good. But he had to admit
life had been better in the years before half his customers died
off and the neighbourhood around Gottingen and Almon
Streets went downhill and the store started losing money—before
he made his plans to sell out to one of the big chains. For a while his
son helped behind the counter and his daughter did the books, but
it wasn't enough, and anyway like all young people they had their
own lives to live. Then Ronny was killed and it seemed to McGowan
that he'd made enough sacrifices for one life.

Some conglomerate was buying up the street looking to demolish
the old buildings to make room for a shopping mall and condomini-
ums, and McGowan was one of the first to take up the offer and sign
the papers. The residents who'd lived there all their lives and some
of the other store owners argued that the character of the neighbourhood was being destroyed for no reason other than greed. But
at the town-planning meeting where the developers were making
their case, McGowan got to his feet and asked what was so damn
special about the character of this neighbourhood that it was worth

preserving? Why would anyone in their right mind fight to protect a bunch of rundown houses and shops that nobody ever went into? The place is a ghost town, he declared. What was the problem with building a home for new businesses that would attract people to the area? When he finished saying his piece, old Emmett Ferguson, who ran the tackle shop, growled an obscenity through clenched false teeth. Then Penelope Stanhope, the bigmouth on the heritage committee, told him to shut up and sit down. Then someone else threw a cup of coffee at him that only just missed its mark. But McGowan straightened his hat and said that they were all just afraid, afraid of progress, afraid of the future. He spat a gob on the floor and, with everyone watching, limped past the plastic model of the proposed development and out the door.

They were afraid, and he couldn't find it in himself to even fake respect for people who refused to act out of fear. Where would we be if nobody did anything because they were afraid? He counted on his fingers: the Polynesians who sailed across the ocean in boats made out of reeds; the Scots who fought the English; that Russian guy, the first one in outer space; the Germans who knocked down the Berlin Wall with spoons and screwdrivers. Even Rhonda Ellison, bless her soul, who didn't want her guts cut out, didn't want chemo or radiation either—she wasn't afraid to tell the doctors to go to hell. Cancer all through her and she gets on a plane and flies to Greece and buys a house. That's something he could admire, having the nerve to play chicken with death.

His apartment gave him a clear view into the window of the building where his store used to be. The development project died on the table, but that was after he'd cashed his cheque, so he didn't really care. Most of the other merchants had hung on to their property and these days business was terrible. The street had declined even further than he could have imagined. Nobody painted or repaired anything. Rot was everywhere. A few doors along someone had set a fire, hoping to make good on an insurance claim, but the police were on to him in a minute and now there was nothing where the house was but weeds and garbage and scraps of charred timber. McGowan's store sat vacant for a few months, but then the space was rented to a skinny young man in denim and a T-shirt who painted the walls yellow and hung paintings and put computers on the tables and nailed up a sign that said Internet Café, whatever that meant. Since McGowan wasn't welcome anywhere else on the street, he spent a lot of time in the Internet Café drinking the house blend.

McGowan's life had revolved around three things: his store, his wife, Rosie, and his children. Now two and a half of these were gone, but this was no excuse for sadness because life still held all kinds of possibilities. All he had to do was figure out what these possibilities were.

"Daddy, you're sure you're okay here by yourself? You know, it's just like last time, there's no food in the fridge and that bulb in the bathroom is still burnt out. You might want to look into getting someone in here on a regular basis."

Gretchen and Alison were visiting, but by now he was accustomed to their banter and took no notice. Either there were old newspapers everywhere or dust on everything or the bread had spots on it or the tub was filthy. He couldn't argue with them because all of it was true, but he didn't mind because every couple of weeks they came over and cleaned the place and tossed out anything rank and did his laundry. Sometimes they even cooked him a meal.

His daughter Gretchen was not one of those lesbians you see on TV, in documentaries and cop shows, who wear black leather and studded collars, who lead big dogs around on thick chains, and who spend all their time oiling their bodies and working out at the gym. There was nothing about her that declared itself either lesbian or otherwise. In fact, she was much the same Gretchen whose childhood photos filled page after page of the album he still maintained. She was not tall and she had a slim build. He loved her small nose and these days enjoyed her hair, which had a subtle ochre tint beneath its chestnut sheen. This was Alison's doing. Alison was a hairdresser with her own salon and when she sat him down and clipped a towel in place around his neck and started cutting his hair, she never forgot to remind him that the same treatment on Barrington Street would cost him fifty dollars.

Why they put up with him, he didn't know. He had seen his own father grow old and cantankerous and never wanted the same thing to happen to him, and here he was at sixty-five, a crabby old slob with a limp and no clean clothes. His father had devoted his life to the old general store on Gottingen Street, and for years as a child he hated going in there. Even the smell of the place caused a lump to creep up his gorge, the merging of dissimilar odours—overripe apples, kerosene, licorice, ink from that day's newspapers—making him nauseous. He'd planned an education for himself, planned to get away and see the world and make a reputation if not a lot of money. But college hadn't worked out, and to escape its blinkered confines he signed up with the army. They sent him to Europe, where he spent three full years of his youth spreading relief and helping with rebuilding efforts in cities and towns that had been bombed out in the war. When he got home his father was on his last legs and his mother pleaded with him to stay and help for a while. A while turned into a year, then two. And when his father died he stayed to give his mother a hand settling the estate and running the store, but only until she found a buyer. But there were no buyers, even though business was good. That was forty years ago. His mother died a few years later and with no reasonable alternatives in sight he carried on working in the store, always with the idea—a sure thing stashed at the back of his mind—that he would eventually sell out and move on. Then one day it came to him that if he didn't do something soon he was going to be a shopkeeper for the rest of his life. By then business was steady and he'd built up a clientele. He realized he was making a living and that he really rather enjoyed it and that he could be doing a whole lot worse. Then he met Rosie.

Gretchen placed some bread and a bowl of hot beef and vegetable soup before him on the table.

"Daddy, we have to talk."

He tore the piece of bread in half and dunked it in the soup. Her tone of voice made his whole body feel hot. Gretchen was always talking, but mostly it was just her sounding off about her job and how her boss still bought her flowers and chocolates and invited her out to dinner even though she'd told him she was gay.

"Eat something first," he muttered between mouthfuls. "Then we'll talk."

Gretchen and Alison exchanged glances.

"What is it then?" He knew what they were thinking. They'd been through it before. "Look, girls, I'm not crippled or senile yet. I'll know when I'm ready for the old geezers' home. I still got my faculties. Maybe this place isn't the greatest and I don't clean it up like I should. But it doesn't mean I need spoon-feeding and someone to wipe my ass for me."

Gretchen wasn't smiling and this more than anything else set off the alarms in his head.

Alison tapped her shoulder. "You have to tell him."

Gretchen released a lengthy sigh. When she spoke, her tone was earnest.

"Daddy, you remember how when we were growing up you were always saying to Ronny and me that we should get out and see the world." She looked up at him and smiled. "You wanted us to know that the world was a big place and that we shouldn't feel tied down just because we were born here. I know you weren't trying to get rid of us, or anything like that. You just wanted us to be curious about what was out there."

"So?" McGowan said. He was conscious of a sudden touch of lightheadedness—or maybe it was more than that. A tingling in his extremities and a shortness of breath.

"Well, you know I'm not happy with my job. It's been like that for a while. So I've been applying for other things. Well, I found out a few days ago. It's through UNESCO. They need teachers overseas and I said I'd do it. I'm going to Africa—Namibia—to teach English."

McGowan's mind raced. Somehow her words didn't quite register.

"It wasn't easy to make this decision." Her eyes dropped a few tears on her cheek and she wiped them away. "Alison can't come. She has her business. And I feel like I'm abandoning you. But I've decided I have to do this. It's just something I have to do."

He looked at her, couldn't take his eyes from hers, which seemed huge and childish and which seemed to plead for understanding. He could handle this. After Ronny's murder. After Rosie's grindingly laborious departure from this life, which he'd followed step by step, every inch of the way. After all he'd been through, he could handle this.

"I didn't want to say anything until I was sure. But now I've signed the papers and they're sending me a plane ticket. I leave next month."

He tried to think. Namibia. Was there a war going on there? Where exactly was Namibia? Africa. But Africa's a big place.

"It's what you want?" he asked.

She nodded.

"But it's not forever. They bring me home twice a year. I get furloughs, so I'll be able to travel around a bit. Alison's promised to come over to visit. I was hoping that you could come to visit too."

"Oh, I'm too old to visit a place like that," he protested. Yet, even as he spoke, it entered his mind that what he was saying was not necessarily true.

"I know it might be hard, but it's a chance to see something different."

"That's for sure."

"I'll have my own apartment," she continued, smiling now. Her eyes darted. "So I won't have to room with anyone. And they'll pay for my food and other expenses. And I get a salary on top of that. It's not much. But it's something."

"Is it safe?"

Again, Gretchen and Alison exchanged a meaningful glance. He looked from one to the other.

"Well, it's not exactly a war zone," Gretchen said. "But—"

"Yes," Alison interrupted. "It's safe. It's very safe."

"As Africa goes," Gretchen added after a thoughtful pause, "it's as safe as it gets."

McGowan nodded. It was almost as if she were asking his permission, giving him an opportunity to exercise a parental veto. But he knew this wasn't the case. Whether or not he endorsed her plan, she was on her way. Only he couldn't imagine the translucent pallor of her skin beneath a relentless African sun. Couldn't see her leading a class of ragged malnourished children through a recitation of the Lord's Prayer. Couldn't see her smile surviving more than a few days amidst the poverty and dilapidation that his mind conjured at the mere mention of the word Africa. What had got into her? Was this happening because twenty-five years ago he'd brought a globe and a set of encyclopedias into the house and made her and Ronny study a different country each week? He'd wanted his children to grow up enlightened and interested in everything that was going on around them. He wanted their view of the world to encompass the whole instead of the part, not just the trees in their own backyard and the school bus that let them off outside their front door, but also the citron trees that grew in rich abundance in Umbria and the shaggy-haired goats that carried supplies over the Taurus Mountains in Turkey. Was this payback for trying to be a good parent?

"As long as it's safe and what you want," he said. Determinedly, he finished his soup.

McGowan still received letters from people he'd met during his army days. That was the thing about McGowan. You remembered him, even if you'd met him briefly forty years ago. It was not that he was always clowning around; it was not that he was the most boisterous one in the group, or even that he told memorable stories or had much to say at all. But he was reliable and he told the truth. People liked him because they could count on him. He drank with the crowd, but mostly in moderation, and even on those occasions when his drinking crossed the line, he never actually seemed drunk. He was a good listener and made friends because when people needed someone to talk to, they went to McGowan. Even in an emergency he maintained a steady demeanour and an uncluttered vision. When you went somewhere with McGowan, you knew what you were getting into.

You would notice his blue eyes and wild hair and how the blue seemed to deepen when he was speaking about some topic that interested him. He could be passionate about the oddest things, like how arsenic is used both as a poison and as a medicine, or how the seeds of a sunflower grow in an arrangement that reflects the Fibonacci series of numbers, or the compression of sound waves that accounted for the difference in pitch of the train's whistle between its approach to and departure from the station. "Look! Look at this!" he was known to say as he bent the highest branch of a bush down to show you a red-winged horned beetle or an elaborately striped caterpillar that was making a meal of a leaf. You're going to be a scientist when you get home, people told him, but the truth was that he'd come overseas to escape all of that, the organized pursuit of new knowledge, the formulation of universal theories, the stultifying principles of inquiry that choked the life out of any truly inquisitive mind. He was the first to recognize that his brainpower could not be reined in or contained, that his intelligence refused to conform to the standards demanded by empirical science, that his thinking was slapdash and muddled. He wouldn't survive a minute in a laboratory, where balance and reason prevail. He was no better than the rankest enthusiast, the amateur with no standing. He wouldn't have fooled anyone, himself included.

So it didn't matter that others thought so, he wasn't going to be a scientist. His return from Europe was heralded by his family as the return of a conquering hero, but he knew otherwise, though he stifled his misgivings beneath gaudy and excessive displays of affection. But the future scared him half to death because he could not see any role for himself that could entice him away from the store and his family for a second time. The needs of his parents seemed to supersede his own, and he easily caved in under the weight of their demands, not just to appease them in their new and shocking frailness and vulnerability, but to save himself the agony of having to make a decision about his own life. It was cowardice that kept him there, the cowardice of a young man who uses as an excuse for inaction the guilt of knowing exactly what kind of hardship his absence will impose upon his aging parents.

But he still had the wild hair and the blue eyes, and after both his parents were dead and buried he became esteemed locally as an eligible bachelor of the highest order. After all, he owned and operated a successful business; he was not known to indulge in any conspicuous vices. He was friendly and well spoken. The store was neat and he refused to stock those glossy magazines full of obscene photographs that were just then coming into vogue. And so the young women came knocking, some on their own, some reluctantly propelled along by their mothers. Rosie was just a girl then, and she entered the store with no purpose in mind other than to purchase flour and sugar for her mother, who was in the midst of Easter baking. Her family had only recently moved to the Gottingen Street neighbourhood and it was her first shopping trip, her first chance to examine the offerings of the local merchants. He could tell she was not impressed. Judging her by her fine clothes and the way she wrinkled her nose as she surveyed his goods, he gathered she was accustomed to better things, certainly to having people at her disposal to take care of tedious chores like this. Possibly she was used to a way of life less burdensome than he could ever imagine, and perhaps even to the trappings of wealth. But despite her haughtiness, he was smitten. It was late afternoon and the yellow light angling through the front window illuminated her childish features and the sheer length of black hair that hung to her shoulders. He raised his eyes and observed her as, weighted down by several large parcels, pouting and angry about having to make another stop, she gazed with annoyance at his meagre wares. He decided that before she left his premises he would see her laugh. And he was right.

He had also guessed correctly. Rosie's family had suffered reversals. Her father had inherited his money and never felt encumbered by the necessity to prepare himself for a career of any kind. When his investments soured he tried to cover his losses through borrowing, and then gambling. At fifty and suffering the pinch of want for the first time in his life—and with the added burden of a sizeable family under the care of the docile, uneducated woman he had married—he indulged his taste for liquor and had soon lost the country house along with the heirlooms and artwork. His fall was precipitous and tragic and, trying to find a place for herself in a way of life that lacked even basic comforts let alone the luxuries she had known for fifteen of her sixteen years, Rosie could summon no compassion for the man. She recalled for McGowan's benefit the day the family was evicted from their ten-bedroom home on Young Avenue and evoked with her fury as much as with her words the crushing humiliation of being sneered at by a servant girl to whom she had always been generous and bullied by a waitress at a restaurant where she learned that her father owed an accumulated bill of more than three thousand dollars. When he finally settled up with the bank the family's depleted resources left them with the most common of middle-class means, which in those days meant a modest house in a decent neighbourhood but which also required a stable income to cover ongoing expenses. Rosie shared a room with her two younger sisters. Her eldest brother, the family's shining hope for the future, was to attend university. The rest of them would get work of some sort when they reached sufficient age. Her mother sat in her room and stared out the window, rousing herself periodically to assemble meals, and her father, when he wasn't drunk, occupied his time plotting ways to get his money back from the people who, he claimed, had stolen it.

After weeks of clandestine meetings and furtive kisses Rosie told McGowan she'd never intended him to fall in love with her, just as she had never planned to fall in love with him. In her company— with her slender body in his arms and her perfumed scent like an opiate dispelling his reservations—there was no question in his mind that they would marry; when he was alone he considered his options. She was sixteen and still a child under the law, but she possessed maturity beyond her years and a profoundly lucid, unromantic vision of life that matched his own. In all likelihood she would not demand luxuries he was in no position to provide, though he would do everything in his power to see that she had within her reach the comforts any wife could reasonably expect. He wanted children, and she seemed healthy. She had the strong white teeth and clear skin of someone who has lived with the nutritious offerings of a master chef always waiting for her on the table yet who has never overindulged. He put it to her that she would work in the store, for a wage. No one need know they were romantically involved. On her eighteenth birthday they would get married.

He was surprised when she—and, shortly thereafter at a formal afternoon tea, her parents—accepted this proposal without hesitation.

Her schooling was important to him and he made sure that her hours in the store never interfered with her classes. He helped with her assignments. Soon she was spending more time with him than with her own family, a circumstance that he thought might trouble only the meddlesome old biddies who had thrust their homely daughters under his nose, impassive lures that had failed to tempt. But gossip spreads like wildfire and in a small community rumour quickly becomes fact. When Rosie was subjected to taunts and jeers at school, when she discovered an anonymous note accusing her of indecent behaviour inserted into the pages of one of her books, when he had too often tasted the salt of her tears, and when the Presbyterian minister in the taciturn company of a female officer

from the Department of Social Welfare arrived at the store to discuss
the concerns of his neighbours, McGowan saw that he had grievously
underestimated the depths to which humankind could sink.

They were married immediately. She moved in and planned to
complete her education in the evenings.

These days he looked back on those early years of married life as
a sort of golden age. The store did well. They expanded, began selling
clothes and furniture and housewares. They renovated and added
a tearoom. A year after the wedding Rosie's younger sister Vanessa
started working for them, and then her mother began stopping by,
rolled up her sleeves and pitched in. It was 1960 and a time of growth.
Money flowed freely and they reaped the benefits. Always conscious
of Rosie's lofty origins and of her family's snobbish attitudes, which
could manifest themselves at any moment—in a haughty turn of
phrase or an arrogant gesture of dismissal—McGowan also found
himself charmed and utterly seduced by their wit and their elevated
tastes, the latter of which proved useful in the discovery of new
and esoteric items with which to stock the shelves. Rosie's mother
retained her overseas contacts, people who had no idea the family's fortunes had suffered, and she exploited these without mercy.
Still known as McGowan's General Store, their enterprise gradually developed a reputation among the more fashionable sector of
local society as the only place where they would be likely to find the
Welsh linen or Dutch cheeses or Eastern European crystal they'd
been searching for. They received orders by phone, packed the items
in tissue paper and cardboard, and had them waiting when the driver
arrived to pick them up. At the height of their prosperity, McGowan
and Rosie could boast a staff of thirty-five eager and enthusiastic
employees and an income that approached six digits.

Today was rainy and McGowan limped up Gottingen Street,
heading for home. He'd done his shopping and carried with him in
a plastic bag a can of minestrone soup, a package of all-beef wieners,
and a loaf of brown bread. He was tired of beans, his standard fare.
Life was long and beans were plentiful and cheap, but you couldn't
eat them day in and day out. Even he knew that. So for lunch he
would enjoy the soup, with its bits of softened pasta and pungent

tang of wine vinegar. Then for supper he would chop up the wieners and fry them until they'd blistered and blackened and he could taste the charcoal in them. The bread would do for lunch and supper.

Now that Gretchen was gone his thoughts lingered in the past, and he didn't like that. He'd survived this long as a practical man and for him the past was a dead thing; he'd lived through it once, so why dwell on it? Over the years his father had delivered innumerable lectures to him on some vaguely defined yet illustrious past that he just couldn't let go, always making it clear that the present day didn't measure up. But old people were sometimes like that. His father's trouble was that he never really seemed to understand that the past was gone and the present was here to stay, and maybe that was why he was always so unhappy. Well, maybe today was no damn good, but there was always tomorrow and surely this was McGowan's realm; it was where he belonged. The only problem with tomorrow was that it was faceless and scary, like a hooded figure wielding a scythe in its bony hand. Who could say what the future would bring? He'd seen able-bodied men and women reduced by diseases of the mind and heart to slobbering wrecks in only a few months, pissing and shitting themselves, blissfully unaware. And he was getting to that age, the age when each day was either a blessing or a curse depending on how your body was holding up.

He passed the store—well, where the store used to be—and paused before heading on. Then, enticed by the aroma of coffee, he turned around and went back. The store—the café—was not busy this morning. He took a seat at a small table with no computer and placed his groceries on the other chair. Soft jazz filled in the background and masked the street noise. One other table was occupied, by a young woman with spiky yellow hair who was smoking and writing in a notebook with a stubby pencil. The aroma of coffee was strong. When the young man who ran the place came and asked what he would like, McGowan ordered the house blend and a cinnamon twist. Then he sat back and looked around. He didn't mind change. Over time all things changed, usually for the better. His store didn't belong here, in this space or on this street. The café was just the right thing for this place and this period in history. The yellow walls, hung with abstract paintings like bolts of brightly coloured cloth in a fabric shop, spoke in a language arcane and unfathomable to the likes of him, but he could still enjoy the way it all came together and the statement it made, even if the sentiments of that statement eluded him. He bore no grudges and regretted nothing.

He accepted his coffee with a smile and bit into the pastry.

It was difficult for him to say exactly when their fortunes began their decline. From the perspective of thirty years later it seemed they were expanding their operation and taking money to the bank by the truckload one week and cutting back on inventory and borrowing to cover their losses the next. More likely it was a gradual process. His one big mistake was agreeing to open a second store and leaving the management of it to Rosie's brother, the college graduate. The boy was certainly intelligent, but he had no business sense and the store lost money for three years before they decided to shut it down. But by then the business was hemorrhaging money. Nothing could stanch the flow. They held sales and stocked cheaper items, hoping to appeal to a less affluent crowd, but they had been tagged as a store for rich people and the strategy backfired. They alienated every segment of their existing clientele and attracted no new customers. To avoid bankruptcy or having to take on a partner, they went back to selling dry goods and penny candy and kerosene and newspapers and the odd garden hose. They made enough to keep themselves afloat and the bank happy and by slow degrees crawled out of the hole of debt.

When Gretchen was ten and Ronny was five, Rosie got sick. At first he thought it was flu. Even at her best she had been delicate, and he suspected childbirth had weakened her system. But he wasn't prepared for the agonizing process of wasting away. When they finally discovered that cancer had spread from somewhere else into her lungs, it was too late to do anything. He took her home and with the help of her mother and sister nursed her through an illness that seemed to him God's revenge on the unwary. Her suffering was absolute and unremitting. She lived for more than two months after telling him she was ready to go and would he please help her along. Selfishly, he refused to do this, wanting to keep her with him as long as possible. In his mind if there was still breath in the body there was a chance, if not of recovery then of something almost as good, remission perhaps. This did not happen, though her colour returned and she seemed at times lucid and eager to get on with things and even happy. But this, as he later learned, was symptomatic of the progress of the disease and of the drugs she was given to ease her distress. He was with her when she died, on a warm Sunday afternoon in early spring, a day of dazzling sun and full of things growing and coming into life and the sounds of children playing in the street. He remembered asking in all seriousness, How could someone die on such a day as this? But, unable to provide an answer, people turned away.

He stayed in the store and brought up Gretchen and Ronny. He often asked himself how he had reached this state of affairs, running a general store and raising two children on his own, given his ambitions, his learning. But this question too remained unanswered. He pushed his children along, placed them in private schools, brought home the globe and the encyclopedias and recordings of Italian operas, other cultural artefacts that he thought might lend them an advantage when the time came for them to head out the door and into the world. Their apartment above the store was littered with books, they each played two or three musical instruments, they painted and recited Shakespeare on rainy afternoons. But he was not satisfied. One day, as Gretchen sat watching cartoons on television and Ronny searched the closet for his baseball glove, he saw, as if a door had been opened and a light switched on, that they were as ordinary as nuts and bolts, as ordinary as himself.

From that day forward he let them evolve as they would and was not disappointed by the result, though he could have done without the homosexuality. He also wondered why each of them had felt compelled to come to him with it, as if to a confessor. It was none of his business. On the other hand, he'd always billed himself as the kind of parent with whom they could discuss anything, and so he had no right to complain. But still.

The young man was hovering over him, his face creased with concern.

"I'm sorry," he said, "but you were saying something and I thought you were talking to me."

McGowan noticed the girl with spiky hair watching him, though there was nothing antagonistic in her gaze, just bland curiosity—a momentary distraction from the poem or story she was composing.

For all he knew, he'd earned himself a place in that story or poem. The gauzy stream of smoke from her cigarette drifted lazily upward.

"Did I ever tell you that I ran a store for over thirty years, right here in this very spot where you're standing?" He spread his arms in a grand, inclusive gesture. "Right here in this very spot?"

The young man's eyebrows twitched. McGowan could scarcely believe the words had escaped from his mouth. Why was he trying to pump life into the past? And why would it have even occurred to him that this young man—faced with all the tribulations of running a business in the present day—would be interested in his tale of another business that had failed in spirit, if not in actuality, years before he'd finally found the courage to shut it down?

The young man absently stroked his neck and cleared his throat. "You don't say?"

McGowan shrugged.

"Well, it was a long time ago."

He finished his coffee and paid and then retreated out the door, his back bent in defeat like someone who has been shouted down in a public debate.

Gretchen's first letter arrived a few days later. It confirmed the best but also the worst of what he'd suspected she'd let herself in for. It bore the date of a Saturday three weeks ago. The stamp pictured a long-necked bird wading through a scruffy wetland habitat.

"Daddy," she wrote, "I'm holding in my hand a gift, a necklace made from human bones by one of my students, a boy named Aki. He's five years old. He told me the bones come from a skeleton he and his friends found at the bottom of a pit that used to be a quarry, near the old zinc mines. The skeleton could have been years old, or the body might only have been left there a week ago and picked clean by ants and hyenas. Aki lives in a small village that has a single water tap for two hundred families.

"I'm working with Dr. Drayton, who has a degree from Oxford. The other teachers here are from places like Australia and Hong Kong and New Delhi. They are all younger than me. We're near Tsumeb, which is a strange town, old and new at the same time, though even the new buildings have a sad look of neglect about them. The school is more run down than I expected it to be and there are no modern learning tools, like computers or anything like that. Some days there is no running water. Everything is dusty, I feel it in my hair and on my skin all the time. People here speak German and the local dialect. It's nothing like home and I was prepared for that, but I didn't know it would get so cold at night. I'm using all the blankets in the apartment already and it's not even winter yet. If you think of it, please send some wool blankets and heavy socks...."

He couldn't read any further.

It only upset him if he thought about it, and so he wouldn't think about it, not for a while anyway. His child, at the ends of the earth freezing to death, eating God only knows what. No, he didn't want to think about it. He put the letter in the kitchen drawer and made himself a cup of tea.

Then there was the other letter, this one from Rhonda Ellison. He turned his attention to that.

Rhonda had lived in the neighbourhood for years and lived comfortably because she'd been wise about investing the money from her divorce. For a few of those years she'd owned the building where McGowan moved after selling the store. She'd done her best with the place, though ultimately there was no saving it from the previous fifty years of neglect and botched repair jobs. She'd even backed his efforts in support of the new shopping plaza, the only person in the area to do so. But when the cancer came she decided to sell up. In her decision to leave the town where she'd lived most of her life, where she had married and divorced and raised three children, McGowan detected not a hint of resignation or regret. She was sixty and she'd always wanted to do something like this, something brash and life-changing, and since the doctors were telling her she had a year to live, maybe two if she was lucky and had her guts removed and let them attach a plastic bag to the outside of her body where her shit would go, there was, in her view, no time like the present. Her ex-husband was Greek and had gone back home, but she had kept her passport up to date. She could still claim Greek citizenship and, judging from the light of passion that flared in her eyes as they discussed the subject, McGowan suspected that any bureaucrat who tried to deny her that right was in for the battle of his life.

He thought she'd be dead for sure by now. His one and only experience with cancer had convinced him that the afflicted rarely got off lightly. A few months after she left town, a letter arrived from an island called Chios letting him know that she'd bought a house and that he was welcome to visit. The photograph made it tempting, if not practical, showing a clear sky of crystal sapphire brilliance suspended over water that was dead calm and that stretched all the way to a perfectly flat horizon; and to one side, almost as an afterthought, there stood Rhonda beside a squat two-storey whitewashed structure with green shutters, her slender limbs tanned a deep brown and her looking as healthy as he'd ever seen her. She'd always been on the skinny side, but attractive nonetheless. The illness, or perhaps its gravity, had in his mind only heightened her appeal, as if somehow unmasking a depth of loveliness, leaving her vulnerable but open to anything. An undercurrent of erotic conjecture had always subtly shaded their interactions, the tension of what-if rendering each conversation edgy and exciting. But he only kissed her, chastely, on New Year's Eve and on her birthday; the single time he embraced her was just before she left. Had she expected more of him? What had held him back? Why had he never attempted to get any closer? And how was he supposed to construe the fact that she was still keeping in touch?

"Dear David," he read. "I'm still alive. Does that surprise you? It's all right if it does because it surprises the hell out of me. There's no doctor here but there are plenty of people with remedies for what ails you. How are you? How is Gretchen? What is the weather like where you are? Please tell me it's grim and awful. (I almost wrote 'What is the weather like at home,' but I keep forgetting, this is home for me now.) I'm happy though I wasn't at first and thought maybe I'd made a terrible mistake. But visitors make a big difference and my son and daughters have all been here at one time or another and have promised to come back. I live alone and that's both good and bad because I get tired easily and what if I fall on the floor and can't get up? But I like my privacy, as I'm sure you remember. An English woman named Gracie (she's a writer) lives nearby and she knocks on my door most days to make sure I haven't expired. I won't lie to you, I'm not well. But they gave me two years at the most and so how can I complain now? Every sunrise is a bonus. When are you coming?"

There was more, but he folded the letter back into its envelope and placed it in the drawer on top of Gretchen's.

The sink was piled high with dirty dishes. A rank smell emanated from the four corners of the room. Years ago he had envisioned himself living out his dotage in a chaotic but comfortable old house surrounded by a family of devoted and energetic children, a loving wife, a dog (a bull terrier?), and maybe some cats. So how had this other reality come to pass, this threadbare existence that was both crippling and demeaning? How had he come to inhabit a world of aches and pains and bland food that dribbled out of a can into a metal pot, and hours to fill and nothing to fill them with, a cardboard apartment that had at the crux of it a television in one corner and a musty pile of newspapers in the other? Why did he live like this when a world abounding with strangeness and beauty lay largely unexplored outside his front door? What could he have done differently in order to avoid such an undistinguished fate? If people hadn't died on him, maybe. If Rosie were still here she wouldn't have allowed this to happen. God, he could still remember the day they put her in the ground, the sun so bright it hurt his eyes and him thinking only of the obscenity of a bright sun on that day, as if someone up there were having it on with him and taking pleasure in his loss. He knew it wasn't fair and that she should have been alive to see the sun come up that morning and hear the day's sounds and smell its smells. To breathe your last on a spring day, it seemed against the laws of nature somehow. Then Ronny. The police called it a hate crime. God only knows, he loved his son. But Ronny was a handful and followed his passions headlong, recklessly, without fear of failure, never once slowed down by practical considerations. But he couldn't focus on one thing and always ended up sidetracked, by the promise of romance or some misguided conviction that he was wasting his time. He dropped out of college to follow his humanities professor to Europe and when he arrived home with someone else altogether, McGowan lent them some money to open a restaurant. That venture failed when Ronny's new friend and business partner discovered he wasn't at all fond of working for a living. Ronny drifted then, supporting himself for a while as a journalist, then as a sales clerk, then enrolling in college and dropping out again a month later, involving himself in one doomed relationship after another. But all the while, and McGowan didn't even know it, he was painting, producing work that, though amateurish and undisciplined, displayed a riotous appreciation of colour and texture. His only show was in a dingy little coffee shop downtown, but the coverage it received fed his ego just enough to make him cocky. McGowan liked the paintings and admired the scumbling technique and mottled backgrounds and startling chimerical and hooded shapes staring out from the canvases, but, more than this, he began to suspect that his son perceived the world uniquely and understood for the first time that Ronny possessed hidden reserves of insight and wisdom and a profundity that he, his father, was unlikely to fathom for as long as either of them lived.

McGowan never learned how Ronny had ended up all alone and miles outside of town at a seedy roadside tavern, a dark noisy place where his shrill voice and splashy clothes and effeminate mannerisms were bound to attract the unappreciative attention of the wrong sort of people. Ronny was thunderously drunk by the time the biker crowd arrived and by all accounts wouldn't leave them alone. Finally, one of them knocked him flat with the butt end of a pool cue and heaved him out the door. The police figured Ronny staggered around for a while and then collapsed in a grove not far from the parking lot, but far enough that it was two days before anyone came across him lying stiff and cold in a hollow under an oak tree, dead from exposure and loss of blood.

McGowan buried his only son on an afternoon that was dazzlingly and frigidly bright, cloudless and eerily calm.

He sat up in the middle of the night, sweaty and wheezing. His apartment was at ground level and he heard sounds, but it was only the whisper of tires on wet pavement and the guttural reverberation of engine parts straining against one another. Nothing more than this. So what had awakened him? What had sent the blood cascading through his veins and started his heart thudding like a battle drum? Was he dying? No, that wasn't it. He got out of bed and unthinkingly, as if blindly heeding instructions, made his way to the kitchen. He opened the drawer and took out both letters. He switched on the light. That was it, probably. He'd been dreaming, and Rhonda and Gretchen had both been there. He closed his eyes and tried to summon the image. There was water and a boat. The vegetation on the island was lush; everything was green and backlit by silver moonlight. Strangely—it was how dreams unfold—they were a family, the three of them, catching their food in the sea with nets and cooking their meals under the stars over an open fire. But they couldn't talk, that was the really odd part. Their only means of communication was gestures and grunts. And Rhonda was trying to tell him something, pointing toward her neck. Her eyes had widened with the urgency of her message and she made a slicing motion across her throat. Was it her, then? Was she the one who was dying? Is that what she was trying to say to him? He took her letter and this time read it through to the end. He didn't put much store in dreams, but if there was a subtext of despair beneath the surface of what she'd written, he wanted to find it before it was too late.

When the sun came up, he was slumped in the easy chair. He'd been through her letter a dozen times, but he wasn't getting any help from Rhonda. The letter was cryptic in the extreme, optimistic and forward-looking, jaunty even. A single reference to her health, which was either failing or unchanged depending on how you chose to take her meaning. He sat and considered the yellow light filtering through the thin fabric of the curtains as it grew ever brighter, listened as the morning traffic on Gottingen Street snarled and wailed in its unending race for downtown. Surrounding him were the keepsakes and mementos he'd found himself unable to part with when he sold out and moved across the street. Rosie's collection of porcelain birds, a couple of old clocks that had come from his mother's family, his parents' wedding picture, Ronny and Gretchen's graduation photos, one of Ronny's paintings, a dozen studio portraits of Rosie in the bloom of youth. He still had all of her jewelry and a few pieces of clothing in a box under the bed. With advancing age he'd developed a weakness for such things, for trinkets and reminders of other times and other places. Just a day or two ago he'd pulled a magazine out of the pile in the bedroom closet, and on first glance it didn't appear old to him at all. But when he examined the cover and discovered a date more than twenty years gone, he pitched it out along with dozens of others. He'd lectured his opponents at that town-planning meeting and made his stand based on the pointlessness of living mired in the past, and here he sat, a hypocrite, buried in it up to his eyebrows. He'd known all along that his excuse for not becoming involved with Rhonda was his long-standing loyalty to Rosie, as if she were in any position to appreciate such a gesture. He stood and very carefully lifted a photo of Rosie down from the wall above the TV and blew the dust off it. No wonder he'd fallen for her: how could anyone resist the childish beauty of her lips and nose and mouth, and the humour, kindness, and wisdom he'd found once he'd cracked her facade of haughty reserve? How would she feel knowing that he doted on her still, that he was unable to let go of someone dead almost thirty years? What would she say if he were to ask her what he should do?

And in the inexplicable manner in which random and unforeseen events take charge of our destiny and the imagination is brought to bear on the decision-making process, he heard a voice telling him to go; and though it was faint and reached him over the distance of many years, he recognized it, after all, as the only voice that had ever made a difference in his life.

His impression upon leaving the 747 in Athens was of a massive burden of heat and the vaporous density of the mid-afternoon air. For just a moment while lugging his bag across the tarmac to the waiting bus, unable to catch his breath, he'd felt panic creeping up his throat, as if he'd awakened to find someone holding a pillow over his face. Once inside the building his alarm faded, but the flight from Toronto had taken eight hours, and now, after waiting a further six hours for another plane to take him to the island of Chios, he'd grown drowsy enough that the only physical need he could reasonably respond to was the one for sleep. The travel agent had recommended he skip Athens and head straight for the island, a suggestion that sounded fine to him, lounging in a plush armchair, and coming as it did from a supremely confident young woman, whose sandy blond hair, red lips, and casual air of authority allowed no room for doubt, and who occupied a desk in a brightly lit office, every wall of which was covered by illustrations of stately European capitals, snow-topped mountains, and sun-soaked beaches, complete with palm trees and the bluest skies and water he'd ever seen. But after six hours in Athens airport, his butt flattened by a rigid seat of moulded plastic, his eyes drooping, his lungs ready to burst with cigarette smoke, he wasn't sure anymore that she'd had his best interests at heart and was beginning to suspect that she was new to the game. For one thing, she'd never heard of Chios. That should have tipped him off right there.

In heavily accented English the voice on the loudspeaker called his flight. He roused himself and, surrounded by parents leading sulky children by the hand, old men and women, people loaded down with overstuffed plastic bags and heaps of on-board luggage and cardboard boxes wrapped with packing tape, made his way to the departure gate. Here, while the process of taking tickets and issuing boarding passes kept him waiting another thirty minutes, he had leisure to reflect upon the mission that had brought him to this strange place so far from home.

Renewing his passport had taken two weeks. The very day he picked it up he'd made his flight arrangements. He phoned Alison to inform her of his plans. Not surprisingly, she seemed only mildly interested and did not try to talk him out of it. His efforts to reach Gretchen by overseas phone had been fruitless, so he wrote her a letter, which she would not receive until he was well on his way. He had no means of contacting Rhonda other than by mail, and writing to her seemed a waste of time since he would likely be standing at her front door long before the letter arrived. So he decided to just go and take the chance that she would still be around when he got there. What, after all, was the worst that could happen? If she was dead, he'd find a hotel and take in the sights. If she was still alive, they could take in the sights together.

The flight was more expensive than even his most liberal estimation, but he'd always been better off financially than he let on. Why he lived as if hardship and despair were just around the corner was anybody's guess, maybe so people would leave him alone. Not that he was rich, but even after paying for the ticket he could still afford a small suitcase and some new clothes—shorts, sandals, T-shirts, the things one took on vacation. He'd been putting money away for years and never paid much attention to what it came to, intending to leave it all to Ronny and Gretchen. Because his needs were modest, the money just sat there.

How long was he planning to stay in Greece? The travel agent had put the question to him, but he hadn't given the matter any thought. Two weeks? Three? He didn't know what to tell her. Since his confusion was genuine, she left the return date open. He could stay up to six months she said, and then she giggled, as if the very idea were preposterous, though he was thinking, Well, wait a minute, why not? Now, inching toward the departure gate, his body numb with exhaustion, famished, besieged on all sides by noisy conversations in a raucous language, jostled by hips and elbows and children stamping their feet and whining, six months seemed like a very long time.

But the flight to Chios was brief and uneventful. The bus from the hotel was waiting for him and some others, and he was able to lay his head on a clean pillow and close his eyes shortly after midnight.

He was not prepared for the heat, or for the noise of the port, the island's main town, also called Chios. A temperature creeping toward ninety and the raspy whine of motor scooters awakened him at seven. His fourth-floor room offered a view of the busy harbour and the street, which was already choked with vehicles. The sky hung like a translucent veil between him and an astonishing blueness, something vast and primordial that communicated the purity of blue in terms with which he was unfamiliar. Voices reached him from below. For what seemed like the first time in his life he was struck by the frightening oddness of waking up in a foreign country, of having to contend with things as commonplace as language, as mundane as placing money into another's hand in exchange for goods. But there was also delight in the sensation that swept through him and tensed his bowels: joy at facing the unknown and a palpable sense of release, as if restraints that had held him in place for most of his life had melted away. Here, in Greece, the habits and routines by which he'd fashioned his days and taken meaning from his nights would serve no purpose. He would have to work at discovering new ways of doing things and find some system for making himself understood.

The young man at the front desk greeted him with "Kalimera" and eyed him expectantly.

"Um...breakfast?" McGowan ineptly mimed the act of eating with a spoon.

"The dining room is straight down the hall, sir. Breakfast is complimentary."

McGowan followed the man's gesture and saw the metal sign declaring "Restaurant" and an arrow pointing in the direction he'd indicated. His flawless English, spoken with only the faintest hint of an old-world inflection, seemed to McGowan like a gentle rebuke.

"Um...thank you."

After eating, McGowan left the hotel and walked along the quay. Already the concrete sidewalk shimmered with the heat. The town's activities visibly converged upon the waterfront. Trucks whizzed by, stirring up the dust, followed by small, boxy cars and a legion of sputtering motor scooters driven by men and women of every age and description. The desk clerk had provided directions to a bank, which he located without a problem. He changed some money and in less than five minutes was back on the street. That everyone readily and eagerly addressed him in English assuaged his more practical concerns, but their ease with his language was also the source of a mild disappointment, as if by flying from one continent to another he still hadn't travelled very far after all. It almost seemed that in the more than forty years since he'd been anywhere, the world had collapsed in upon itself and cast off the variations of speech and manners and collective memory that attest to one society's distinctness from another. Something seemed watered down, as if no effort had been spared to render the local culture unthreatening to foreigners. Mingled with relief at finding himself in a safe corner of the world was this vague sense of having been cheated, lured abroad by the promise of difference only to find the differences puny indeed.

But this was not why he was here, and he wanted to move on to the purpose of his visit without further delay. At a newspaper kiosk he used these strange new euros to purchase a map of the island. He took a seat at an outdoor café, realizing he would very soon have to buy sunglasses and a cap with a visor. The waitress came (again, perfect English) as he was unfolding the map. He ordered a Greek coffee. He'd done no research and so the irregular crescent shape of the island, its mountainous interior, the zigzag pattern of roadways, were all pristine concepts, additions to this dazzling sense of newness. In a bookstore at home he had glanced through a bewildering array of travel guides, but faced with prices he judged excessive and by a near certainty that he would be engaging in little that required guidance—that, if the need arose, Rhonda (or someone) could show him around—he committed himself to none of them. He ran his finger along the island's concave eastern coast, established his current location, and then ascertained where he wanted to go, making a crude estimation of the overland distances with his eyes. Having arrived unprepared and uncertain of his motives, he now recognized his ambivalence for what it was. In his own mind his excuse for being here had lost a good deal of its plausibility. What could he possibly hold out to her that would be of any value? If his purpose was one of courtship, how could his clumsy embraces make the least difference, faced as she was with her own impending mortality? And if he thought he could offer a distraction from the miserable finale awaiting her, then he was surely granting his crusty personality too much credit as a source of amusement.

But despite a profusion of nagging doubts and a sensation in his stomach that was like wings flapping, he found himself a few hours later in a taxi heading south. Rhonda lived in Komi, a tiny beach settlement near the southern tip of the island. The village was not served by bus routes. So, once again taking the advice of the desk clerk, whose name was Christoph, McGowan accepted the services of a taxi driver. "My cousin Hector," Christoph assured him cheerfully, "is a very good driver." They headed inland, ascending steeply into the mountains, but after driving for no more than ten minutes Hector pulled over and pointed out his side window, making a camera gesture with his hands. McGowan had no camera but at Hector's urging he stepped from the car anyway. Maybe they were a few hundred feet up, McGowan wasn't sure, but the spectacle of land and sea caused the breath to halt in his throat. Far below them, blotting the landscape like paint splatter, was the town of Chios, its hustle and bustle silenced by the distance. The line of the sea was crisply drawn. Beyond the water lay the hulking mass of undulating terrain that was Turkey. Capping it all was the shimmering ever-cloudless sky. McGowan felt the sun on his back, the flaming intensity of its heat drawing perspiration instantly to the surface of his skin. A faint movement of air disturbed the small oval leaves of the trees, olive he guessed, that sprouted from the rocky soil. With one arm, Hector motioned grandly toward the panorama, as if showing off some personal creative triumph of which he was immensely proud. "Nice, eh?" he said. It seemed to be all the English he knew.

They set out again, but in a very short time were descending toward water and leaving behind the sparsely populated interior of the island. At an unmarked junction Hector veered sharply from the paved road onto a dirt lane that followed a straight line toward the sea.

Sleepy was the word for Komi, which appeared to consist of a single row of structures facing a pristine beach. McGowan had brought with him the photograph of Rhonda outside her house, and he'd had the foresight to explain to Christoph why he'd chosen this obscure village as his ultimate destination, reasons which Christoph had translated to Hector. But now that they were here, McGowan didn't know what to make of his chances of actually finding Rhonda. A few people tanning themselves on the beach raised their heads at the approach of the taxi, but their lack of interest was palpable. Nobody else was in sight. Hector took the photo into the open door of one building where some white plastic tables and chairs sat out front awaiting customers. But he came back shaking his head. For a few moments they both rested themselves against the taxi, staring past the beach into the distance. Hector lit a cigarette and offered one to McGowan. He shook his head.

"Well." He looked at his companion. "What should we do now?"

Hector smiled and nodded.

McGowan wiped the moisture from his brow and studied the photo, trying to tally the actual scene before him with the one pictured. He wondered now if this whole enterprise wasn't a preposterous miscalculation, a misguided and costly attempt by a lonely old man to recapture some vestige of his youth. He could see that he had never allowed the possibility of not finding Rhonda to intrude upon his blissful vision of what would take place once he got here. And what was more, he realized that he had shut his eyes and mind to an inescapable contingency: that her illness was incurable and that if it hadn't already killed or incapacitated her, it was sure to do so sometime in the months, or weeks, to come. He'd been stupid to entertain hopes of discovering in Greece some elusive Eden, and yet, even as he nodded in agreement with Yeats or whomever it was who'd said there is nothing in this world more foolish than the foolish dreams of a foolish old man, he could not find it within his heart to altogether abandon them.

He heard a voice. Hector turned and said a few words in Greek. A woman had emerged from the restaurant and called out to them as she hurried over. Hector snatched the photo out of McGowan's hand and gave it to the woman. She was young, forties perhaps, wearing all white. Dark hair. She spoke rapidly, as did everyone in this country. She gestured over her shoulder, toward the way they had come. Hector passed the photo back to McGowan and indicated that her business was with him.

"My husband," she said, her eyes flashing with annoyance. "He's an idiot." She pointed at the photo. "That American woman is here all the time. She lives in that house by the water. There is a dirt road. I told him how to get there. He will take you."

In a few minutes they were bumping along what was no more than a donkey track. The clamour of his heart was almost audible as it banged out a disorderly rhythm in his chest. She wasn't expecting him, so what would she say? Would she be angry? Maybe she already had someone in her life. Maybe she was only being polite when she suggested he visit. He glanced at Hector, the command to flee ready on his lips, but he could see by the grim set of the young man's jaw that there was no turning back.

It was the house in the picture, whitewashed with green shutters, sitting on a bluff exposed to the sea but shielded from view of the main road by a thick curtain of foliage. Sensing in his limbs that he was leaving civilization behind for good, he climbed stiffly from the taxi. Hector got out too and stretched himself. He lit another cigarette. McGowan approached the house, alert for signs of occupancy. Beneath his feet was sand and shoots of yellow grass struggling toward the sun. The house, a simple brick or cinder-block construction splashed with a veneer of mortar, had received its coat of white paint not long ago. The wood of the door and shutters was aged and weathered, but the green paint covering them was recent as well. He sensed Hector watching as he banged his knuckle against the door, making the whole thing clatter on its wobbly hinges.

He was truly sweating now, his body drenched and tingling.
"Rhonda?"

The door was not locked. He nudged it open and peered inside.
"Rhonda?"

The white tile floor gleamed. There was a heavy inner door, made of fine-grained wood with a dark lacquer finish, but this stood wide open. To the right was a living area, to the left a kitchen, straight ahead a steep wooden stairway. The door was ornamented with a bronze knocker. He banged this a few times, but there was no response.

He stepped back out into the sun. Meeting Hector's questioning gaze, he shrugged. He ached for this to be over, to no longer be standing around trying to guess how Rhonda would react to his unexpected presence. At this point he was willing to accept anything. Indifference, annoyance, even open hostility—any of these would be perfectly understandable. As long as Hector lingered within sound of his voice, an unobstructed path of retreat was available to him.

Waves breaking on a shoreline filled his ears with a rhythmic murmur. He followed the sound along a pathway worn through the undergrowth. This was possibly his last resort, the place where he would complete his search. He signalled to Hector and took off along the path, hobbling as fast as his legs would go. His canvas shoes were soon filled with sand. The path descended through rocky outcroppings toward a small crescent-shaped beach. He seemed to know, or miraculously to intuit, that she would be here, that the beach came in parcel with the house. He thought vaguely about having cancer and spending hours buck naked in the sun, wondered if it wasn't courting disaster or thumbing your nose at the fates. On the other hand, if you've already received a death sentence, what was the worst that could happen? He spotted her from a turn in the path that left him exposed on a rock overlooking the water. The waves striking the rocks showered him with spray and in the air was the briny reek of life. She wasn't naked. Reclining on a plastic beach lounge chair and reading a book, she wore a white dress that reached to her ankles, her arms concealed by long sleeves. Concealing most of her face was a broad-brimmed straw hat with a white ribbon around the dome. Large dark glasses. As he rounded the bend in the path and emerged onto the rock, she turned, distracted perhaps by his movements. But he wasn't sure she could see him. He looked up, trying to determine the angle of the sun. In a recurring fantasy he had watched the two of them sprinting across a grassy landscape and finally clasping each other in a passionate embrace. Utter nonsense. He carefully made his way down the path, watching for rocks and anything else that could trip him up. He heard her voice.

"David? Is that really you?"

When he reached the bottom she was approaching him. Her face told him nothing of what she was thinking.

"I was in the neighbourhood. Thought I'd drop by. See how you were."

Then she was standing no more than a foot away. She removed her glasses and her hat. Her thick hair, a pleasing fusion of silver and black strands, fell almost to her shoulders. Her expression was tender, and he saw she was as he remembered her, only browner, possibly thinner. The sudden realization that he was standing on a beach in Greece with a woman he loved erased from his mind any words he might have found to share with her. But the truth of the matter was that he hadn't really planned to say much of anything.

She was smiling.

"Well, you've come a long way. Aren't you even going to kiss me?"

He leaned over and positioned his lips against hers and felt, along with the delightful pressure of her response, an agreeable sensation of coolness. Her kiss was ardent, and he grew aware of her fingers caressing his neck. Then they parted and stood gazing at one another. For a moment their tongues seemed stilled by disbelief. Her features were not youthful, but it had come to him lately that youth was not what he was seeking. What did he need with youth, when the years had brought him his own fractured species of wisdom and a willingness to surprise himself? Her cool slate-grey eyes searched his features, for what he couldn't imagine. She was everything he wanted, but how did he appear to her, with his sunburnt face, his rumpled shirt, his bandy white legs protruding gracelessly from a pair of wrinkled blue shorts? Could she possibly overlook such grievous shortcomings?

The rhythm of the surf rolling along the beach returned to him like a song he couldn't forget, reminding him of the forces that had delivered him to this spot, taking the search for it out of his hands and leading him it seemed by the nose, as surely as a horse is led to water. He had tried to understand these forces, but there were too many unfathomables, too many questions that could never even be posed let alone answered. He had spent a good portion of his life utterly stationary, free of ambition or expressible needs, accepting payment in exchange for goods that people could have doubtlessly lived without. His wife and son were dead, his daughter had sought refuge at a far-away corner of the earth, and he was standing beside the sea transfixed by this dying woman's beauty, standing on a tiny, windswept island at the edge of the largest continent on earth. How was he supposed to assemble from these pieces a truth that he could live with?

He started to open his mouth, but Rhonda spoke first.

"Come," she said, taking his hand. "You must see the house."

In a short while he was in another car, speeding up a hill, heading once more into the mountains. The car, an ancient Toyota, belonged to Rhonda's English friend Gracie, who was driving. Rhonda sat beside her in front. McGowan had the back seat to himself. Their destination was a monastery situated at the exact centre of the island.

His first order of business was to pay Hector and see him off, but he'd hardly had a chance to drop his bag on the bed in the spare room before Gracie drove up, honking her horn and yelling, "Hallooo? Anybody home?" She was a tall, casually elegant Englishwoman, with a long nose, a peremptory manner, and a big floppy hat, who had evidently taken upon herself the task of organizing activities for her neighbour. But Gracie had charms of her own, and if either shock or dismay were part of her reaction at McGowan's sudden appearance, she hid it well.

"I finished my writing for the day," she declared to Rhonda after shaking McGowan's hand, "and I thought we'd go for a drive." She turned to him. "Of course, you're welcome to come along, Mr. McGowan."

"Thanks. Please call me David."

Rhonda left them for a moment and as McGowan followed Gracie out to the car she leaned in so close to him he could feel her breath. "You realize she's ill," she whispered.

"Yes," he said. "We're old friends."

"She's doing very well though," Gracie confided, giving him a look. Then, taking him altogether by surprise, she grasped his hand in both of hers. "It's quite a miracle she's alive." She nodded and scrutinized him keenly. "Quite a miracle."

In the car he watched the landscape drift by. Gracie chatted away to Rhonda and occasionally drew to his attention items of interest.

"These mastic trees, Mr. McGowan, don't grow anywhere else. They harvest the resin and make all sorts of things out of it. Gum and oil and whatnot. It's the island's biggest export."

"That so?"

"David knows all sorts of things like that," Rhonda interjected. "He's an encyclopedia on legs."

Picking up the thread, Gracie asked, "And what do you know about our humble little island, Mr. McGowan?"

"Not much," he admitted. "You'll have to fill me in."

"Did you know," Gracie went on, glancing at him in the rear-view mirror, "that Chios is the birthplace of the poet Homer?"

McGowan raised his eyebrows but said nothing.

"And...Mr. McGowan? Chios is also said to be where Christopher Columbus was born."

"I'm impressed," he said. It had suddenly come over him that he'd had little sleep the previous night and that he was very tired.

Rhonda had turned around and, resting her chin on the back of her seat, fixed him with a steady smile.

"What?"

"I'm so glad you're here," she said.

At the monastery, Nea Moni, they paid a small fee and proceeded through a gated entrance. The grounds were littered with loose stones. From the pamphlet McGowan learned that the original monastery had been constructed almost nine hundred years earlier, but in 1822 the Turks had crushed a rebellion by invading and sacking the island, murdering thousands. At Nea Moni they set fire to the buildings and slaughtered the entire population of monks. The year 1881 brought further destruction with a devastating earthquake. But each time the structure had been rebuilt and today it remained one of the world's most significant Byzantine monuments.

Rhonda linked her arm in his and together they toured the dilapidated chapel while Gracie chatted with some English tourists. When they re-emerged into the light Rhonda said, "You know, I never get tired of coming up here. The air has that serenity you only find in holy places. It's like you're breathing in the holiness. And when you look around you know they never gave up. Almost everyone was killed, and they never gave up."

"Do you want me to stay with you?" McGowan asked when she remained silent for a moment. "Because if you don't I can find somewhere else."

They shared a glance.

"Don't be silly."

Another pause preceded his next question. "How are you?"

She tugged on his arm. "Come over here," she said, deflecting his concern by drawing his attention to another small building. "I want you to see this."

She opened the door and led him inside. Judging by its appearance the room was a library: book-lined, filled with large rectangular tables encircled by chairs. The air was faintly musty. The stone floor had been worn smooth by thousands of feet.

She led him further inside. He found himself facing a tall wooden cabinet with glass doors. On the other side of the glass, arranged neatly on shelves in stacks and rows, were at least a hundred human skulls. Most of them lacked the lower jaw, which, he guessed, would have made stacking them easier. In some, a gaping hole had pierced the curved surface of the cranium.

"These are the skulls of the murdered monks," Rhonda explained.

McGowan could not remove his gaze from the grim display, at once a monument to a tragic past and a prescient reminder of what was in store for every man, woman, and child on the planet. To his amazement he felt an upsurge of tears overflow his eyes and dampen his cheeks. Annoyed, he rubbed them away with his fingers. Somehow, crazily, everything he'd ever been seemed to fuse with this moment. It was all here, from his years as an insecure teenager to his time overseas to his final days as the weary and disillusioned proprietor of a general store. Rhonda came to him and touched his wet cheek. She drew his mouth down to meet hers. They kissed, and along with the rhythms of an indomitable life force, her body conveyed to him a startling and invigorating euphoria. He caught himself thinking that some miraculous intervention had allowed them, together, to out-manoeuvre death.

Maybe he was just a sentimental old fool, but if he truly believed that being here completed a circle and transformed what was surely an ending into a beginning, then who could say he was wrong?

# THE UGLY GIRL

//

When I say Karla was ugly, I don't mean that she was plain, or homely. Or that she had a scar, or that she walked with a limp. Or that she had bad skin or rotting teeth or that she had fallen prey to some disfiguring illness. I don't mean to imply either that she was simply unattractive, in the sense that her features were not to my taste—that from another perspective or to someone else she might have appeared charming or even lovely. What I mean is that she was ugly, ugly in the innocent and helpless way that newborn babies or perhaps some tropical amphibians can be ugly. Ugly in a sense that speaks of the brutality of nature yet is in some strange way beguiling and even heartening.

Some things are so completely alien to us that they rouse a spirit of dread. We encounter them in our dreams and in daylight hours shudder at the recollection. Yet there is a familiarity about them that is truly frightening, almost as if we are gazing into a mirror and getting to know ourselves for the first time. The moment Karla entered my life I felt my hands tremble and my breath quicken. I suffered a seizure of distress and bewilderment, as if I'd just discovered that someone for whom I harboured a special regard had betrayed me. I lifted my gaze and studied her across the desk. She was one of my new students coming to see me for the first time, and I gawked at her with the mute transfixed stare of an imbecile. My back stiffened, and I felt the breath solidify in my lungs. The hair on my chest bristled. To my shame, I was unable to conceal my agitation. She saw my struggle, I am quite certain, and was perhaps amused, though she may have found it tiresome, I can't say for sure. Finally, I pushed the words up and out of my throat, asking what I could do for her, how I could be of help. Before opening her mouth to speak she drew in a long breath.

It was a winter unlike any other in my memory. The bad weather came early and thwarted my resolve to make peace with the circumstances of my life. My office had become a sort of refuge, occupying as it does a remote corner of a sprawling stone building with windows overlooking two sections of the campus. Its walls are lined with heavy oaken shelves and the wood itself has been treated with oil, possibly linseed, darkening the room to a sumptuous tone and leaving behind an aroma of turpentine and ancient eminence. I was working on a book, a study of modern poetry, in which I argued among other things that many young writers these days retreat too far into themselves, abandoning the traditional role of the poet, which is to disclose us to ourselves afresh, show us ourselves in a different light. By the time I met Karla I'd been stalled for weeks at a critical juncture in my argument and had despaired of ever getting started again. Day after day that autumn when I should have been writing I wasted my time watching the trees drop their leaves and litter the grass with the red, orange, and brown of their surrender. The barren trees speared the frozen sky and their tiny branches seemed to shatter the horizon. Out beyond the campus, the city where I made my home appeared puny and vulnerable. With the leaves gone I could even see the apartment building where I now lived, its brick facade set with rows of square windows like teeth and exposed in a defenceless way I'd never noticed before. Immediately beneath the window where I sat immersed in my pedagogical anguish, Karla clutched her books to her heart as she strode along with the meditative poise of one who has no conception of herself and no desire to hide anything. I was used to seeing her by now, and as always she paused here and there to engage in silent communion with nature. Other students walked by, saying nothing, greeting her with a stiff nod or else ignoring her completely. She may have had a social life and been acquainted with some of these people. I don't know. But for a long time she stood alone, watching the jittery antics of a squirrel. Possibly she suspected I was observing her, or that someone was observing her. But in her mind such things appeared to make no difference. People stared at her all the time. She seemed to understand that brazen curiosity and morbid fascination did not excuse rudeness, but she bore all this in a detached manner, as if it had nothing to do with her. When she met another's eyes and saw that person shrink away in the first instant of blind revulsion, she merely let her face relax into a smile—as she did that day in my office—drawing attention away from the initial moment of dismay and confusion.

Her ugliness was not apparent unless you got up close. With her back turned she looked the same as the rest of us.

My poetry seminar was not the only course she was taking, though she told me it was more important to her than the others. She came to see me often, but I tried not to get too involved and I had no desire to become someone she could depend upon, a mentor or a special friend. I did not want to become the object of her affection. After reciting the usual mundane pleasantries, our conversations normally focused upon her research, what paper or assignment she was working on now, or on poetry and what I thought she should read. I held strictly to my office hours and was often not available. I was chairing a university committee on academic planning and had a number of departmental activities to keep me busy. It was exactly what I needed, to be busy and distracted. But I was not busy enough.

Usually I look forward to the cool weather as a kind of stimulus, but this year before I had any chance to prepare myself the season turned from a warm dry autumn to the severest kind of winter. A cold drizzly shadow cast itself over the city and lingered there, spreading the sort of gloom that causes damage and ruins lives. I was spending more and more time alone, treading an aimless path here and there, my steps upon the damp pavement echoing back to me a strange and disquieting message of spiritual destitution and moral decay. One afternoon I found myself outside a local strip club, watching an intermittent but steady procession of gentlemen about my age—heads bowed, hands in pockets—slink through the door. With a shudder I hurried away from the scene of my almost crime and in my best leather shoes went for a vigorous hike through the park, following the twisted pathways, until many hours later I made my way home, sweaty and exhausted.

After our separation, my wife, Lisa, remained in the house with our two daughters, Sarah and Lucy. I made plans to live on my own, in the same spartan conditions that years before had distinguished my undergraduate days. My apartment offers few comforts, much like a downtown street on a chilly day when everything is shut up tight. But in the beginning I'd looked forward to the hours of solitude as one anticipates a lengthy respite from unwelcome pressures. Free of the distractions of a family, I would work on my book and finish it in record time.

I discovered, however, that after fifteen years of marriage my ability to tolerate my own company had been seriously impaired. Silence itself was an irritant—a constant childlike presence that plucked and grabbed at me until I was compelled to find some way to appease it. I had no television, so I switched on my radio and listened to its tinny whine. I opened windows to let in some noise, but not many sounds that are worth hearing make it all the way up twenty floors. These tactics did work for a while, allowing me to imagine that I existed at the hub of a busy creative community and that my efforts were part of a collective work in progress. But as the rains descended and I was forced to seal myself in against the weather, I discovered there was only myself and that I was alone and that I didn't like it. What else was there in my life now but four blank walls, a bed, a felt-tipped pen, and a stack of loose-leaf? I tried to concentrate my energy on the jumble of ideas in my head, to arrange them into sentences and preserve them on paper. But like a dimly recollected childhood memory, my argument had grown hazy and elusive, and then one day to my alarm began to seem untenable, even absurd. In a panic, I relocated my base of operation to my office, hoping that the company of colleagues and students—and the clutter and the smells and sounds of work continuing as usual—would make it possible for me to re-establish contact with my critical faculties. But no such connection took place. The leaves fell and someone came and gathered them up. Then for a week or two there was frost on the grass in the morning and rain most afternoons. I met Karla. After a while, I ceased my struggle and drifted into a routine of teaching classes and marking assignments, of waking and sleeping and dreaming. I became an animal with no inner life to speak of.

It was perhaps unfortunate that, other than my obligations to the university and to my students, I was not required to be at any particular place at a given time. I suppose this was a choice I made, but considering that I'd only recently abandoned any pretence of being an adequate husband or father, and had elected to relinquish the comforts of home and family rather than face an inevitable reckoning, I can't see how I could have done anything else. Very soon after moving out of the house I realized that my state of mind was too fragile to bear the strain of regular social interaction. I was behaving oddly, even by my own lenient standards. I sometimes remained in my office throughout the night, and there were many days when the only person I spoke to was the one staring at me from the mirror. I ate impulsively, almost by chance, selecting bruised fruit and wilted lettuce leaves from among the discounted leftovers at the student cafeteria or raiding the vending machines down from my office for coffee, pastries, and chocolate bars. Sometimes I wore the same clothes for several days in a row. I can't deny that I missed Lisa and Sarah and Lucy with a fierce longing that, when it took hold of my mind, pushed everything else aside until I could think of nothing but my own pain. But my conduct was not the sort of thing I wanted them to witness first hand. Several colleagues offered me advice—for it was quite evident I was "troubled"—and I was reminded of the role I'd spent years fashioning for myself: that of the scholar, the serious student of literature, the enlightened and responsible member of society whose opinions mattered. But I knew in my heart that when I stopped working on my book I became little more than an eccentric individual who had discovered a wealth of available time and who was accountable to himself and nobody else.

Outside it had grown dark. A mid-afternoon haze had lifted, leaving behind a high clear sky that was by this time dotted with stars. I'd earlier been toying with plans to go to a movie this evening, and had even leafed through the paper to see what was showing. But then Lisa had interrupted, calling to say she wanted to get together to discuss a few things. She proposed meeting for dinner, at some neutral site of course. I was surprised to be hearing from her and not from her lawyer—who would surely have advised against her contacting me—and wondered as we spoke if she was doing this on her own, without counsel, as it were. It would be like her to retain a lawyer and then ignore advice that made her feel confined, that set limits, erected barriers. There was something in her voice too—a quickening tremor, a penitent lilt—that told me she was puzzled by what had happened to us, emotionally frayed, and quite possibly smarting from the breakup. So I tried to remain open to suggestion, though I admit my conversation was guarded. After all, our mutual silence had by now extended over many weeks. I was not so far gone that I failed to see merit in talking, but I really had no idea what she was up to. I fully realized that we soon had to sort out our differences and arrive at an agreement. We were both living a temporary life, suffering the kind of stress that comes from not knowing what to do next, waiting to see if we would emerge whole or in pieces as if from some test of will. And though I'd become to a degree settled, I was not prepared to spend the rest of my life crammed with my belongings into a bachelor apartment, estranged from my own children.

But I suspected also that she was seeking to make the split permanent, and I was not convinced that our dispute was of such profound magnitude or so deeply irreconcilable. I was quite certain there remained common ground on which we could meet, though locating it on any map that I knew of would be a challenge. On the day I moved out, the air in our house had turned shrill with accusation, fraught with grievance. Her enumeration of my failings had been exhaustive and unforgiving. She counted my offences on stiff little fingers and, holding up her hands, showed me the result of her tabulation. She made me feel as if my very existence were a compromise. As if by leaving impressions of my feet in the carpet I was deliberately fostering an atmosphere of confrontation. This afternoon, as I listened to these initial attempts on her part to be reasonable, I felt on the contrary that I had every reason to be uncooperative. She had become an adversary and I could see only what she had deprived me of: my family, the pleasure of her company, the simple convenience of residing in a place I could call my own. And the decision had been hers; my offer to stay and try to work things out had been soundly rejected. I discovered at that moment, while speaking with her on the phone, that in miserly fashion I'd been hoarding my resentment all along, keeping it out of sight and mind, but letting it accumulate just the same. And so I informed her in a priggish tone that I was already doing something for dinner, but she was welcome to come down to my office to meet with me anytime she liked, though I couldn't guarantee that I'd actually be there. She made an angry noise and hung up.

Once outside I followed a familiar route, the meandering paths from building to building inscribed in my mind like figures etched in glass. I recalled with a certain fondness the ease with which I'd been filling my mornings and afternoons of late—the meetings with students, the discussions of research topics, the recommendations and proposals. I should have been left with a myriad of impressions with which to occupy myself over the supper hour. But instead, all that remained to me was the sound of Lisa's voice telling me to go to hell, the softly inflected tones turned ugly and hateful like piano keys being pummelled at random. To my surprise, I now found it easy to admit—if only to myself—that much of it was my doing, that her years with me had sucked the sweetness out of her and left a bitter rind. I'd always been much too selfish, setting family priorities according to my academic needs, quite happily leaving Lisa to explain my absence whenever something I considered more important suddenly called me away. Even when I was around, my mind was too often occupied by concepts that existed only in the abstract. Toward the end I developed a habit of reacting to attempts to bring me down to earth with peevish displays of temper. I remember seeing my two children tiptoe around the house, speaking to each other in whispers, watching television with the sound barely audible. I could scarcely believe it now, but at the time my behaviour had seemed to me perfectly reasonable.

Thinking back, I could still see Lisa's face as she once had been, her sensuous and eager smile, and feel her skin as I traced with my fingers the intricate web of creases encircling her eyes. I remembered what it was like to be married, to be warmed by the nearness of living creatures who were my own flesh and blood. I remembered the easy monotony of sex and sleep, the simple rhythms of a life lulled by certainty and repose. After months without these things, what did I want but solace? What did I need but a hand to grasp and eyes to tell me I was not, after all, deranged?

I clutched at the collar of my jacket. Tonight, the air had turned unnaturally cold; my breath clouded before me, and as I crept from one darkened building to another—seeking shadows like a fugitive— I found myself fighting back the humiliation of tears for the first time since the separation. It was the thought, I suppose, of this prison I'd constructed for myself, this contemptible bulwark of isolation that in my present disordered state I would defend with the last drop of blood in my body. I'd thought solitude was the cure, the very thing that would heal my soul. But any happiness it had provided had been purely delusional, any peace of mind fleeting. I'd conceived all sorts of illusions about myself, imagined reserves of strength and pillars of fortitude where in reality what existed were frailty and yearning. My failure to cope on my own was pathetic and quite obvious to anyone who cared to look.

I leaned into a sudden wind.

In the cafeteria Karla sat by herself, engrossed in some book or other. Students drifted in and out. Some spoke and laughed loudly, but most were intent on their studies or working on assignments. After getting some coffee and a cinnamon roll, I took a seat at the far end of the cavernous room, quite apart from Karla, who sat near a window. I had no trouble admitting that my own problems appeared trivial next to hers; that in fact they made me feel somewhat conceited and foolish for acting as if they were the stuff of tragedy. I was doing my best to come to terms with the situation but had so far been less than successful. Now I wanted to enlist Karla in my struggle. It was a selfish notion, full of hazards and promising severe embarrassment for everyone. But it seemed the right thing to do, which gives an indication of how far I'd strayed from the rational logic of everyday life.

Watching her from this private vantage point, hidden among the crowd, I was struck by something ethereal, an ambience of unearthliness that enclosed her and kept myself and the rest of my world safely at a distance. She was gravely calm, detached, as if living this life were something she did incidentally, in her spare time. She seemed to desire nothing, from me or anyone else. It was so strange, I wanted desperately to get to the bottom of it. And so, as I sat taking my last bite of cinnamon roll and thinking maybe I should have another, I began in my mind a curious process by which Karla was transformed from a mere student into an angel of deliverance, sent to earth to rescue me from the depths to which I'd sunk.

I gave Karla an 'A' on her first paper, and also on her subsequent assignments. Whether or not she actually deserved these marks I don't know, because I didn't read anything she passed in. I couldn't bring myself to deal directly and honestly with this game I was playing, the rules of which I made up as I went along. I'm not even certain what I hoped to accomplish by any of this, other than to satisfy an earnest craving for her to like me and trust me in ways that a few weeks earlier I would have discouraged and recoiled from in breathless horror. I suppose she already did like me, but only in the sense that as a student she had no problem approaching me whenever she wished to discuss something. I wanted more than this. I found it distressing to think she could exist independently, that she could go about her daily tasks and not want at odd hours to confide in me, that there were not times when she wished she knew more about me. I found it difficult to accept that I was just one of many people who touched glancingly upon the fringes of her life for a few moments each week but who left no lasting impression. Why this should have mattered so much, I can't say. I was not seeking any physical union between us because, in pure truth, I still found her grotesquely unattractive, though much less so than on our first meeting, the initial shock having dissipated. So my motives were hardly clear, even to myself. I seemed to be giving in to any urge that arose, allowing my actions to be driven by nothing more substantial than waves of feeling. Residing at the back of my mind throughout this period was an image of Lisa and I reunited and living together harmoniously with our daughters as we had for many years, restored to the settled comfort of willing cohabitation, resigned to each other's weaknesses and oddities. This remained my ultimate goal, I believe, though I did manage to lose sight of it upon occasion. How Karla was supposed to aid in the attainment of this goal is a mystery, for I rarely thought beyond the present moment, and I never gave even perfunctory consideration to the effect my behaviour was having on her.

On the surface nothing changed at all. Karla attended class, made her contribution, passed in her assignments, and went away. When we spoke, she never referred to the grades I'd given her, or to the fact that I'd made no comments or corrections on her latest paper. Now and then I tried to steer the conversation away from schoolwork and around to matters of greater and more profound consequence to us both—her future, for example, or my quarrel with Lisa—but subtle inquiries and casual remarks had little impact. The surface of her serenity remained untroubled. With a kind of studied indifference she remained impervious to my attempts to probe the inner workings of her spirit or to coax her to move in the direction I wished her to go. She gave nothing away, asked nothing of me. The only progress I can report at all came one afternoon when, as she was leaving my office, I offered to accompany her on her walk home, or wherever she was going. It was a question asked in all innocence, for I had no plans whatsoever and merely felt a need for some fresh air and a bit of physical activity. But the confusion that flashed across her face was piteous, and I was left with the impression—as she declined and hurried away—that until this day nobody had ever presented her with such an offer. I may have been wrong, but this did appear to be something upon which I could build: I'd glimpsed a part of her that I'd never before been permitted to see. In that instant the defences had melted away and she'd revealed more of herself than in the previous two months combined. A kind of perverse delight swept over me, for not only had I been given to understand that my objective, which was to get close to her, was a practical one—I'd been granted a valuable clue how to go about attaining it. Of course, my elation was tinged somewhat with regret. I'd obviously caused her distress, and I suffered some uneasiness over whether or not I may have driven her away for good.

As it turned out, I worried needlessly. In a short time, Karla was again in my office and we quickly settled into a now familiar routine: I would ask a few questions that touched upon personal matters, and she would avoid answering them. Then we would talk about poetry. But I was no longer discouraged by this. The little I'd glimpsed had given me hope. Emboldened by renewed confidence, I expected that in time I would be permitted to see more.

Christmas was a dreary affair. I spoke to Lisa once or twice concerning gifts for the children, hinting strongly as I did so that I was available for dinner that day and would very much enjoy and appreciate being invited home. When she played ignorant, coyly evading the point, I apologized for my snippy behaviour the last time we'd spoken and asked if I could spend the afternoon with Sarah and Lucy on Christmas. She said I could talk to them on the phone. When I suggested that it was not fair of her to deny my request, she hung up. I did some half-hearted shopping, but in the end gave the money I'd saved to one of the young women in the office and asked her to buy things that would be of interest to two girls, aged twelve and fourteen. On Christmas Eve I took the packages over to the house in a taxi, ready to leap into the role of extravagant father and play it to the hilt.

Nobody was home. The magnitude of my disappointment left me almost tearful. Clearly, I should have called before coming over. But, damn it, today was Christmas Eve! I was still a member of this family. They should have been waiting for me. Was Lisa expecting me not to bring presents? Did she really believe I would allow our disagreement to spoil the holidays? Or that I'd forgotten? I knew it was the last minute. But that's how I dealt with Christmas every year and I'd never heard her complain before. Did she think I was going to change now?

I let myself in and waited for nearly an hour, spending the time examining the interior of the house as if it were a text I was going to have to interpret before a class. The photo of Lisa and I from our wedding remained in its place on the dresser. This was something of a comfort, indicating—or so I thought—that I was still very much a part of her life, if just for now. My inspection took me through each room. I didn't realize until after I'd started that I was actually conducting a systematic and detailed search. An odious thought had crept into my mind, and I understood that my greatest fear was of stumbling across evidence of an infidelity—such as unfamiliar men's shoes in the closet or a strange brand of aftershave in the bath-room—something I could neither deny nor excuse. When I was done, and had discovered nothing, the relief that swept over me with the realization that she had not thrown me out in order to accommodate some other arrangement was almost tangible. I felt a new buoyancy lighten my step and in celebration I brewed a pot of coffee. I realized that Lisa's problem was mostly with me personally, with my sloppy lifestyle and befuddled ways. If she'd ever been inclined to seek out someone else in order to gratify emotional or sexual needs that I'd neglected or to which I'd failed to respond, I'm sure she would have done so before now. Certainly, I'd never been aware of harbouring any suspicions of such a sordid nature, though I suppose the thought could have arisen at some point and been thrust to the back of my mind where it would have lain untouched and forgotten. I often did that with things I didn't want cluttering up my head, like appoint-ments with doctors or social engagements with people I didn't like. This was one of Lisa's foremost complaints about me.

The Christmas tree stood in the same corner of the living room where we always placed it, and I couldn't help but wonder who had dragged it in from the car this year and rigged it up in the stand. The table was set for dinner (for three), and a thawing turkey sat in the roasting pan in the refrigerator. I'd enjoyed a few moments of euphoria, but my mood began once again to darken when I came across two small wrapped parcels on a shelf near the front door and addressed to me in adolescent script as "Daddy." I'd picked up a few simple things for Lisa—some soap, earrings, a box of chocolates—and had dropped them in with the presents for Sarah and Lucy. But evidently Lisa had seen fit to get me nothing. I felt a demented urge to rummage through the bags for Lisa's gifts and retrieve them, per-haps return them to the store and get the money back, or maybe give them to someone else. To do this, however, would have been petty and would have defeated my purpose in coming here, which was to appear magnanimous. Besides, I was beginning to sense that maybe

I should get moving before they returned from wherever they'd gone. For one thing, I'd lost track of my coffee cup, which Lisa would sniff out and which would make her suitably irate. This was another of the things she detested about me. As well, I was no longer certain I could count on myself to behave in a reasonable fashion once she turned on me her disapproving eye. I had no desire for the girls to witness anything I'd later regret.

As I prepared to go—deliberating over whether to leave a note, deciding in the end not to—I spent a few minutes looking the tree up and down. A spiteful notion had invaded my head, slithering up from some dark recess in my heart and filling my mouth with an acrid tingle. Lisa always took such elaborate care decorating the tree, and with an aesthetician's eye would balance colour and light and texture to great effect. This year was no different (which also troubled me—so much remained the same while so much had suffered irreparable damage). I examined the tree closely, searching for the one ornament I knew she treasured above all the others, a plain red glass ball that I'd purchased for her at no inconsiderable expense from a street vendor. Years ago, before we had any children, we'd taken a trip through the southern states, and in our wanderings through one small town came across an amateur artisan peddling home-fashioned glassware in front of an abandoned movie theatre. He sang a Christmas carol for Lisa in the midday heat, and as a reward I bought the most expensive and delicate piece he had to offer. Ever since, it had occupied a privileged position on each of our Christmas trees. When I located it, I lifted it gently from the tree limb, dangling it by its nylon string, then held it cupped in my hands. The glass was thicker at the bottom than the top, and the shimmering burgundy swirls and tiny oval bubbles proved that it had indeed been crafted by hand and was probably unique and worth a great deal more now than it had been when I bought it. I then watched, as if at one remove, as I let it slip from my fingers and tumble down the side of the tree. It smashed against the floor with a muted explosion, sprinkling fine shards about in a polite and graceful manner.

Having now struck back where it was likely to hurt, I waited, hoping to savour the full essence of this act of retaliation, the only one I'd so far allowed myself. I expected the warm and pleasurable radiance of contentment to embrace me and a voice from somewhere to congratulate me on my ingenuity. Or, I assumed, at any rate, that I'd at least feel free to emit a brief chuckle of satisfaction as Lisa's perplexed and wounded response played itself out in my imagination. But nothing of the sort happened. Instead, with my thoughts in chaos and my stomach rioting at the irretrievable horror of what I'd done, I gathered up the presents from Sarah and Lucy and quickly left the house to walk the two or so miles back to my apartment in the crisp winter air. On the way I decided I would stop at a nearby liquor outlet so that for the next few days I could stay safely bombed and not have to think about what I'd let myself in for.

Shortly after Christmas I was served with divorce papers. I suppose I should have seen it coming and done something to prepare myself, or else tried to persuade Lisa that reconciliation was still possible. There were likely a number of routes I could have followed, each one pointing away from divorce as the next logical, inevitable, step. But I did nothing. I held myself aloof from the entire business, as if it were someone else's problem and no concern of mine. I did emerge from my pit of agony long enough to make contact with my family over the holidays, but only briefly and only by phone. Sarah and Lucy each thanked me for the presents, and for this I was grateful. But, far from providing comfort, their voices cut me with a shy formality of tone, evidence, I could see, that they had been quite unwilling to speak to me at all and had likely been browbeaten by Lisa into making this gesture, either out of compassion or for the sake of propriety. Whatever the case, the conversation left me shaken and morose. After only a few months I'd become a stranger to them. I'd allowed myself to drift to the periphery of their young lives and was now someone—like the pious neighbour or senile aunt—to whom a reluctant show of gratitude is made in the hope that it will satisfy some obligation but also discourage them from trying to get any closer.

My own life seemed squeezed into tiny crevices, stuffed into the cracks between larger, weightier issues. Neither my time nor my thoughts were my own. I wanted with a desperate longing to start writing again, because that's what I was supposed to be doing all along and it's what always brought me into contact with myself. I felt also that I needed a vacation—a suggestion that had initially been broached by my department head, who handled me now with the sort of exaggerated delicacy usually reserved for combustible materials—but feared that if left on my own for too long I'd be tempted toward a more drastic and conclusive course of action. As a survival tactic, I maintained a rigorous teaching schedule and as well continued to meet with Karla, and other students too, on a regular basis.

I did not try to contact Lisa.

Eventually, circumstances forced me to hire a lawyer and to appear against my will at a number of tedious meetings. I tried to approach all of this casually, firm in my belief that, though it may scar me and lay me low, it would surely not destroy me. But when, at the close of a lengthy and disheartening procedural song and dance, I finally encountered Lisa—seated at that smooth, flawlessly gleaming consultation table, looking vigorous and young and trim, and accompanied by her youthful female lawyer who appeared equally flush and healthy—I could not see otherwise but that I was exposing to the harsh light of impartial scrutiny my rumpled drabness and mouldy academic disarray. I almost wept to think that she was going to such exhausting lengths to disentangle herself from me. After the meeting, in which I agreed to all her terms and conditions—I wished only to escape and get back to my office—she came up to me and we spoke alone and face to face for the first time since the day I moved out.

"How are you, Barry?" she asked, formal but not frosty.

"How do you think I am?" I asked in return, no longer certain how to behave in her presence. My peevish retort made her shake her head.

"You should get some help," she suggested earnestly, her brow creased. "Is there anyone you can talk to?"

I almost asked if she was offering, but wisely reconsidered. Being facetious now would win me no points and was unlikely to generate long-term good will between us.

"We'll see," I told her, and managed a weak smile.

Even at my most grief stricken and remorseful, I'd never imagined it ending like this, with the two of us facing each other in a sterile courthouse corridor, speaking in that artificial manner of people who were once friends but who now realize they have nothing in common. It seemed incredible to me that this woman, with whom I could barely bring myself to make eye contact, had been my wife for more than fifteen years.

"I'll see you sometime. Okay?"

How do you wind up a life together? What words bring a period of profound intimacy to a fitting and dignified conclusion? I suppose I wanted her to apologize, or at least to make a display of sympathy even if she felt nothing in her heart. She could see what a wreck I was. She could see how this affair had twisted the gumption out of me and left me shell shocked and bewildered. I felt myself standing before her, teetering on the edge, wondering if she would catch me.

"Okay," I said.

We left it at that. I watched her walk away, joined by her lawyer, and distinctly heard the word "lunch" spoken by one of them. Who, I wondered, could have an appetite for food after this?

Lisa rounded the corner and disappeared from view without once looking back.

Suddenly I found myself surrounded by strangers, a sea of them; each and every one a face I didn't know. Their eyes skimmed the surface of me but seemed unable to probe deeper, a sign, I hoped, that I would survive this, the worst life had to offer. As if from miles away hundreds of footfalls formed a clattering echo in my head, I heard phones ring and doors slam, and a multitude of voices drifted over and swarmed around me, not one of them speaking words I was meant to hear. It seemed another realm, and I realized all at once it was precisely that: the realm of the living. I remained where I was for a few moments, just to gather strength. But then I began to notice an expression of uneasiness settle into the faces of the men and women who approached where I stood, noticed too that they were all following the same wide arc around me, as if I were an obstacle placed mischievously in their path or a reminder of some unpleasant thing they would rather not think about. So with a decisive movement, my first in quite some time, I pulled on my gloves and headed off in a direction that seemed, more or less, the right one to take.

I may have misjudged Karla and the role she was to play in my life, but I have to believe my attempts to communicate caused her no harm. I realize I may have pushed for a degree of intimacy that was never meant to exist and that would have left her shaking her head, regarding me as mad, had I told her what I was thinking. But we did manage to pull each other through. We spoke often and at length, using the obscure and arcane idiom of literary analysis to express the suffering we shared. I believe she was sympathetic to my grief. And I know she suffered each day the burden of her ugliness, of attracting attention for the wrong reason, of seeing people ogle her and turn away, ashamed and dumbfounded. We never discussed it. But the reality of it was there every time our eyes met. I admit, certain of her features were not unattractive—her full lips, the blue eyes set far back in her head, the delicately recessed chin—but they worked against rather than with each other. The totality was unsettling if you were not accustomed to it. But I began at an early stage to read this face in terms of the message it conveyed rather than its immediate effect. With not much effort at all, I was able to redirect my attention beyond the physical—which had no literal meaning anyway—and reach in toward some essential crux of her, wherein everything of consequence would reside. As a teacher of literature I suppose I place too much store in lofty interpretations and seek nuances of meaning where simple reality sits obdurate and brooding, steadfast in its lack of meaning. I want to believe, however, that Karla was not simply a fetish, that I did not fasten myself to her as a convenient means of steadying myself upon the shifting foundation of my life at that moment. I want to believe that she was someone whose welfare would have mattered to me regardless, that our shared interests would have brought us together under any circumstances. But the fact is that we met at a time when I was being taught a painful lesson in the volatile nature of human relationships, and I clung to her and her message of serenity at the heart of chaos as if my life depended on this message being true. Perhaps it did.

After the divorce became final I felt a mantle of oppression slip away. For many months I'd been sustaining myself on the meagre hope that something of my former life could be salvaged. But now that I'd been forced to recognize that dream for what it was, I was shocked by how easily I could open my hand and let it go. It was, after all, a tuft of smoke, a shadow with only scant traces of actuality holding it together. And so I entered a new phase. Quite suddenly, certain things didn't matter so much. I waited a few weeks after our disastrous meeting at the courthouse and then phoned Lisa. Our conversation was in every way amicable. I was not in the least deterred when she began teasing me about some of my old habits, because all of those things belonged to the past. When I confessed what I'd done to the Christmas ornament, she said only that she'd cried when she found it. In a strange way, talking like this, I felt closer to her now than at any point during the past year or so. But I harboured no illusions about us getting back together. That too belonged to the past.

I read Karla's assignments in earnest and found that she deserved the marks I'd been giving her. There was little time for us to meet now, because she was studying for exams and also preparing to transfer to another school. I decided not to talk with her about what she meant to me, about how I'd derived sustenance from her strength of character. I was unable to conceive of a simple utterance that would adequately describe the magnitude of my debt without making me seem harebrained or juvenile or, even worse, insincere. So I remained silent in the hope that I'd managed to make a gift of something meaningful in return, even if it was only a warm office in which to relax and escape the annihilating grip of winter.

My book took care of itself. One day I realized I had an idea. I wrote it down. From then on the flow maintained itself with little abatement, almost as if my brain had all along been labouring at the problem at a subterranean level I'd not been aware of, some profound and remote depth of myself I'd never before had the wit to tap into.

In the cafeteria, Karla sat with a group of people. This was the first time I'd noticed her in the company of others. I'd intended to return to my office, but now felt compelled to stay and observe what was going on for a few moments. I got my coffee and took my newspaper to a seat near a window, where the spring sun cast its warmth full upon me. I recognized in Karla's group a few from the poetry class and some others who I was fairly certain were English majors.

One girl appeared especially striking, with an anaemic complexion and a long sheaf of glossy black hair pouring down her back like tar. I'd never seen her before. Karla seemed to be concentrating her own attention on the book she'd laid out before her on the table, sipping quietly at her juice or tea or whatever. When she spoke, her remarks were addressed to the young man seated next to her, though the others tended to listen in. In a moment, they were all laughing. Wishing to conceal my curiosity, I barricaded myself behind my newspaper. Eventually my attention wandered and I began to idly gaze out the window, listening still, trying to keep their voices distinct in my head from other background noises, the general chatter and clamour of eating. Outside, people walked the concrete pathways. The snow had by now melted and seeped into the earth, leaving it mushy and unreliable, and the grass had that sick straw-coloured look about it that made you think it was too much to hope that it would ever turn green. The sky hung distant, radiant, clear—rippling like a curtain disturbed by a breeze. Down near the cluster of evergreens that defined the heart of the campus a young couple walked along, hand in hand, talking, unhurried. Lisa and I had met this way, on a college campus, many years ago. We'd taken our share of midday strolls, cheerfully neglecting our studies, immersed in each other and what we perceived as our future together. I was amazed to think that we had actually lived that future and that now it was over.

In the brief moment of my distraction the others had left and Karla and her young man were now alone, speaking together in low tones, intimately involved in their conversation, aware of nothing but each other. Karla's face appeared lit as if by a fever, her eyes large. Beneath the table they held hands.

I left them and went outside, where the motionless air still bore traces of our last winter freeze. But this would pass very soon, possibly by tomorrow or the next day.

I found the path I wanted and set out across campus.

# ON THE BEACH

//

There were six apartments, three stacked up on either side of the building. We lived in the basement, though I'm sure that if anyone were to ask, my mother would tell them we were on the ground floor because it sounded better. Our windows were right at eye level and they looked out over dirt and grass and the little brick wall that hid the yard from the street. An old lady named Hazel lived across from us with a dozen cats and she was always complaining to anyone who would listen about leaks and smells and noise and bugs and anything else she could dream up to complain about. My mother said she was crazy and no damn wonder the place smelled and that we should keep clear of her. But it wasn't easy when she lived right across the hall.

Not too long after we moved in we woke up in the middle of the night because of someone yelling.

"What's that?" Julie moaned.

"I don't know." I rolled over and stared up at the ceiling waiting for it to stop. The security lights from the parking lot washed our whole room in an eerie subterranean glow.

I lay there thinking that my mother would be mad. She was always saying that people were stupid and ignorant when they yelled at each other or played loud music at two in the morning. It was one of the reasons we'd moved from our last apartment; there was always noise of one sort or another. Finally my mother said she'd had enough, she had to get out of there before she murdered someone. So we moved down the street to a building that someone told her was quiet. But it was only a week later and already the people and their noises were back. It was like they were following us and we were never going to get away from them.

My mother opened the door and stuck her head in our room.

"You kids sit tight. I'm putting an end to this right now."

"Mom!"

I got out of bed and followed her to the living room, but she was already out the door. During a pause in the yelling I heard her slippered feet thumping the wooden stairs.

It was a man's voice. I couldn't make out any words, even when I went into the hall and up three or four stairs. The hall was empty and faintly lit by a bare bulb that hung from the ceiling on a wire.

My mother was pounding on the door.

"Will you be quiet in there? People are trying to sleep!"

I came around the landing and up a few stairs until I saw my mother, wearing her housecoat and her fuzzy slippers, slapping the door with the flat of her hand. This was the only noise now. Everything else had gone still and silent. I noticed the door across the hall was open just a crack.

"I'm going to complain! You'll be sorry then! I'm warning you, I'll get you tossed out of here...."

There was clattering and banging from inside, then a crash like something overturning and shattering on the floor. Then voices and some cries.

The door opened.

"You crazy bitch! I'm Jesus bleeding!"

My mother moved aside just in time. A man with long straggly hair backed out of the apartment. He had on a plaid shirt with none of the buttons done up. The buckle of his belt was undone too. I could see something in his hand that I thought was a knife but turned out to be glasses with wire frames that he was trying to unfold and fit over his face.

A woman's voice said, "You're breaking my heart."

"Fuck!"

My mother just stood there. I couldn't see her expression from where I was. The door across the hall was closed now.

The woman emerged from the apartment while the man fumbled first with the glasses and then with the buttons on his shirt like he couldn't decide which was more important. She was very thin in a short gauzy nightgown and she held a carving knife in her left hand.

My mother took a few steps back and I shifted my position to stay behind her out of sight. I'd never seen anything like this before in my life. It was almost as good as TV.

The man turned sideways to the wall and stooped over to shield himself as the woman approached him with the knife. High up on his forehead a small gash was seeping blood.

"Get away from me, Rachel!"

"Why don't you say hi to the neighbours, Gerry?" She turned to my mother. "This is Gerry. He's leaving now."

He looked at her. He'd finally gotten his glasses on.

"You're fucking crazy."

She turned abruptly and ran back into the apartment. Gerry straightened himself and watched her, and I could see something like hope flash across his face, like he was thinking maybe she wasn't kicking him out after all, that he still had a chance to make things good between them.

But this only lasted for a second. He had to be quick to jump out of the way when something big and black flew out the door and hit the wall where he'd been standing. My mother flinched.

"Jesus, watch it! I paid a lot of money for that."

He picked it up and started pulling it on. It was a leather jacket.

"I've had enough of this crap. You can keep the booze and the fucking pizza coupons."

He pulled some keys from the pocket. There was blood all down the side of his face and he kept dabbing at the wound with his fingers as if checking to make sure it was still there. Rachel watched from the doorway, her eyes cold, her features rigid. She was smoking a cigarette now, but her other hand still gripped the knife and I could see the tip of it sliding up and down against the doorframe.

"You're an asshole, Gerry."

He didn't answer. But as he made his way along the hall to the front door he said, "You're crazy, Rachel. You're out of your sick fucking mind."

He disappeared down the flight of stairs and I heard the door open and close. Rachel stood completely still in the doorway except for when she raised her hand to place the cigarette between her lips. She drew the smoke into her lungs, lifted her chin, and calmly expelled the smoke into the hallway where it rose and collected around the light. My mother didn't move or do anything, and I hardly dared to even breathe. I felt like I was watching a play and waiting for the next line of dialogue.

The silence was broken by the deep-throated revving of a motorcycle. He gave it some gas and cranked it again and again, probably more times than he had to. Then I heard the roar as it shifted into gear and hit the road. The sound droned into the distance and then everything was quiet again.

Rachel shook her head.

"What an asshole," she muttered, hardly moving her lips.

"Are you okay?" my mother asked, taking a cautious step forward, as if Rachel's comment had broken a spell. Rachel still held the knife, though I got the feeling the threat of her actually using it on someone had passed. When she finally glanced toward my mother it was with a lazy vagueness that made me think she'd forgotten that other people could see and hear what she was doing. In only a minute the muscles of her face had lost their tautness. Her whole manner seemed hazy and out of focus.

"We sure made a lot of noise, didn't we?" she said, and then giggled.

"A bit. Yes."

"What time is it?" Rachel asked in a panicky voice, all at once very concerned. She looked at her wrist as if she expected a watch to be there. "What time is it?"

She hurried back into the apartment, taking the knife with her. My mother followed as far as the door, but when she turned to look in she spotted me crouched on the stairway. Her expression grew stern as she marched toward me mouthing, "What are you doing here?" and gesturing for me to go back downstairs.

But then Rachel was at the door holding a bottle and saying, "I'm celebrating. You want a drink?"

I almost think my mother was tempted by the offer and that only the late hour and the fact that I was there to see prevented her from going into Rachel's and joining the festivities. She eyed me narrowly, as a warning, and said, "Not tonight, thanks." We started down the stairs.

"Hey, but maybe later. Okay?"

My mother called back, "Just keep it down. I've got children. We're trying to sleep."

She pressed her hand against my back, urging me along as we rounded the landing.

"I'm sorry about the noise!" Rachel called after us. "Hey, I'm really sorry!" And then, following a brief pause, she hollered, "Hey, everybody, I'm sorry about the noise! I'm really sorry about all the fucking noise!!"

She slammed her door so hard the whole building trembled.

My mother pushed me into our apartment.

"What do you think you're doing?" she hissed. "Those people are dangerous! You could have been killed!"

I didn't say anything. I just hung my head and waited for her to send me off to my room, which she did after taking a minute or so to tell me how stupid I was. Julie asked me what happened and I said I'd tell her about it in the morning.

But I was too hot and excited to sleep—greasy with sweat and not tired at all. I put my hand on my chest and felt my heart thumping, its rhythm galloping out of control. In my mind I replayed the quarrel that had just taken place, letting myself imagine the events leading up to the confrontation my mother and I had witnessed. I saw furniture overturned, curtains ripped from windows, ashtrays and lamps flung the length of a room, heard voices raised in fury and terror. I fell asleep after a while, still listening to Rachel and Gerry fight it out, watching the blood pour from his wound and her sneering smirk of demented satisfaction as he escaped down the hall.

I still didn't like these people and I planned to avoid them whenever I could, but it seemed a wonderful place to live, with crazy neighbours and someone whose life was high drama living right upstairs. What would happen next? I wondered.

And then what came into my mind was that I'd never find out because we were probably going to be moving again very soon.

The next morning came earlier than usual, or so it seemed. Rain pelting against the window woke me up. It was still raining while we sat around the kitchen table. Julie and I ate our cereal while my mother sipped her coffee and nibbled on a piece of plain buttered toast. None of us spoke. It was just after seven-thirty and the radio was turned low; the weather forecast was for more rain, days and days of it. "April fucking showers," I heard my mother say once. Only it wasn't April, it was May. People were walking around overhead, and I saw my mother glance upward when the treads became frequent and vigorous, as if someone had decided to practice their dance steps. But she didn't seem annoyed so much as completely wrung out.

The dreamy glow I'd felt from last night's events had dimmed. Instead of revelling in the strangeness of it all, I felt a heaviness weighing down my limbs and dulling my thoughts from knowing that we'd have to listen to more fights and more yelling, day after day and night after night, until we finally packed up and left this building for good. I couldn't imagine where we'd go from here, and I could sense within me a growing resentment toward these people who seemed to think they had every right to impose their undisciplined lives and obnoxious habits upon others at any time of the day or night. All we wanted was a quiet place where we could sleep and read and eat and watch TV in peace, and it didn't seem to me that something so simple should be so difficult to find. But since moving out of our house we'd had to put up with parties that spilled into hallways, loud music all night long, screaming and fighting at two a.m. It had already forced us out of one building and into another. But what bothered my mother the most was that nobody seemed to care; not the superintendents, who were supposed to make the tenants behave, and certainly not the people responsible for the noise.

I looked at her. She noticed my glance and smiled.

"Sleep well?" she asked.

"No."

She shrugged.

"Neither did I."

I knew she couldn't do anything to help the situation, but still her indifference stung.

Then she said, "Is that someone at the door?"

I hadn't heard anything. Julie and I both turned to look, as if we expected the door to open on its own.

"I'm sure I heard something," she said as she got to her feet. She smoothed her housecoat and fiddled with her hair briefly before peeking into the little hole that magnified people's heads so they looked big and round like beach balls.

I heard a knock, a scraping sound really, small and tentative.

My mother sprang back from the door.

"You two—" she snapped her fingers at us and pointed— "go to your room! *Now!*"

"But Mom—"

"*Just do it!*"

Her eyes were huge and her normally soft voice boomed the way it did when she wanted us to know she meant business. We got up and shuffled the short distance down the hallway. Julie was snuffling like she was going to start crying any second. She whimpered, "I didn't do nuffin'."

Behind us I could hear my mother pulling back the chain and unbolting the door.

Julie plopped down on her bed and screwed up her face for a good bawl. I hung back and swung the bedroom door until it was almost closed. I put my finger to my lips and motioned for her to be quiet.

By now the apartment door was open all the way and my mother was discussing something with someone in a low voice. I couldn't catch any words, but her tone was rock-hard and no-nonsense. She stood with one hand on the doorknob, the other firmly on her hip, and spoke to the person around the partly open door. I couldn't see her face.

I turned to Julie.

"Shhhh. Come here and see this."

She lowered herself off the bed and joined me at the door of our room. Her eyes were puffy and she snuffled loudly.

We watched as my mother opened the door all the way to let someone in.

"Who is it?"

"It's that woman from last night, the one who lives upstairs."

Rachel came in, directing a timid smile toward my mother and wiping her nose with the back of her hand. My mother shut the door and invited her to take a seat at the kitchen table. She took the box of tissues from the counter and placed it on the table in front of Rachel, who pulled one out and blew her nose. My mother leaned forward and said something, then reached out her hand and touched Rachel on the shoulder. Rachel nodded.

Rachel was wearing jeans and a knitted sweater that was so big the sleeves swallowed up her hands. Her feet were bare and she sat daintily with her heels off the floor and her toes bent forward. She'd pulled her mousy hair up and fastened it with a barrette, but it was a messy job: clumps stuck out all over.

My mother came down the hall to our room.

"C'mon out, kids, and meet our neighbour."

She said this in her normal voice, but as we followed her up the hall she whispered over her shoulder just loud enough for us to hear, "Be nice."

In the kitchen she stood off to the side and presented us to our guest. Rachel smiled broadly, as if she'd never seen anything so cute in all her life.

"Rachel Mae Wheeler, this is Julie, and this is Sara."

"Hi," she said. She didn't stand up or offer to shake hands or anything. There were alarming grey shadows beneath her eyes and she clutched the tissue in her fist as if there was something folded up inside it that she was going to need, something that would save her life if she could only hang on to it.

I tried to smile.

"Hi."

Julie stared at her and didn't say anything.

Rachel twined her fingers together and, looking serious, lowered her eyes.

"I just came by to say sorry about last night, all the noise and everything." She smiled weakly. "It won't happen again."

"It wasn't so bad," I said.

"But I woke you up," she countered adamantly, as if I'd tried to argue with her. "It's not right. Children need their sleep. I know that. I have a daughter. She doesn't live with me, but I have one."

She shook her head and raised her face to my mother. There were tears in her eyes.

"I'm so sorry," she whispered, and then choked something back into her throat. She covered her eyes with her hand and bent her head down and wept silently.

Julie and I just stared. I'd never seen any adult except my mother really cry before, and it made me feel guilty and panicky all at once, like I'd done something to cause it even though I knew I hadn't. My mother seemed embarrassed, and after a moment or two she tried to distract us by organizing us for school, retrieving our lunches from the fridge, getting our coats and boots out. We left Rachel by herself at the table, blowing her nose and clearing the tears from her eyes. I looked over at her once and saw her watching me, though she might have been staring into space, it was hard to tell. In the watery morning light her slight figure was almost eclipsed by shadows. She didn't get up or offer to help with anything or say she had to leave, but she came and stood beside my mother at the door to see us off with her eyes red and weepy, looking for all the world as if she lived there. My mother kissed us and said to be careful and to look both ways and "don't dawdle," but I didn't like it when she and Rachel exchanged a smile just before closing the door on us. It didn't seem right.

"You know, your mom's about the best friend I have in the whole world," Rachel said.

This was a few days later in front of the apartment building. I was coming home from school and she was sitting on the front steps smoking a cigarette. I didn't want to be rude, so I stopped when she spoke to me. She had on a pink corduroy shirt over a wrinkled T-shirt, the same jeans from the other morning, and little tan sneakers with no laces. The same shadows filled the hollows beneath her eyes and she sat with her back stooped, looking frail, like someone who was recovering from something.

"She's been so nice, just helping me get myself together."

"Uh-huh."

Squinting against the sunlight, she took a drag off the cigarette and let her gaze wander. There wasn't much to see. The street was kind of ugly, the houses squat and drab and mostly in need of either repair or demolition.

"Have you been living here very long?"

She flicked ashes into the grass.

"About a year. It's not a bad place. I know it doesn't look like much from the outside, but Bill keeps it clean and fixes things when they break. I can't complain."

Bill was Mr. Abernathy, our superintendent.

"C'mon, Sara," Rachel said, patting the step next to her. "Sit by me and we'll talk for a while."

I was wearing my best plaid skirt and I had to go to the bathroom. And I didn't really want to sit and talk. I had nothing to say to her. But then I thought if I didn't she'd tell my mother I was rude. So I sat down, clamping my knees together and setting my books across my lap. The concrete was warm from the sun and I could feel the heat in my rear end.

"What do kids your age do for amusement?"

I shrugged.

"I watch TV and I read a lot," I said. "I like going for walks. Sometimes I hang around at the mall with my friends."

Then I looked at her.

"How old are you?"

She laughed, showing me her teeth, which were stained yellow.

"I'm twenty-six," she said. "So I've been around a while. I know a thing or two."

"Like what?" I asked.

"I know you can't trust men. I learned that the hard way. You can't believe a thing they say. They only want one thing and once they get it you can forget about them being any use to you."

"Do you have a boyfriend?"

I thought she was going to laugh again, but instead her expression became serious and she lowered her eyes. She puffed on the cigarette and blew the smoke away from me out the side of her mouth.

"I used to have all kinds. But none of them were any good. I have a knack for attracting useless men. The kind who make promises. Do you know what a promise is, Sara?"

I nodded.

"That's when you say you'll do something and then you do it."

Rachel stared at me so long I began to feel like I'd said something incredibly stupid and she couldn't believe I was serious. She shook her head.

"Nope. I'll tell you what a promise is. A promise is a worthless thing because it's the easiest thing in the world to make. Anyone can make a promise. It's like magic. You can make one out of thin air. You don't need to know anything and you don't have to buy anything or build anything, or give part of yourself away. So a promise is worth nothing. Less than nothing." She looked at me. "If you're smart you'll remember that."

I nodded even though I didn't understand what she was talking about.

"Your mother doesn't have a boyfriend, does she?"

"No," I said. "She's married to my dad."

"And where does your dad live?"

I was starting to feel funny, almost like there were things crawling on me. This was getting too personal, too close to the stuff that really mattered. I didn't like telling anyone about my father, and my mother had made it clear I didn't have to because it wasn't anyone's business but ours. The only person who knew anything was my teacher, Mrs. Grant. My mother had phoned her to explain the situation in case anything came up in class, like one of those dumb show-and-tell sessions where you have to tell everyone what your parents do for a living.

"I don't know." I shrugged.

This didn't seem to bother her. She stubbed her cigarette against the side of the step and flicked the butt into a bush.

"Yeah, I know all about it. I should have guessed. It blows me away how they feel they can just walk out like that. You know?" She pulled a cigarette pack and some matches from her shirt pocket and lit another one up. "Fucking blows me away. The people I know who let men screw up their lives for them. Ella, this other friend of mine? She's got three kids, all with different fathers, and none of them give her a thing, not one bit of support, not a cent. She works too, downtown in a bar somewhere. I don't know how she does it."

I couldn't tell if she was saying this to me or to herself. She was staring off into space, taking drags from the cigarette and blowing out the smoke. Then she was quiet, and for a while her eyes followed each car as it passed by going down the road, as if she was wishing they'd stop and take her with them. I thought maybe it was a chance for me to get away, but before I could stand up she asked, "How do you feel about it, being a kid and not having your father around?"

I shifted my body. I had a feeling she was asking the wrong kind of questions, but I wasn't sure. After all, she was a grown-up; she had to know what she was doing. It didn't seem like she was prying or being nosy. Maybe all she wanted was to be friends. I wished that she was being really obvious about pumping me for information. Because it made me feel so small and mean, that she was talking to me as easy as anything, and I didn't want to talk to her or tell her about myself or have anything to do with her, when all she wanted was to be my friend.

"I don't know." I shrugged again. "I can't remember much about when he was around."

"He's been gone a while, huh," she said nodding.

"Yes."

"It's rough on kids when that happens. Sometimes they get pretty wild. I was like that. I was always talking back to my mother, giving her grief, staying out late drinking and shit like that. But you and Julie seem pretty straight. And your mother—sheeesh!—she's so together I can hardly believe it."

I wasn't about to tell her what my mother was really like; I wasn't going to mention the tears or the yelling or the time I heard a noise in the middle of the night and when I got up, there was my mother in the dark kitchen on her knees cleaning the oven and talking to herself.

"Sara, how old are you? Nine?"

"I'm ten."

She nodded and seemed to think for a moment.

"You know, when I was sixteen, I was pregnant."

She blew smoke out her nose, flipped her hair back, and glanced at me casually, like talking about this was something she did every day. The sleeve of her shirt had slipped down and along her arm I saw a row of small purple bruises.

"Bet you didn't know that, did you? That I had a baby when I was sixteen. I don't know why I let it happen. I guess I was just too young and stupid to know what I'd gotten myself into."

I didn't say anything. A shiny black beetle went scuttling across the concrete step. When he bumped against my foot I moved it so he could keep going.

"My mother wasn't too happy about it, that's for sure. And my dad wanted me out of the house. He actually said that. 'I want her out of this house.'" She sniffed. "Can you imagine?"

She'd turned to face me and seemed to be waiting for a reply. But I didn't say anything. I watched the beetle crawl off the concrete and into the grass.

"So anyway, we went down to somewhere in the States. My mom and me. But it was too late for an abortion. I had to carry it full term and when it was born it was retarded. Well, not retarded exactly, but really slow. I named her Katie and took her around the block in the same stroller my mom had used with me. It was so weird, having a baby and still being that young. I wanted to go drinking and stuff with my friends, but I had this kid. I couldn't even go to the movies."

I stood up.

"I have to go to the bathroom," I said.

"Your mom's not home. I lent her my car. She went to get groceries."

"You have a car?"

"Not a very big one." She squinted and shielded her eyes from the sun.

"Do you have a job?"

"Oh God, I'm not in any shape to work." She laughed, as if I'd suggested she perform some menial chore that was beneath her. "It's my back. It goes out on me. I end up in bed for days and it hurts like hell."

I nodded. I was going to ask what she did all day if she didn't work, but I decided I didn't want to know. I already knew more about her than I figured was safe.

"If you want to you can wait for your mom in my apartment. Use the bathroom. Help yourself to a glass of milk or—"

"Thanks, but I just want to go home," I said. "Bye."

"Bye, Sara."

I pulled the door open and ran down the stairs feeling like I'd escaped from something. The door to the apartment stuck when I unlocked it and to get in I had to ram my shoulder against it. My throat tightened and almost took my breath from me when the door didn't give the first time. It was like she was closing in on me, and in my mind I saw her discovering me stranded outside the apartment and leading me back to her place, making me sit and listen as she talked on in that breezy, insinuating manner of hers, on and on until I knew everything there was to know about her and could no longer deny that we were best friends after all.

For some reason my mother liked Rachel and they spent more and more time together, mostly playing cards and watching TV, or just talking. My mother didn't know any card games and Rachel taught her how to play Crazy Eights and 45s and Go Fish and something else that involved yelling "Hit me!" a lot. Rachel seemed to really like it at our place, even though my mother made her go outside to smoke. But I don't think she minded doing this because she always went, unless it was raining, and then my mother would open a window and Rachel would blow her smoke out through the screen.

The first time Rachel showed up at the door cradling a forty-ouncer in her arm my mother let on there was nothing different and they sat down at the kitchen table as usual. My mother's drinking was an off and on thing. She mostly didn't drink in front of Julie and me, but all it took was a setback of some kind—losing something or not getting a job she wanted or a bad report card from one of us—and she'd go on a binge. When she was on a binge she spent hours either in bed or in the bathroom. The first few months after my father's accident were the worst, full of long silences and crying fits and lots of swearing. And even after she got her first temporary job and started feeling better about herself there were still days when she did nothing but drink and get sick and sleep. But I knew she was trying to do better. And lately things had levelled off.

So when she started inviting Rachel around it made me uncomfortable even though what they did seemed harmless enough. I think it was because of a look that Rachel had about her: a haunted, spindly, needy look, sort of like a small animal that's been whipped and after that is always watching out. She had small grasping hands too. I didn't like her touching me. She and my mother talked for hours and hours, sometimes long into the night, and once Rachel was there sleeping on the couch when I got up at six in the morning to pee. I remember standing there thinking that I'd rather wet the bed than wake her up—because if I woke her up I'd have to talk to her. If I wet the bed I wouldn't.

Rachel plunked down the forty-ouncer in the middle of the kitchen table and went to get a glass from the cupboard.

"Time you were in bed," I heard my mother say.

I was just sitting there reading. It was only eight-thirty.

"I won't bother you," I said. "I promise I won't."

But I could see she wanted me out of there. Now. Julie was already in bed. Tomorrow was another day, and all that. I grabbed my book and trudged down the hall to our room. Rachel hadn't said a word to me, hadn't even looked in my direction. As I closed the door I heard the bottle being opened, glass clinking on glass, liquid sounds. They spoke in whispers, laughed huskily beneath their breath at some shared joke. It made me feel weird, like they were keeping secrets. Later the laughing got so loud it sounded more like screeching, but I managed to fall asleep anyway.

In the morning Rachel was gone, the empty bottle was in the garbage, and my mother's bedroom door was closed and locked.

They went out together, "shopping," my mother said. As far as I knew we didn't have any money. That was why she couldn't buy us new shoes or raincoats this year; that was why she stopped giving us an allowance. All we got was lunch money and a bit of pocket change. So it didn't make any sense to me that she'd go out shopping with Rachel, especially when Rachel was even poorer than we were, or so my mother said. But I was busy with homework and after-school stuff and I didn't think about it very much. Things were the way they were. It was none of my business what my mother did with her time or who she spent it with.

Then I began to notice things—new things that would suddenly be there. Earrings, cosmetics, a shiny GE toaster, a blaster for playing tapes and CDs. We began to eat better—roasts, fresh vegetables instead of canned. Once we all went out to a restaurant. But my mother still wasn't working. I didn't understand where the money was coming from but I didn't say anything.

Somehow Rachel became a fixture in our apartment, showing up at odd times and staying for as long as she liked. She and my mother discussed things, but they kept their voices low. Notes were made and pieces of paper were passed across the table. Even though I was busy with schoolwork I noticed a shift in their relationship. My mother didn't laugh or joke around much anymore. The only voice I ever heard raised above a level pitch was Rachel's, and it was a sharp voice, the voice of someone barking orders. Between Rachel's visits my mother seemed anxious and depressed. Sometimes, when we were alone, she spoke vaguely of moving again, but mostly she just sat in the kitchen drinking coffee and leafing through glossy magazines. When I asked what the matter was I always got the same answer: "Nothing."

When school ended in June I was dreading another summer stuck at home with nothing to do. Last summer had been awful. My mother was in a bad temper the whole three months, yelling and swearing. But this summer looked like it might be different. The only part I wasn't keen on was spending time with Rachel. But if Rachel being there meant my mother didn't yell at us, then it seemed a small price to pay.

We hadn't made it to Oceanview Manor to visit my father for ages. By now he'd been living there for a couple of years. Julie and I had been to see him about three or four times, for Christmas and birthdays, but it was depressing, with all those old people slouched in their wheelchairs drooling and mumbling and staring out the windows at the trees and the parking lot, because you couldn't see the ocean after all. My mother sometimes went to visit him, but it was a long way out of town, well beyond Eastern Passage, and on the bus it took almost two hours to get there. So it was easier to not even think about going. And since he didn't know who any of us were anyway, it didn't seem to matter very much.

But Rachel had a car, and my mother got it into her head that we should all go to the beach and then on the way back stop in to visit with Dad. There was a look-off near Cow Bay—you could see all the way out to Devil's Island—and close by was a beach where you could walk for miles and listen to the surf and where the sand was the colour of cornsilk and soft like satin between your toes. There were millions of stones all different colours made round by the water. We used to go there when I was small, before the accident.

I didn't find out for sure that Rachel was coming with us until the morning we were supposed to go. I was hoping my mother had arranged to borrow the car. I was hoping we'd leave Rachel behind for once. But she showed up at the door around eight in the morning while Julie and I were helping my mother make peanut-butter sand-wiches and ham sandwiches for a picnic lunch. She was carrying a canvas bag with a big hokey sunburst on it and she had on sunglasses and a baseball cap and shorts. Her bare legs were lean and white and decorated with little scrapes and bruises.

"Jesus, that's a good idea," she said as she took a seat at the kitchen table. "I didn't even think about bringing food. It's a wonder I haven't fucking starved to death. The only time I think about eating is the middle of the night."

She crossed her legs, took out a cigarette, and started to light up. I'd never seen her do this in the apartment before—just light up a cigarette, without asking—and I was surprised that she seemed so at ease, like she'd been doing it all along. I glanced at my mother, but she appeared to be trying very hard to ignore the fact that Rachel was smoking.

"Well, it's supposed to be a nice day," was all she said.

Rachel smiled and released a stream of smoke into the air.

Julie coughed.

By nine we were all done with the preparations. Rachel chattered on, but my mother wasn't talking very much; it was almost like she was sick, or disappointed in something. We went out the rear of the building to the parking lot, which wasn't paved. Rachel's car was a subcompact white Toyota with no hubcaps and patches of scaly rust that looked like a skin disease, and one headlight missing. The inside was dirty and the upholstery was gashed and the foamy yellow stuffing leaked out through the holes. It smelled like cigarettes and the floor was littered with old butts.

Rachel tapped the hollow headlight socket.

"Gotta get that fixed one of these days," she said.

She opened the hatch and we loaded our plastic cooler into the back. The way my mother was being quiet made me think that something was burning away inside her. When we got in the car she switched on the radio first thing. "I want to get a weather report," she said, even though the sky was a high, clear blue. Rachel settled herself in behind the wheel and Julie and I got in back. Julie pinched her nostrils and made a face and I tried not to laugh. The car gurgled and sputtered as Rachel cranked the ignition and jerked the clutch back and forth. When she stepped on the gas the car lurched forward, gasped, and then wheezed to a stop.

"Shit," she said.

"What's wrong?" my mother asked.

"Oh, I don't think there's anything wrong," Rachel said and then smiled oddly. I could see something was going on between them. "I think everything's going to be just fine."

After another try she got it going, and a minute later we were on the road.

I wonder about adults and especially about my mother when she does something that I know she'd yell at Julie or me for doing. If either of us had turned the radio up as loud as she did we would have heard about it, that's for sure. Without asking what anyone else wanted she tuned in to the most obnoxious rock station she could find and set the volume sky high. The jagged screech of electric guitars steamrolled over the silence.

"What are you doing?" Rachel hollered. "You don't even like that kind of music."

My mother just looked at her. Rachel shrugged and began an intricate series of movements as she attempted to drive and light a cigarette at the same time. At one point she had neither hand on the wheel.

I rolled my window down part way to let the air rush in. It didn't take long to get out of the city. For a while we passed subdivisions of new houses and brick apartment buildings, but then the houses became fewer and more rickety and the apartment buildings smaller and more run down. Soon there was nothing but trees. When we passed a large oval sign that read "Oceanview Manor" my mother didn't say a word. The road clung to the shore and between the trees I was soon catching glimpses of water. I saw a few fishing boats tethered to wooden piers, and grey weathered shacks, some with little chimneys. Every now and then we passed someone walking along the roadside and they'd turn to stare at us like we were driving through private property. When you live in the city you forget this part of the world even exists, and it seems impossibly quaint, like a picture postcard of some far-off place you'll never get to visit. Gulls circled above us, hovering effortlessly, their white wings spread to full span. Suppressing a giggle, Julie tapped my arm and pointed: in the middle of a cleared spot was a small square green building with a sign above the entrance that said "General Store" An old guy with a big belly, in a white T-shirt and suspenders, sat on the front steps smoking a pipe.

Eventually the signal from the rock station faded and my mother switched the radio off, and soon after this she told Rachel to watch for the turnoff to the beach. It was mid-morning and the sun hung almost directly overhead, shimmering, thickening the air with its heat. Julie sighed and shifted in her seat. Rachel eased the car onto a narrow dirt road and I began to wonder how we'd ever found our way here to begin with, all those years ago.

The car heaved and shuddered over the potholes. Bushes closed us in on either side. It looked like no one had come this way for a long time. Rachel said to my mother, "You're sure about this?" and my mother nodded. Then I saw a cabin squatting just off the road in the bush. A Jeep was parked in the driveway and laundry flapped on the line out back. And in another minute the trees were gone and just on the other side of the tall grass I could see the beach, the rolling surf, an endless expanse of sky. It was like a photograph, one that had been touched up to make it seem more real.

Rachel pulled the car to a stop and we all got out and started unloading. The murmuring surf chanted in my ears, a soothing message, a lullaby, a softly shushing voice. And the salt sea scent in my nostrils drove out all thoughts of the city, our life there, the things that I'd left behind at home. We could have driven a thousand miles, the beach was that far removed from the kitchen where I'd been standing less than an hour ago.

My mother and I carried the cooler down the grassy slope to the sand and found a shady spot for it. Julie ran ahead with a plastic pail and a little shovel. All I'd brought was a book and sunglasses. My mother had thought of sandwiches and juice but I didn't notice her with anything else, except towels and some magazines. She had on a loose shirt over a bathing suit and shorts. After setting the cooler down, she went back to the car for something else.

Rachel dropped her bag on the sand, unrolled a towel, and spread it flat.

"You kids run along and have fun now. We've got real important stuff to talk about here. Adult stuff. You'll just be bored if you stay."

I looked back at my mother who was reaching through a side window into the car. All of a sudden she seemed a long distance away.

"Why don't you go check out the water? I bet it's warm. Or go for a walk up the other end there or something. I bet there's all kinds of neat stuff out there, shells and stuff. Maybe there's buried treasure. If you dig in the sand you might find some."

"There's no treasure," Julie stated as if she'd already looked. She lowered her eyes and nuzzled her toe into the sand when Rachel turned to her.

"And how do you know?" she asked crossly.

"How do you know there is?" I asked.

Rachel's eyes narrowed, and at that moment I understood how profound and indelible my aversion to her really was. I'd been confused up until now because my mother actually seemed to regard her as a friend and enjoy spending time with her. But I was beginning to see that something was at stake here, and whatever it was it had nothing to do with friendship.

She grabbed my shoulder and pointed her finger at my nose. I squirmed, but she dug her fingertips in.

"Listen, Missy!" she hissed. "If you know what's good for you you'll take your fucking sister and get as far away from me as you can. I've got something to work out with your mom and I'm not letting you mess it up. I'll let you know when you can come back. And I'm not having you treat me like shit either. I'm not your fucking servant.

I see you looking at me. You think you're so special. Well I got news for you. I'm as good as you are any day."

She let me go and I stumbled backward. My shoulder throbbed with a raw, bottomless ache and tears flooded my eyes. I hated her as deeply as I've ever hated anyone, before or since. I hated her bony, underfed waifishness, her spotty complexion, her breath soured by cigarettes. I hated the down-slant of her brows and the way her eyes invaded me. And I was furious at myself for being small and helpless and overwhelmed by all this hatred.

Through my tears I could dimly make out my mother approaching, her bare legs swishing through the grass. I felt dizzy, giddy with hate. I took Julie by the hand and walked away, kicking sand as I went. Julie didn't resist—her hand was flaccid in mine, like the hand of a plush toy I could drag anywhere I wanted.

Behind us I heard words exchanged as my mother returned from the car. She asked a question and Rachel responded with a brief comment and a laugh. I don't know what she said and at that point I didn't care. I just wanted to put distance between us. My mother called, "Sara, Julie don't go too far!" and I sensed Julie turn her head to look back. But I refused to do that. I wasn't about to let Rachel see what she'd done to me.

The beach curved to form a crescent, and in a minute we were out of their sight. The air was warm and a steady breeze drifted in over the water. Julie flexed her fingers in mine. Both our hands were sweaty, but my feet were dry and the sensation of hot sand slipping over them reminded me of why I'd wanted to come here.

After we walked a bit longer Julie asked, "Where are we going?"

"I don't know," I said sharply. But I didn't want her to think I was angry, so I added, "Not too much further," in a softer voice. My tears had dried up by now, and with the surf a calming presence and the sand and the bright morning sky, I was beginning to feel better, though my shoulder was still sore. "Maybe she's right," I ventured, trying to present the situation in a positive light. "Maybe there's treasure out here and if we start digging we'll find it."

Julie looked at me.

"You're dumb," she said.

"Why am I dumb?"

She sighed.

"She was only saying that to get rid of us. There's no treasure. Don't you know anything?"

I shrugged.

"What do you want to do then?"

We rounded another bend. The beach continued uninterrupted before us, a ribbon of glistening beige, until it ended at the foot of a hulking promontory of stone and earth that extended into the ocean. The high yellow grass rose like a wall on one side of us. The water washed over the sand on the other.

"Let's sit over there," she said, pointing at a tree trunk lying flat on the sand. The wood was streaked and grey. The branches flowed from the trunk like shoots of liquid mercury I'd seen during science period at school.

She dropped her plastic bucket and, using the branches as supports for her feet, climbed up and perched herself on the fallen trunk. Her chubby legs dangled. I shielded my eyes and squinted down the length of the beach. There was nobody else around, only a few birds circling. We could have been the last two people on earth.

"Why is Rachel so mean?" she asked.

"Rachel's a bitch," I said without thinking.

"Rachel's a bitch!" Julie echoed, her voice rising to a shout. "A bitch! A bitch! A bitch!"

Normally I would have shushed her, but what she was saying seemed appropriate and worth repeating. I climbed up on the tree trunk and sat next to her. The old wood was hot from the sun.

"What do you want to do?" she asked after she'd grown tired of yelling.

"I don't know. I might go down to the water and get my feet wet. But I don't want to go swimming."

"Me either!" She made a face.

For a few moments I occupied myself picking at a wormhole in the wood, chipping splinters away with my fingernail. I was still doing this when a gull flew over and landed close to us. It strutted around and cocked its head and focused one beady eye on us and stood waiting, as if it thought we had food that we might be persuaded to share. When we didn't do anything it spread its wings and lifted itself into the air, crying as it did this, probably calling out to the others that they didn't need to bother with us. We had nothing to give them.

I jumped down from the tree trunk.

"Where are you going?"

"Just down to the water," I said.

Julie stayed where she was. The sun was almost directly above us and I could feel its heat on my head and across my shoulders. It hurt my eyes. I'd left my sunglasses with my mother and Rachel and there was no way I was going back for them.

I hadn't expected today to be like this; I hadn't expected to be alone with my sister. In my mind I'd seen lots of people and imagined going for a long walk on the beach with my mother, listening to her tell us stories about when we were younger or about her own childhood, which she sometimes did, and watching her hair sway in the sun. The whole day would be pleasant and relaxing—nobody would cry or yell or whine. We'd have something to eat and then lie down for a while and read, and then we'd get in the car and go visit my father. Then we'd go home.

In my fantasy, Rachel hadn't figured at all.

I found some smooth rounded stones and tossed them into the water. They disappeared beneath the surface with barely a murmur, causing only the faintest ripple. The horizon was a white foggy smudge, but above me the sky was a shimmering blue, disturbed by only a few wispy clouds. I let the water wash over my feet. The chill shocked me at first and sent a shudder through my entire body. I clenched my teeth against it, against the frigid tingle in my legs. When I moved again I couldn't feel my feet. It was like I was floating above the water, and as I walked the weightless sensation stayed with me. I waded out further, until the water reached my knees. The water was clear like swirling glass, and I could see seaweed drifting beneath the surface and bits of broken shell embedded in the sand. When my feet returned I sensed them squishing in the soft bottom, felt the water's dancing currents eddying around them. I walked carefully so I wouldn't fall or step on anything rough or jagged.

I wondered what my mother and Rachel could be doing, what they could be talking about that was so important. Now that I was thinking clearly again, Rachel's anger seemed extreme and unreasonable.

And it occurred to me, not for the first time, that maybe she was crazy. I certainly detected an oddness about her—a subdued hysteria, a lopsided way of expressing herself, as if she hadn't quite figured out how to arrange her thoughts before turning them into words. But there was a possibility this impression was left over from the first time I'd seen her: that night in the hallway when she'd been reeling drunk and dangerous. Maybe she was just as lost and helpless as the rest of us, a grown-up child who needed someone to look out for her and steer her in the right direction. Maybe she'd been hurt so often she didn't know how to trust anyone anymore.

I couldn't find it in me to like her, though, because I knew she didn't like me or Julie. She wasn't interested in us, in what we were doing or in what we had to say. The only reason she ever spoke to us was to put on a respectable show, to pretend to my mother that she did like us. In the evening when she came over she usually asked just enough questions to make us squirm and then my mother would shoo us away. Other than that one time on the front step I hadn't spent any time alone with Rachel. I avoided her whenever I could and I ignored her when I saw her outside. She ignored me too. But it didn't matter because we both knew she was only interested in my mother.

I lowered my hands into the water. When I stood absolutely still the sun made me woozy like it sometimes did; I felt like my brain was being baked in an oven. But I was still happy to be here, even with Rachel. Though it seemed like a wasted opportunity. We hardly ever did anything together anymore. Sometimes it seemed like we weren't even a family, just three people who happened to live in the same place and share the same toilet. I liked being on my own sometimes, but I also liked the feeling that someone was nearby who would actually care if something happened to me. My mother was supposed to be that person, but ever since Rachel came along I'd had a feeling that she cared about other things more. She seemed content to let us spend time out of her sight, to go visiting friends without telling her beforehand and to come home late from school without any explanation. She wasn't asking us the kind of annoying questions that mothers usually ask their kids. A few months ago we were like three children living on our own, depending on each other for everything. But overnight she'd grown up and left us behind.

I heard Julie's voice calling me.

"Sara! Sara!" she said, running across the sand. "C'mon and see this!" She stopped at the rolling line that marked the furthest reach of the surf, breathless with excitement. "C'mon! You gotta see this!"

I followed her beckoning gesture and headed back in, toward dry ground. The water slipped away, exposing me to the air. My skin felt shivery and tight.

"C'mon!" she urged, her voice rising.

"Okay!"

She took off toward the tall grass, her brown hair bobbing as she ran. I followed across the hot sand, which clumped on my feet. Julie scrambled up the bank and turned to make sure I was still behind her, then she waded into the grass as I'd waded into the water. A few birds calmly circled overhead.

I passed the fallen tree, stepping into the depressions Julie's feet had left in the sand. The sand banked upward sharply where the soil gave out. I crawled up and grabbed some grass at the edge so I could pull myself the rest of the way.

Julie was standing a few paces ahead of me, staring at something lying on the ground. The blades of grass were coarse and spiny, prickly against my feet.

"What is it?" I parted the grass as I stepped forward.

"Look," she said, pointing.

Something furry lay sprawled on the ground. It looked like a dog, or what was left of a dog. The ears could have been dog ears, but since most of the head had been squashed it was hard to tell for sure. A huge gaping wound had ripened almost to black. The body was long and lean, but it looked deflated, like all the flesh had been drained out of it. Through the coat of amber fur I could just detect a shadow of ribs. The tail stuck out from the behind like the poor thing had been wagging it when it died.

"Gross, huh?" Julie said. She stood frozen above the carcass as if she thought any second it might move. "I've never seen a dead thing before."

I couldn't remember if I had or not, but at the moment it didn't seem like an important question. I was noticing how quiet it was and how a breeze wafted in from the water, making the grass tremble. The little cabin with the Jeep was visible from here. The clothes on the line were being reeled in by someone I couldn't see.

"Touch it," she said. "I dare you to."

"What?"

She was watching me, her expression purposeful, impudent.

"I dare you to touch it."

I was conscious just then of the distant rumble of a vehicle's motor starting up. And it occurred to me, as I stood rooted to the spot, that my mother and Rachel were going off somewhere together and, finally, leaving me and Julie on our own. I tried to assemble my thoughts, but I was groggy from the heat and had drifted into a state—a kind of lucid dream, a frenzied calm. I didn't seem capable of the effort needed to make sense of anything. Instead, I crouched and laid my palm flat upon the dead fur, which felt like fur and nothing else. I was repelled by its warmth, though I understood that the heat had been drawn from the sun and had nothing to do with any viable life force. But I kept my hand there nonetheless, as if I'd made a promise of comfort to this poor dead creature. However, I wasn't thinking of that, or anything. My mind was like a hollow shell, resounding with the surf. Cool saliva collected in my mouth; I could feel a bitter sharpness rising in my throat and a spinning sensation in my head, a roaring in my ears. I was sweating. The water from my brow trickled into my eyes. And when I finally heard Julie emit a sound, a squeal of revulsion, I looked down and saw a busy horde of tiny red ants swarming over my hand and marching with evident purpose up my arm.

"Mom, Mom! Sara's gonna throw up! Sara's gonna throw up!"

I realized only then what was happening. I leapt to my feet and turned just as my knees buckled and vomit surged up my throat and poured out of me in an acrid torrent. My stomach convulsed again as I stumbled forward, and then a pair of arms was circling my waist, preventing me from toppling over into the steaming puddle of my own puke. A hand braced my forehead. Then weakness overtook me and I closed my eyes and let it all come out, let my stomach empty itself into the tall grass.

My mother led us in a slow progression back along the beach. I placed one foot in front of the other, but that was about all I could manage. The sun bore down on us with a relentless burden of heat.

"I can't let you two out of my sight for a minute. What were you doing poking at a dead dog? Who in their right mind would do such a thing?" She shook her head. "I don't know. I just don't know."

I was going to argue that it had been Julie's idea. But at the thought of exerting myself to open my mouth and utter the words, I decided I couldn't be bothered.

"I mean, things like that, they're full of disease. They're dirty, filthy, crawling with God only knows what. I don't even want to think about what you might have picked up just being near it."

"Aw, Mom," Julie whined.

"Aw, Mom, my foot! You don't go fooling with that sort of thing. You never know what you're dealing with."

She led us around the last curve in the beach. The cooler was sitting where we'd left it, only it wasn't in the shade anymore. The sun had shifted and was now directing its rays full upon it. I imagined the sandwiches inside sweating, turning mushy and poisonous.

"Where's Rachel?" Julie asked.

My mother sighed.

"Well…" she drawled vaguely as she stopped walking and turned to gaze out toward the sea. She reached up with both hands and gathered her hair behind her head into a golden sheaf and lifted it away from her back. Then she let it fall again. She didn't turn to face us.

"We've got a little problem," she announced.

"She's gone, isn't she?" I said. "She took the car and left."

We waited, listening to the surf rolling into the shore. My mother appeared unconcerned as she bent over to retrieve a handful of sand in her cupped palm, which she then examined as if expecting to find an answer hidden within. Her features betrayed no anxiety, only an odd detachment, as if none of this were any concern of hers. It was an expression I'd seen on her face before. But there was something magnificent about her at this moment. Her ability to withdraw and conceal herself from us while standing in plain view was truly amazing. I had no idea what she was thinking, what plot wriggled

embryonic in her brain. Yet I had every confidence that she'd find a
way out of this mess—that, whether they knew it or not, someone
somewhere was waiting to rescue us.

We got out of there. We walked back along the dirt road that
led to the highway, my mother and I hefting the cooler between
us. I was still queasy from the heat, so we walked slowly. As we
went my mother admitted that she and Rachel had been shoplifting together for a couple of months. Their system was simple but
effective. Rachel entered the store and pretended to browse. My
mother followed a few minutes later and diverted the staff by faking
some sort of attack or fainting spell. While everyone was occupied
reviving her, Rachel filled her pockets. Rachel sold the stuff afterward and they split the take. So far they'd avoided detection, but
my mother hated the risk. She got headaches after each episode
that felt like her head was clamped in a vice, and she couldn't stop
thinking about what might happen the next time. Two weeks ago
she decided to quit.

"All I want is a real job," she said, conviction hardening her voice.
"I want to get up in the morning and go to work like a normal person.
I want to walk down the street and know that I don't owe anybody
anything."

But Rachel didn't see it that way. She threatened to expose her to
me and Julie if she refused to go along. The thought of us knowing,
she said, was worse than actually going through with it. So they did
a few more jobs, and at the last one they almost got caught. A sharp-
eyed store detective was ready to drag her into the office and put the
question to her, but she came up with a story and managed to get
away. That night she told Rachel she'd had enough. She didn't even
want any of the money from the last job. Rachel went wild and made
all kinds of threats, including turning her in to the police.

"I told her she could say whatever she wanted. I'd deny it."

She turned on the loud music on the way out here to make sure
Rachel didn't start talking about it in front of us. And then at the
beach they'd had it out. Rachel got into a snit and took off.

"I know I let you down. I've only ever tried to do my best, but
sometimes things don't work out. I've been a lousy mother. I shouldn't

have to steal to make ends meet. But I had to pay the rent and there didn't seem to be any other way."

She flashed us an apologetic smile and turned her face away. A few tears gleamed on her cheek, but they quickly dried. We kept walking.

A young man and his young wife lived in the cabin. His name was Vern and hers was Melinda. Vern fixed my mother some iced tea and Melinda made cherry Kool-Aid for me and Julie. When I asked if I could use the bathroom Melinda laughed and pointed out toward the backyard. The outhouse was a crooked grey box with a peaked roof just visible at the far end of the property, beyond the patch of freshly turned soil that was going to be a garden when they were through planting, and behind a clump of stunted trees. A path to it had been worn through the grass. I followed the path all the way down but when I came to the outhouse I couldn't make myself go inside. There were so many flies around that I could hear the steady hum they made above the breeze and the murmur of the surf, and the stench brought tears into my eyes. Instead I went further along, to the very edge of the clearing, pulled down my pants, and squatted behind a stump. When I was done I used leaves from a bush to wipe my behind. My head reeled as I bent to conceal my shit beneath a layer of dark forest earth, using a piece of bark to move the earth into place. I felt ashamed until I realized that what I'd done was really no different from the same act performed behind closed doors and was perhaps more healthy and honest, because instead of flushing it away and forgetting about it I'd faced the consequences of my action and covered the remains, as any responsible person would.

Late July. I was walking home from the mall with my friend Angela. We were talking about something, I can't remember what. The apartment building was just coming into view as we reached the top of the hill. A man with long hair stood on the lawn smoking a cigarette. He seemed familiar.

"What's the matter?" Angela asked when I fell silent and stopped moving.

"I know him," I said. I crept to the edge of the road and hid behind a big chestnut tree.

"Who?"

"That man. Remember the woman I told you about? Rachel?"

She nodded.

"He's her boyfriend, the one she threw out of her place in the middle of the night."

We looked down the street again. Gerry faced the building and held the cigarette in his left hand. He lifted it to his lips. His motorcycle was parked across the street. Even in the middle of summer he wore his leather jacket.

"So what?" Angela said. "Are you afraid of him?"

I thought about this.

"No. I guess not. But if he's there then she must be around somewhere."

Her eyes widened.

"Let's go see."

She started up the street.

"Angela!" I whispered, but she wouldn't stop. I ran up behind her and plucked at her hand, but she pulled it away and walked faster. I'd told her about Rachel and some of the things I'd seen, but she'd never actually met any of these people. These days Rachel was keeping to herself. Her car was always in the lot out back, but I never saw her. I sometimes wondered if there was something wrong but I wasn't curious or concerned enough to ask any questions. My mother never mentioned her.

We approached the building. Gerry's hair was tied back from his face in a neat ponytail. He didn't move except to glance in our direction and toss the cigarette into the street. There was nothing in his eyes to indicate that he recognized me. His attention was focused on the building. The discarded cigarette released a slender strand of smoke into the air.

As we passed him Angela said, "Hi," in her most chirpy voice.

He seemed annoyed but replied, "Hi, there," anyway without looking at us.

"Waiting for someone?"

He turned. I could see him assessing us, curious perhaps, wondering if there was a purpose behind Angela's question or if we were just being nosy. He had on the same wire-frame glasses as before. I studied his forehead for a scar and found one high up, near his hair-line. But there were others: one beside his left eye, another shaped like a scythe that corkscrewed into his upper lip. I wondered if Rachel had given him those as well.

He nodded in the direction of the building, drew a pack of ciga-rettes from his pocket, and tapped one out.

"My girlfriend lives here," he said. "Or, I guess I should say ex-girlfriend. She called me to come over and pick up some stuff, but when I got here she wouldn't answer the door. I know she's home though. Her car's around back."

He lit the cigarette.

Angela nodded.

"Is that your motorcycle?"

He briefly followed her extended arm.

"Yeah. Look, do you kids want something? 'Cause I don't have anything."

I tapped Angela's elbow.

"C'mon, let's go in."

We left him standing in the street with the cigarette dangling from his lips. Angela said, "Bye," and waved, but he kept his mouth shut and didn't return the gesture. As we went inside I saw him jab the air with his fist and kick some invisible thing with his boot.

A few days later Rachel resumed her place on the front step. The first time I saw her I almost couldn't believe the person sitting there was someone I knew. She sat hunched over and trembling, a cigarette in her hand, so thin she looked like she belonged in the hospital. Bruises lined her inner arms and wrists and her normally bleached complexion had paled further to an excruciating whiteness. Her cheekbones protruded and the circles under her eyes were like wounds carved into her flesh. I stepped around her to get to the door and when her eyes roamed upward to meet mine she displayed no interest at all. Her glance was empty. I wondered if she even remem-bered who I was.

One day in August we finally moved. We were going to a building on Ogilvie Street, near the railway tracks and close to the shopping malls. My mother supervised the movers as they loaded our things into the truck. Rachel had to get out of the way while this was going on, but she didn't seem to mind. She lingered beside the lilac bush at the edge of the lawn and spoke to my mother for a few minutes. They didn't have much to say to each other. Rachel nodded and smiled. My mother spoke solemnly, in urgent whispers.

When the time came to leave nobody said anything. Nobody waved. Rachel was looking the other way.

My mother joined us in the back seat of the taxi.

"Well, she's as good as dead. I'd give her a month, maybe two."

"How do you know?" I asked, turning so I could see her through the rear window as the taxi pulled away. Mr. Abernathy was standing beside her on the step and Rachel had lifted her head to speak to him, exposing her scrawny neck to the sun.

"My God! Just look at her! She's nothing but skin and bones. She said she feels fine but I don't think she knows the difference anymore."

"What's wrong with her?" Julie asked.

My mother was silent for a moment. Her eyes explored us.

I expected to feel something—sorrow for Rachel and what was happening to her, a sense of loss because someone I knew was dying—but nothing came. I was aware only of the momentum of the moving cab and my mother's eyes upon me.

"I couldn't even begin to answer that one."

There was nothing more to be said. The car rounded a corner, taking us to our new home.

# A DARK HOUSE

//

She noticed how his gaze swerved to avoid hers and understood that he was testing her, lying brazenly but uncertain of the limits of her gullibility.

"So how long do you want?"

"I'll get it done," he replied, languidly surveying her office now as if bored. For the hundredth time he shifted in his seat. "Yeah, I'll get it done. All I need is a week. Or two weeks, say. You can throw me out of class if I don't have it done in two weeks."

"You know, I may do that."

Her offhand remark drew his attention, and she stared him squarely in the face until his eyes withdrew from hers. She observed his smooth young skin and noticed how the flesh around his cheekbones seemed to cling, creating a strangely appealing aura of deliberate or compulsive sacrifice, as if he were starving himself. He swallowed and his throat quivered oddly. She couldn't help but watch.

He coughed before he spoke.

"Are you pissed off at me or something?"

She recoiled from the question and noticed that he was watching her intently. She avoided meeting his eyes in their recessed sockets.

"I'll admit I'm annoyed." She drew in a breath. "You people always show up at the last minute begging for extra time to get these things done when I've already been more than generous to begin with. You're supposed to be adults. It shouldn't be this difficult for you to organize your lives. I'm tired of it. I'm tired of listening to idiotic excuses and frankly I'm insulted that you expect me to believe them. I wish you'd realize that when I set a deadline I mean it."

He muttered something toward the floor.

"What was that, Scott?"

"I said, 'It wasn't my fault!'" He leaned over the desk. The skin of his neck was suddenly, alarmingly, red. "Other people get extensions all the time. You don't yell at them. This is the first time I've ever asked for anything. Christ, it's only two weeks. It's not the end of the world."

He rose to his feet. His request was suddenly so reasonable, she couldn't believe she'd raised her voice. Had she been yelling? It seemed unlikely. Yet there he stood, trembling, shaken by his own temerity, wondering if he'd gone too far. It crossed her mind that perhaps he was violent, uncontrollable in a rage. She could see now that he wasn't in the least undernourished. His body was sturdy and muscular, his hands immense, the hands of a giant. They could snap her neck with no effort at all.

"Sit down," she said softly and watched as he lowered himself into his seat.

"All right," she began, fixing her gaze on a jagged scar in the surface of her desk. "I'm prepared to give you the two weeks. Just get it done this time. Please. And, Scott, if you get stuck...don't wait until the last minute to come and see me."

She forced a smile.

"Thanks," he said.

He got up and opened the door. He was about to leave.

"Uh...."

"Is there something else?"

"I guess I probably shouldn't say anything—"

"Then please don't."

She stared him down, willing him out the door. As he lingered, his fingers rattled the doorknob. The sudden clatter took him by surprise and jarred her nerves more than it should have. He stood regarding her, sadly, she thought, as if she were the victim of some life-altering calamity. She wasn't sure when it had happened but somewhere she'd crossed a line and the distance between them had been diminished. She wondered if he was waiting for an apology, or perhaps a plea for understanding, or if he imagined the vulnerability she'd just now exhibited was an invitation to further intimacy.

Then he blurted, "Okay!" and with an ambiguous smile disappeared down the hall.

As his steps receded her breathing grew easier. Maybe she would be able to laugh about it later, but for a moment, as he towered above her, she'd felt herself become a child again. Fears she thought she'd outgrown years ago—of the dark, of being alone, of the nameless evils that populated her dreams—were suddenly as real as the stack of papers on her desk and as imminent as the weather.

The hours of the day had rested heavily across her shoulders. From the beginning she'd felt herself being observed, taken note of, for some obscure reason singled out. As a result she'd become clumsy and strangely inert, as if drugged. Though she was thin—certain people told her she was too thin—her body seemed to inhabit too much space and her feet defied her commands as if they'd turned to wood. She hesitated before answering the simplest questions, hoarding her words with selfish ardour, hoping to get away with the impossibility of silence. Tight- lipped and irascible, she encountered colleagues for whom she had no use and swept wordlessly by them, giving them barely a glance, ignoring their greetings and no doubt leaving them perplexed and affronted. She languished through two hellish classes, her lectures dulled by the tormented drone of her voice. At last she retreated to the sanctuary of her office in the hope that nobody would want to consult her. But as she tucked some books into her canvas carry-all and prepared to leave, Scott Simon appeared, looking just like him, sounding just like him, using his size to intimidate her and muttering his excuses with the sullen disrespect of a cranky teenager. But surely granting his request didn't make her a pushover. She felt as though she'd been coerced, but she hadn't really let him bully her. Upon reflection she could even feel sorry for him. Wasn't he a tragic figure, doomed by a flawed character to repeat his failures over and over again? Of course she had failed too, by allowing emotion to colour her words and actions. But all she wanted was to be rid of him. She wanted him gone and out of her life. So why hadn't she just given him what he'd asked for at the outset and saved the scolding for another time? Her posturing had prolonged the encounter needlessly. She'd allowed him a clear glimpse around the facade of reason and calm, so that even if he'd only been guessing before, he knew now that something in her life had fallen apart and that she was looking for a way to fit the pieces back together. She talked tough, but it was just for show. Beneath the hard-nosed bluster she was ready to crack.

She pulled on her coat, in the process banging her elbow against the wall and emitting a whispered curse. Her whole head was throbbing; her shoulders ached. Abruptly and unexpectedly her vision was clouded by tears and to get at them she had to remove her glasses. With a vigorous gesture she rubbed the tears away and then wiped her nose. Shutting the door, she scanned the letters etched into the copper nameplate: Dr. S. Parsons. The likelihood of this referring to her seemed remote. Didn't people just call her Sandra? Or Sandy? Wasn't she just some scrawny, not particularly ambitious kid from Arlington Heights who did what she was told? Who never surprised anyone? Growing up, she'd followed all the rules, taken all the proper steps, passed all the exams, managing finally to impress the right people with a critical flair and an ability to weave words tightly into rational, irrefutable argument, never missing a stitch. Implicit in the act of employing her was the admission that, yes, she was intelligent, perhaps even gifted. Dr. Wilkins, the head of the department, directed a benign smile her way as she scrawled her name on the contract, turning herself over to them for three years. Whatever had she done to blind them to the truth? How could they have failed to see what she was? For two years she'd been waiting for them to realize that she had nothing original to offer. That her mind was second rate. What was taking them so long? Or maybe they already knew. They already knew and were waiting for some glaring act of impropriety on her part so they could throw her out without a second thought. That had to be it. Unless she was being spared because she was a woman. They needed women. There were regulations that said so. But how badly did she want to be spared? What, when all was said and done, was she doing here? The notion crept up on her as it had before that she should have married the son of that banker friend of her father's and saved herself the anguish of failing in a profession she loved.

She hadn't seen her mother in weeks, but for some reason today it was her mother's voice that sounded in her head, as usual with no other purpose than to remind her of where she'd come from and to put her firmly back in her place. An image of the pale green house on Mason Avenue hovered in her thoughts: the sagging stone wall, the sloping lawn, the eavestrough hanging like a crooked eyebrow above the front window, a grimy little girl digging in the muddy soil, no shoes, her knee torn and bleeding. She could still hear her mother insisting that it was bad to talk back or spit or chew gum, and did she want to have everyone thinking she was one of those horrible people from Grimsby and did she want to grow up with her teeth sticking out like that?

Voices reached her from somewhere downstairs. She paused in her movements, pressing her back to the wall and sucking in her breath. But her fear—if that's what it was—quickly dissolved when she considered the absurdity of her behaviour, and she compelled herself down the steps, quietly greeting two female graduate students on their way up.

Outside the air bit into her and though the threat of rain pressed her to hurry, she maintained her usual pace. A line of poetry by Sylvia Plath had tunnelled to the surface of her memory and was restless in her thoughts: trees stiffened into place like burnt nerves, and this was followed by something from Hardy, a description, bleak and harrowing, though she failed to recall which novel it came from. Hardy suited her mood. The way he clung to his conception of hopeless anonymity in human suffering. How could he have endured nearly ninety years of life when he knew so early and so well that everyone was alone, condemned to live and to die alone? In his depictions, to live was to suffer. There was nothing noble about it, nothing to provide comfort at the worst moments. His characters were always pledging their hearts to mistaken beliefs and foolish quests. They embraced misery like a lover. And each day people proved Hardy right by casually tossing their lives aside, as if life didn't matter. Nothing had changed since Hardy's day. Everyone was still alone.

Self-reliance was one thing. You could strive for that and not end up feeling sorry for yourself. But being alone was quite another. And she was certainly alone now. Chris had left this morning and there was no question in her mind that it was final. After last night there would be no reconciliation. Things had been said and she couldn't see him coming back. How many times had he walked out on her before? He always came back. But somehow she knew this time was different.

And why did Scott Simon have to show up today? As if he'd had it planned. He looked so much like Chris and even sounded a bit like him. Chris walks out and on the same day the only student in any of her classes who bore him the slightest resemblance barges into her office. No wonder she'd been hard on him and made him defend himself. It was almost as if he'd deserved it. Of course it hadn't been strictly ethical to back him into a corner like that. She'd stung him, quite unfairly, she now realized. Still, for a single instant it had taken her mind elsewhere. And on days like this even transitory relief was enough to justify almost any behaviour.

She crossed the narrow street, looking both ways, just as she'd been taught. Chris had long ago set his mind on marriage. But her, well, she wasn't sure. You'd think she'd know, after all this time, you'd think she'd at least have some idea if she was ever going to consent to marry him. But no. She couldn't tell him anything for sure. Even though she was thirty years old and if she wanted children she'd better start giving it some thought. Make no mistake, Chris wanted a family. He needed that stability, the unequivocal permanence of a home, even though as a musician he was lucky to hold a job for more than three weeks at a time. But still, he didn't want to be fifty and find himself alone, with no one to help him and take care of him when he got old and sick. Which sounded pretty selfish to her. If you ask me, she said. Pretty damn selfish. Okay, but why should he have to waste the most important years of his life waiting for her to make up her mind? They'd been through it all before and it wasn't as if he was asking her to jump off a bridge or rob a bank. What was left to think about? He wanted to know. It was a simple decision. Something people deal with all the time. Sure, it was a risk, but eventually people have to choose. They figure out where they want their lives to take them and they decide what they have to do to get there. Surely, Sandra, he said in a calmly rational tone that drove her wild, surely you know yourself well enough to be able to see where you'll be in a few years and who you'll be with. You must know that you can't bury yourself in that office of yours forever. You're going to have to start looking around and I think you should do it soon because it may not always be this easy. Then he said, with an unpleasant laugh, I can't believe you're being like this. You're no different from those people we used make fun of who want everything they can get their hands on but none of the responsibility. Why can't you just admit that your life is empty and that you're miserable and that things would be a whole lot better if you got married and had a couple of kids?

That was enough from him. The look on her face told him so. He shut his mouth and turned his back to her, perhaps shaken by what he'd said. But then, who could tell? Did he withdraw because he'd had his say, or because he'd gone too far and knew it, or because he was bored?

She pulled him around to make him look at her.

Don't you start telling me what's wrong with my life, and I think it's a hell of a presumption for you to say there's anything wrong with my life! You don't know me, Chris. We've lived together for five years, but you haven't even begun to get to know me. Do you seriously believe that getting married and having children is the answer to anything? Is that really the only option I have left? I don't know why you have to push me like this. Why does it always have to be up to me? You have no idea how ridiculous you sound, spouting generalities as if they had anything to do with what really happens in peoples' lives. Why do I have to be the same as everyone else? What would that solve? Right now I don't have an opinion about marriage or children. I never think about it. Never. But it's all you ever talk about. I wish I knew what the answer was. I really do. But I don't think it's up to me to find it. You're the one with the problem. You probably don't even remember when we first moved in together, how you tried to make me into your little homemaker. God, I was stupid. Then all of a sudden it came to me, what you were up to. I had to make a scene—you remember that?—and you acted like I was crazy because I didn't want to pick up your underwear and clean up your mess. But now it's my life you're talking about, and I like it fine the way it is. Maybe I am miserable and can't see it, but God knows I don't need a bunch of kids running around here. I'm sorry, but that really is the truth. We both know having children would make you happier. But I can't see any point in sacrificing myself for that. And anyway, I'm not sure you'd make a very good father. You never think of anyone but yourself.

Sounds to me like you've made your decision, he said. And then he was gone.

That was last night. This morning he came back and gathered up a few small things—his eyes hollow and veiled in deep shadow, his face strained by lack of sleep—and carried them away without a word. As he moved about in his familiar fashion, she felt an irrational desire to attempt a reconciliation, to extend toward him a mollifying gesture, to plead with him to stay and talk it over. But the impulse to speak faded when she sensed him lingering by the door, waiting for the apology she had against all reason been formulating. She stayed where she was and sipped her morning coffee as she listened to him leave. There were no tears this time. She had to go to class.

She stopped at the drugstore for Tylenol and then continued walking up to Cedar Street. Almost home. She squinted against the glare of a pale grey sky and lowered her eyes. A child chased a ball into the road and she didn't flinch. Didn't pause in her step even when she heard the tires screech, the horn bellow. She hurried her pace. You learn to care for yourself and that's all there is to it. You have to be out of your mind to imagine that anyone is going to do it for you. How else will that child learn not to run into the street? Maybe you have to risk being hurt, and learn what it means to be hurt, in order to put aside the gushy sentiment and get something done in this world. There's no sense waiting for someone to come along with all the answers because that's not the way it works.

She stifled a sniffle.

Damn this cold.

A front door slammed nearby.

She couldn't avoid being seen by Mr. Armour, her neighbour, a tall, angular man in his seventies. In the three years since moving here she'd spoken to him many times, but it had been Chris who was really friendly with him. They played chess sometimes on Saturday afternoons. His wife was not well, that much she knew. He called to her and she felt the muscles tighten in her chest.

"Hello, Sandra!"

"Hello, Mr. Armour. How are you?" She shrank from the note of affected cheer in her voice.

"Can't complain. Nope. We haven't seen much of you these last few weeks. How are you?"

As if deliberately blocking her path, he stepped onto the sidewalk just as she came up to meet him.

"I'm okay. You know. Tired. Classes and everything."

"You work too hard. And you look pale. Are you feeling all right?"

She became conscious once more of the dull throbbing pain that had settled into the space behind her eyes.

"Well…no. Not today. I guess I don't feel all that great." Why was she whining? What did she want with his sympathy?

"Is there anything I can get for you? I have to go over to the mall to get a new rake. Time to rake the lawn, you know."

She noticed as if for the first time the colourful mounds of rotting leaves.

"Yes. I…I guess."

"If there's anything you need at the grocery store, I can pick it up while I'm there. It's no trouble."

"Ummm…."

"You know that old rake of mine I had for twenty years? Finally wore it out." His eyes glinted. "You just don't expect things to last that long. Then, before you know it, they do."

He seemed to pause and she waited dreamily for him to continue.

"You should go in and see May. She's fixing supper. I'll be back in just a bit. You could keep her company. She'd like that. Then, when I get back, you could stay and eat with us."

She gazed without interest up into his face. The skin was sunken and creased. But his eyes shone, as if filled with images of some past that was still very real to him.

"I'm sorry. I have to get home."

"I saw Chris come by with a truck today. We talked."

"Oh? Really?"

"What are you going to do, Sandra?" he asked, suddenly almost grave. "Will you stay on?"

"I..." She encountered a blank spot where the answer should have been. "I guess I hadn't given it much thought."

"It's expensive. That house. The rent you pay. I hope you can manage."

"I'll have to see," she said, shifting her feet restlessly.

"It's going to be a difficult time for you. Getting used to being on your own. You'll need people to talk to."

"I'll be okay," she murmured, letting her eyes wander.

There was a brief silence.

"Well, I'd best be getting along. You get some rest. Think things over. We're right next door if you need anything."

She watched him go.

Turning, her breath caught at the sight of Mrs. Armour standing expressionless in the doorway. She slowly lifted her hand to wave, not certain what was expected of her. But all she could manage was a feeble gesture—a disappointment, even to herself. Backing off, she let her fingers curl into a limp fist. The old woman made no movement in response and, in fact, did not even seem to notice she was there.

The house was dark and cavernous. Yellow sunlight streaked through tarnished windows and scorched the bare floor. She kicked off her shoes and listened to the clatter echo down the length of the hollow entryway. The abandoned look of the place caught her unprepared: things lying haphazard on the floor, like the scene of a struggle. She found it difficult to breathe, so much was missing. Most of the furniture had belonged to Chris, so she could not deny his right to take it with him. And then she noticed the gap-toothed look of the bookcase. He'd searched through it and taken everything that was his. Books she loved, that seemed as much hers as anyone's, books she would have concealed elsewhere had she only known.

Her heart thumped as she crept along, pausing here and there as if trespassing. Life would be different now. Time on her hands, for one thing. In the kitchen she noticed a torn piece of blue paper hanging from a magnet on the refrigerator. Without thinking she reached for it. But her hand froze and she decided not to read what was written there until later. At least until after she'd eaten something. Maybe not until tomorrow.

Later, upstairs, she glanced out a window and saw Mr. Armour raking the leaves on his lawn. It was nearly dark. The rain had held off. She watched as he stopped for a moment to rest, wiping his long face with a rag and leaning the rake against the house. She could not be sure, but the rake looked worn and rusted, held together by nothing more than wire and tape. Twenty years old at least. She tried to recall what he'd said to her only an hour earlier but was no longer certain what it had all been about. His words had made sense as he uttered them, but all that came to mind now was the foolish sentimentality and the flicker of nostalgic yearning in his eyes. And the vast expanse of time and space that seemed to stretch open between them, leaving her dangling, vulnerable, desperate with longing to escape.

Quietly and with exaggerated caution she slipped away from the window and drew the blind. She stood still, conscious of the cold floor pressing on the bones of her feet, the shadows retreating like timid animals, the empty room darkening behind her, the breath stirring in her lungs. Chris had kept his guitar and keyboards in here, the instruments propped on shaky tables, wires snaking all over the floor, but there was nothing in here now. Slowly it dawned on her that she was waiting for something to happen, that a decision hung in the air, heavy and palpable, like a curtain, separating the past from the present. She would soon have no choice but to turn on some lights, find some food, make herself eat. Eventually she would have to confront herself in a mirror. It would be painful and perhaps even frightening to see herself alone. The thought of it filled her with horror, for all she could envision was a wiry commotion of brown hair and the cruel unshielded light exposing her weariness.

She caught herself wondering where Chris had gone and wishing she could talk to him, but she quickly expelled these notions from her head, chiding herself. She didn't need him. She didn't need anyone. It was natural for her to want to know where he was out of simple curiosity, but she'd find out soon enough. Even now he seemed to have lots of friends she knew nothing about—slim and denim-clad with long hair—polite, impoverished, effeminate young men who came, stayed for a day or two, and then vanished. One of these would have taken him in. And anyway, did it really matter where he was when he no longer had a role to play in her life? He'd given up on her. Why should she care what he'd done with himself?

Later, when the phone rang, she flew to the other end of the kitchen to answer it.

# THE MUSIC LOVER

S now had fallen thick and heavy while Annie was indoors, and it was still falling when the time came for her to leave. It covered everything—the street, the houses, the trees, the cars parked by the curb, the sidewalk leading from Mr. Stedman's small red-brick house on Bonnie Terrace to her house in Rockland Estates—softening outlines and making the whole world tidy and perfect. When she stepped outside it was starting to get dark. The cars and buses had their lights on. The snow falling through car lights made her think of angels. But when she began to walk she realized she was walking on the angels that she imagined had been sent to help her on her way. And since she didn't like to think about this, she lowered her eyes and tried not to look behind her, at the tracks her boots were leaving in the snow.

Today's lesson had not gone well and Annie was sorry about that. Whenever she went to Mr. Stedman's she was supposed to be happy, but today she was not happy. Her parents had been out late last night and this morning they were both grumpy and her mother yelled at her when a blob of porridge fell off her spoon and landed on her leg, leaving a wet spot on her favourite black tights. Then her father had told her mother to "shut the hell up" and her mother had called him a "drunken liar." Annie was crying when Mrs. Gladstone walked with her in the bleak early morning light to the shelter with the plastic windows where the school bus stopped. Mrs. Gladstone held her tightly by the hand and said in a hard voice that her parents had "disgraced themselves."

"But you know, Annie," she added a moment later as they rounded the corner to Waterman Avenue, "they don't want to make you feel bad. You must remember that they love you very much. But when people drink they lose sight of the important things and I think your Mommy and Daddy sometimes drink so much they can't remember how much they love you or how much they love each other."

Annie nodded. Somehow, she understood that her mother hadn't really been mad at her. She understood this even before Mrs. Gladstone told her so. But still, it was hard for her to imagine what all the yelling was about if nobody was mad at anybody else.

They stood and waited together without speaking as a crowd of tired children and tired parents gathered and the hard, grey sky brightened. Annie opened her mouth wide and puffed her warm breath into the cold air and watched the cloud float and dissolve. She did this over and over again. When the bus came Mrs. Gladstone handed Annie her violin in its case and Annie fell into line with the other children and got on the bus. Mrs. Gladstone stayed and watched as the bus pulled away from the curb, and Annie waved to her until the bus turned the corner and Mrs. Gladstone was gone from sight.

Annie's lesson started at three-thirty. On Wednesdays she had permission to leave school twenty minutes early so she could take a taxi to Mr. Stedman's house. Her mother had arranged the whole thing with the taxi company, and every Wednesday afternoon there was a car waiting for her that would take her to Bonnie Terrace. She always sat quietly in the back seat and when she got there Mr. Stedman came out to pay the driver. Annie didn't have anything to do with the money. All she did was watch it change hands.

Mr. Stedman started every lesson the same way.

"To play music," he declared rapturously, "you must be happy. Gloomy people make terrible musicians. Always remember this."

Then she had to smile before she was permitted to lift the violin to her chin and apply the bow to the strings, sounding the four notes:

Most of the time she smiled right away, but sometimes if she didn't feel particularly happy, she wouldn't smile for five or ten minutes. When this happened Mr. Stedman let her stand there until she felt so ridiculous it would be all she could do to keep herself from giggling and falling on the floor in a heap.

Mr. Stedman was a tall man with a neatly trimmed white beard and big hands. His house was small, though, and Annie was always waiting for him to bump his head on a doorframe. But he never did. He spoke with an accent and sometimes when she made mistakes he said words in a language that she couldn't understand. Mostly, though, he seemed distracted, usually by other things that had nothing to do with what he was trying to teach her. The television was always on when she arrived and sometimes he left it on all through the whole lesson. Once he had a roast in the oven and kept running to the kitchen to make sure it wasn't drying up. Another time the phone rang and he talked for twenty minutes before returning to the lesson room. Annie didn't think any of this was strange or unusual because Mr. Stedman was the only violin teacher she'd ever had.

Annie always tried to be happy for Mr. Stedman because of all the dead people. On almost every wall of his house Mr. Stedman had put up photographs of people and when Annie asked him who they were, he told her they were his relatives and that they were all dead.

"Look here," he said, steering her toward a grainy black and white photograph of two people bundled up in layers of heavy clothing standing in a snow-covered field beside a wooden fence. The photograph was so old it was yellow.

"These are my parents," he said.

"What happened to them?" Annie asked. They looked so cold in the photograph it made her shiver, and somehow she got the idea that they were waiting in line to go somewhere. They weren't looking at the camera either, or smiling the way people did in other photographs she'd seen.

Mr. Stedman shrugged. "They died." When he looked at her again he seemed very sad. "Annie, do you know what a Jew is?"

She shook her head. The word had a ring of familiarity to it and yet its meaning was like something floating in the air just out of reach.

For a moment as he gazed at her his eyes seemed to fill with tears, but when he spoke again his voice betrayed no emotion.

"It's of no importance. Too soon you will learn."

So today she wanted to be happy for Mr. Stedman. She felt if she could be happy for him, then she could be happy for herself, and then maybe when she got home her parents would be happy too. But when she smiled and lifted her violin, it didn't feel to her like she really meant it, and that was almost the same as telling a lie. She stole a glance at him, sitting in his wooden chair, to see if he could tell. But then she went ahead anyway and placed the violin under her chin and played the first notes of the movement from the Bach partita she'd been assigned. But for no reason at all her fingers seemed twice their normal thickness and felt like they'd been stuck together with glue. She lost her confidence and played so tentatively and made so many mistakes that it took her ten minutes to get through the piece. But Mr. Stedman didn't even seem to notice. This was one of his distracted days and it annoyed her that all the while she struggled through the Bach, he was humming another tune altogether.

It took her almost half an hour to walk from Bonnie Terrace to the edge of Rockland Estates and it snowed the whole time. Sometimes she regretted the violin lessons because she would rather take the school bus home with the other kids and not have to walk so far all by herself. But she still liked Mr. Stedman, and she liked playing the violin, even if she wasn't happy all the time. By the time she turned the corner onto Waterman Street the snow had formed a layer on her violin case and the shoulders of her overcoat and on her pink backpack that had her books and lunch bag in it, and she was having trouble believing the flakes of snow were angels. She walked slowly because she was tired and because she knew that when she got home there would be more of those people there and she would have to be nice to them. She wasn't exactly sure what her father did for a living. He didn't play any musical instruments himself, but he knew a lot of people who did. They all seemed to like him a lot. He was always bringing them over to the house and playing loud music and giving them lots to eat and drink and being nice to them.

Tonight she could hear the music all the way down the street. The house was covered with snow and almost all the lights were on. There were three big cars in the driveway that she didn't recognize. When she opened the front door the voices and laughter met her the way a dog or a cat might, if her mother hadn't been allergic and she was allowed to have a dog or a cat. The porch was full of strange boots and the closet was full of strange coats and the air was full of smoke and voices and loud music.

She pulled off her things and put them away and went as fast as she could down the hall, past the door of the living room where all the noise was coming from, and into the kitchen, where it was quieter and where she would find Mrs. Gladstone. But Mrs. Gladstone wasn't there. Then she heard a sound like something falling over or being moved. It came from the library.

She went back out to the main hallway. It was a large house with high ceilings and dark panelled walls. Her parents always kept lots of lights burning. Down the narrow hall she could see the door to the library was open, and thinking that maybe Mrs. Gladstone was in there, she went to check. But it wasn't Mrs. Gladstone at all. It was her father and a young woman. The young woman had long black hair and she was wearing a black evening dress. She held her bare arms behind her with her hands linked together. They were standing very close together at the other end of the room by the shelves and as Annie's father pointed something out to her he said, "It's signed by Yehudi Menuhin."

"I see," the woman answered in a voice full of amazement that had no hard edges at all.

Annie's father moved closer to her and touched her hair. His hand crept down her back.

"You know, you're very beautiful tonight."

Annie didn't hear the woman say anything, but she could see her cheeks dimple as she smiled.

"Daddy?"

The two adults jumped away from each other as if from a sudden jolt of electricity. The woman saw her immediately, but Annie's father adjusted his glasses and looked around frantically for a moment as if unsure where the voice had come from. Finally he spotted her.

"Annie, how many times do I have to tell you not to go sneaking around the house like that? You could give someone a heart attack."

"I'm sorry, Daddy," she said and looked down at her feet in their dirty socks.

"Well, now, don't sulk." He took up a glass from the desk and drank from it. "I suppose I shouldn't have snapped at you." He held up his hand and beckoned her over. "Come and meet our guest."

Annie entered the room slowly. She didn't like the library because it was full of things she wasn't allowed to touch. Three of the walls were covered with shelves packed with books that went from floor to ceiling. In the corner, where her father stood with his friend, a mahogany display case with a glass top held manuscripts that Annie had been told many times were very valuable. The wall behind the desk was a single huge window that provided a view of the sloping backyard. Looking past her reflection in the window, Annie saw it was still snowing, and now she could well imagine that the flakes of snow were indeed angels.

"Annie, this is Lorelei Severn. She's going to be a famous violinist someday."

Lorelei glanced at him with a mischievous glimmer in her eye as if they shared some secret built upon this very point. "Hello, Annie," she said.

Annie accepted the young woman's hand and shook it. Lorelei had a narrow face that was shaped like a heart, beautiful thick eyebrows like smudged charcoal, and her large eyes were very blue. At her throat hung a small gold pendant that looked like a droplet of water.

"I'm pleased to meet you," Annie recited dutifully. "I play the violin too."

"Yes, I know. Your father told me."

"That's my Annie," he said with a warm fondness in his voice. He drank off the last of the amber liquid in his glass. "The next Hilary Hahn."

"I'm studying Bach with Mr. Stedman," Annie said, unsure what to make of her father's comment and so ignoring it altogether. "We're doing the Partita in E major."

"That's a very advanced piece," Lorelei said, her eyes widening. She turned to Annie's father. "Robert, aren't the Bach partitas too advanced for her?"

"Nonsense," her father said.

"How old are you, Annie?"

"I'm nine."

"You know, Annie, I didn't tackle the partitas until I was twelve. You must be very good."

Annie smiled and folded her hands together in front of her. She couldn't think of anything to say.

"Why don't you run along now," her father told her after a brief but uncomfortable silence. He bent down and as he kissed her on the cheek Annie smelled the familiar musk-scented staleness of his breath. "Your mother and I are going out tonight with Lorelei and her friends. We won't be home until late."

"Where's Mrs. Gladstone?"

"She's out shopping, but she'll be back soon."

"Bye, Annie," Lorelei said. She held up her hand and wiggled her fingers.

"Bye."

Annie left them. But instead of turning down the hall to go upstairs to her room she went back to the kitchen where she dragged a chair over to the cupboard. She climbed up on it, stretched her arm out as far as it would go, and took the jar of peanut butter off the top shelf. She opened the jar and dipped her finger into the peanut butter, retrieving a glob two inches long, which, with a quick glance over her shoulder, she immediately deposited in her mouth. Then she put everything away and carefully replaced the chair where she'd found it. As she was leaving the kitchen, sucking on her finger and savouring the soft density of peanut butter on her tongue, her father and Lorelei emerged from the hallway leading to the library. He had his arm around her and she'd rested her head on his shoulder. Annie stayed where she was, and they didn't see her.

"But it's much too difficult for someone her age," Lorelei was saying. "She'll get discouraged and then she won't want to play anymore."

"That," Annie's father said, "is precisely the point."

Lorelei raised her head and looked at him. "Why? What do you mean?"

"I'm afraid you've caught me out," he said. "It's a terrible thing to admit, but the girl has no talent."

"But how can you—?"

He touched his finger to her lips.

"Lori, you haven't heard her play. I have. And I can tell you there's no hope. Absolutely no hope for her in music."

"But why make her take lessons?"

"She wants to! Her mother wants her to. And God knows I'm not about to interfere with the wishes of her mother."

"But if there's no hope...."

Annie held the dissolving blob of peanut butter still in her mouth.

"I know. I know. But it keeps her occupied. Her teacher's an old family friend, a hopeless drunk, but he knows what he's doing and, believe me, he's being paid handsomely for the privilege of doing it."

Annie watched as they embraced.

"I hope you don't think less of me for having a dull child."

"Never," Lorelei said.

They kissed, and after a languid moment or two spent gazing into each other's eyes, they parted, their hands remaining linked until the last possible second. Annie's father returned to the library and Lorelei walked very slowly all the way up the hall. She pushed open the elaborate French doors of the living room and went inside. A moment later Annie's father followed, holding his empty glass in one hand and straightening his tie with the other.

Annie checked to make sure there was nobody around and then, to launch herself, darted up the hall, skimming the rest of the way on her socks along the gleaming hardwood floor, past the door of the living room. The voices were louder now, but someone had turned the music down. She grabbed her violin case and her backpack and hurtled up the stairs. Her bedroom was at the end of the corridor, across from her mother's room. Her father had a much larger room than either of them in the other wing of the house.

She turned on the light and then went and stared at herself in the mirror, holding the muscles of her face absolutely still. She tried not to think about the things she'd heard her father say, and after a few minutes she'd almost succeeded in putting it out of her mind. She smiled, and then frowned, and then stuck her tongue out at herself. Sometimes she imagined what it would be like to live in a smaller house with a normal family, like the ones she saw on TV, with brothers and sisters and a dog or a cat. Her friend Naomi King, who lived on Fortescue Street, had three older sisters who talked very loud all the time and wore lots of makeup and cooked their own meals. All three had part-time jobs and boyfriends, and whenever Annie went over to visit, one or the other of them was just coming home or just rushing out the door. Mr. King sold refrigerators and once she and Naomi got into trouble for taking the bus out to the mall to visit him. Naomi was always talking about going to church and playing field hockey and eating at McDonald's, things that Annie wasn't allowed to do. Annie's mother wanted to send Annie away, to a private school in New Hampshire, to "get her out of that atrocious environment," but when her parents told her they were going to do this Annie stopped eating, and after a day or two they took her to a doctor who told them to let her stay at Springhaven Elementary with her friends.

Annie heard a sound like the clinking of glass coming from her mother's room. This was unexpected because she'd assumed her mother was downstairs with the others. She got off the bed and went out to investigate. The paired doors to her mother's room were set off from the corridor in a small arched alcove a few feet further along from Annie's room. Her mother hadn't always occupied this room. Back when Annie was small her parents both used the big room in the other wing as their bedroom. It had a whole bathroom in it with a pair of matching sinks and tiles made of Italian marble and a whirlpool bathtub. But a year or so ago her parents had a big fight and her mother moved in across the hall. She hired some carpenters to come and knock down the wall between this room and the one next door, making an even bigger room. Then she added a bathroom, with a pair of matching sinks and tiles made of Italian marble and a whirlpool bathtub, just like the one in her father's room. Her mother laughed when the carpenters finally left, but to Annie it seemed silly to go to all that trouble to build something that was already built.

The door to her mother's room was ajar and the lights were on but turned down low. By prodding it open a little bit further with her big toe, Annie could just fit her nose into the slender chink between the two doors. As she tried to see what her mother was doing, she searched her mouth with her tongue, lapping up the last bits of peanut butter trapped between her teeth and stuck to the very top of her throat. Her mother was seated at the dressing table with her back to the door and all she had on was a slip and a pair of high heel shoes. She was drinking out of a glass, but it didn't look to Annie like she was getting dressed or doing much of anything. All her effort and concentration seemed focused on the glass in her hand. She lifted it and took a drink and put it back on the table, but she didn't take her hand away, and after a few seconds she lifted it again and took another drink. Other than that, she didn't move. For a moment Annie thought of Mr. Stedman and it seemed to her that her mother would never make a very good musician. She was a heavy woman who hardly ever smiled and even when she did smile it always seemed to be for a reason that didn't have anything to do with being happy.

When she heard the living room doors open and voices and laughter spill into the hallway, Annie ran back to her own room and jumped up on the bed. She sat still and wiggled her toes. Sure enough, her father was coming upstairs. She heard his heavy steps in the hall and the tap of his knuckle on her mother's bedroom door.

"Mary? Are you ready?"

He let himself in.

The exchange of voices that ensued, though brief and muted, was passionate, and in only a few seconds her father retreated from the bedroom, pulling the doors shut behind him with a bang. Annie heard him pause and draw in a long raspy breath. Then he knocked on her door, which she hadn't closed all the way.

"Annie?" He leaned through the doorway just far enough for her to see his head and one shoulder. His face was pink, like he'd been holding his breath. "I'm going out now. Your mother isn't feeling well, so she's here if you need anything. But it would be best if you try not to bother her. Mrs. Gladstone will be back in a few minutes."

"Yes, Daddy."

"Goodnight, sweetheart. I'll see you in the morning."

"Goodnight, Daddy."

Annie listened to the chatter and commotion of the people leaving the house. When the front door finally closed for the last time she hopped off the bed and went to the window. It was dark now, but with all the lights on in the room behind her she couldn't see outside very well. It was still snowing and people were getting into cars and slamming doors, but there were so many of them she couldn't tell which was Lorelei or which was her father. Then one by one the cars pulled out of the driveway and drove off, and even though she tried very hard to think of them as angels, the flakes of snow falling through the beams of the headlights looked like nothing more than flakes of snow falling through the beams of headlights.

Annie didn't see her parents together in the same room at the same time for a whole week. When she came downstairs in the morning for breakfast either her mother was there or her father was there, but never both of them. In the evening when she got home from school, her mother stayed in her room and her father stayed in his room and she ate her supper in the kitchen with Mrs. Gladstone. Most nights both of her parents went out, but they left at different times and Annie guessed they went to different places. That Saturday in the afternoon her mother took her to a movie, and on Sunday she went to a recital with her father and Lorelei met them at the auditorium. Even though her parents were acting as if nothing were the matter, it seemed to Annie like she was suddenly living in two different but identical houses, one that belonged to her mother and one that belonged to her father.

The following Wednesday was sunny when Annie walked down the front steps of the school and climbed into the taxi that was to take her to Mr. Stedman's. All week she had been working diligently on the Bach partita, particularly the movement that was giving her trouble. The truth was that she liked the violin; the sound it made when she drew the bow across the strings appealed to her in the same way that the aroma of a shiny apple or the sudden warmth of the sun on her skin appealed to her, as something she didn't necessarily crave but the loss of which would most definitely leave a void in her heart. Each evening after completing her school assignments, Annie carried her violin downstairs to a small room adjacent to the dining room, where her mother had installed the grand piano that nobody ever played. Her mother had played the piano at one time in her life, but this was before Annie was born, and so instead of music all she heard were stories of concerts performed to packed halls and standing ovations that lasted for fifteen minutes. But her mother had given it up when she married her father. And so the piano stayed silent, and most nights it was her only audience when she practiced her violin. She put her music on the stand and stood very straight and smiled and drew the bow over the strings as she'd been taught, in a motion that was deliberate but not aggressive. She had been taken once to see a virtuoso violinist perform, a young woman who gestured wildly and spun herself around so that her skirt flared and her hair stood straight up in the air and drops of sweat flew off the end of her nose. But Annie didn't like to move her body when she played, and Mr. Stedman had told her that anyone who engaged in such antics was probably a fraud—not a real musician. The best musicians expressed themselves through the music, not with their bodies.

So Annie practiced because she liked the sounds that came from her instrument and because she looked upon this as another way she could make Mr. Stedman happy. On Wednesday and Thursday she had practiced all alone. On Friday Mrs. Gladstone had joined her, sitting on a chair in the corner and nodding her head in time to the music while she sipped a cup of tea. Annie practiced for only a few minutes on Saturday, after she got home from the movie, and she didn't even take the violin out of its case on Sunday. But on Monday she resumed her routine, and to her surprise her mother came into the room and sat with her as she played. This made her nervous, but she managed to get all the way through the first minuet without a mistake, and at the end her mother clapped lightly and said, "Bravo." Then her mother kissed the top of her head and went back upstairs to her room.

Sitting in the taxi, Annie held her hands up and looked at them. The violin was a big instrument and her hands were very small, and she wondered how her hands were ever going to make the violin do the things she wanted it to. She worried about her hands, even though she knew it was silly. Mr. Stedman had once told her that she'd grow into her talent, that small or large, her talent, when she

found it, would fit her like a glove. She liked the image of herself as
a grown-up woman, wearing her talent like a pair of white gloves,
and whenever she thought of this she didn't worry so much about
her hands. But today, in the back seat of the taxi, her hands looked
pale and soft and very small.

When she got to Mr. Stedman's, he came out and paid the driver
and they went inside together.

"How are you today, Annie?" he asked as he helped her take off
her coat. "How has this week been treating you?"

"I'm very good, thank you," she replied.

"You are ready to show me what you can do?"

She nodded.

As always, he allowed her to precede him down the hall, past
the gallery of photographs of his dead relatives, and to open the
case and remove the violin and bow. Two years ago, once she'd mas-
tered the proper sequence and technique and learned to approach
her opportunity to make music with reverence, he refused to give
her any further help with these preparations, even making her tune
her instrument and stroke the bow with the little amber-coloured
block of rosin on her own. These acts, he claimed, were essential
for the musician to perform in order to become intimate with the
instrument.

Every week now, like a ritual, she went through these steps while
he looked on and regarded her very seriously.

She had just placed her sheet of music on the stand and smiled
her stage smile and was ready to begin playing when there was a
knock on the door.

"Acch, who is that now?" Mr. Stedman left her and went down
the hallway. The knocking continued. "I'm coming," he muttered,
"I'm coming...."

Annie stayed where she was, not shifting a single muscle or relaxing her posture. She heard him open the door.

"What do you want? We are just beginning the lesson."

It was a man's voice that replied, but Annie could not make out
the words. The voice was rich and deep and it sounded to her like
her father's, but she couldn't be sure. Normally she would be grateful
for such an interruption, but not today, because today she was ready

to play the whole partita, and the longer she stood waiting and the more she thought about it, the more likely it seemed to her that her performance would somehow fall short of either her expectations or Mr. Stedman's.

"You cannot speak to her now. We are busy."

There was a pause while the other man said something.

"Then...then I will do it for nothing."

Annie heard the thump and clatter of a brief scuffle. Then steps.

"She's my daughter, goddammit, and I'll talk to her if I want to!"

"Do what you want then. Don't listen to me."

Her father burst into the room, his long black coat swirling behind him like a cape. His coarse grey hair was standing up as if in a wind and his cheeks glowed with the same pinkish blush that Annie sometimes noticed during parties or late at night. He knelt before her and gripped her shoulders with his big hands so that she had to lower the violin and release her body from the stiff pose in which she'd been holding it.

"My Annie," he said. He seemed to be crying, but there were no tears. "My girl."

"Daddy, what are you doing here?"

Mr. Stedman appeared in the doorway. "Don't upset her...."

"Please go away," her father pleaded in a fractured voice, directing his remarks over his shoulder. "Let me talk to her alone."

Mr. Stedman shrugged and walked away.

Her father turned back to her. He sniffed and straightened his glasses.

"Annie, I have some news."

He was smiling, so she smiled too. But she didn't say anything.

"I won't be living at home anymore. Your mother and I have agreed to a separation."

"Are you getting a divorce?" Lots of her friends at school had parents who were divorced.

"Well, we might." Her question seemed to have unnerved him. "We might get divorced. Or maybe things will work themselves out and we'll get back together."

"Are you going to live with Lorelei?"

He hesitated before lowering his eyes and nodding.

"Yes, I'll be staying at her place. But only for a little while. Until I find a place of my own."

"Are you in love with her?"

He smiled sadly and stroked her hair, but he didn't say anything. He was silent for so long it was almost as if his attention had wandered elsewhere.

"I don't know, Annie," he answered finally. "I don't know."

"She's nice," Annie said. "I like her." Then she asked, "Can I come and visit?"

"Of course you can," he said. "But only if your mother says it's okay." Then he drew her close and hugged her tightly until the warmth of his body flooded into her, but Annie couldn't hug him back because she was holding the violin in one hand and the bow in the other.

When he released her Annie felt dizzy yet very calm, and when the spell passed she found she was crying. But she wasn't sure why. Her tears seemed to leap from her eyes of their own accord, arriving suddenly and without any warning.

He wiped the tears from her face.

"When will I see you again?" she asked.

"Soon. I'll come and pick you up and we'll go for a drive. Would you like that?"

She nodded.

"Now," he said, "I have to go. But I know you're going to be a brave girl." He reached into his pocket. "And the best brave girls don't tell Mommy that Daddy interrupted her violin lesson."

He retrieved some money and showed it to her.

"Do they?"

"No," Annie said.

"Now, where will I put this?" He quickly scanned the room. "I know." With a dramatic flourish he made a show of carefully folding the bill and inserting it down the inside of her winter boot.

When he was done he winked and kissed her cheek. "That's for later. Okay?"

He stood and smiled at her and then turned to leave. Annie followed the sound of his steps all the way down the hall. Then she heard the front door open and close.

It was a few minutes before Mr. Stedman returned to the lesson room, and at first he didn't even come all the way in. He shuffled his feet in the doorway and moved back and forth, glancing at her and stroking his beard and running his hand over his head.

"Your father is a selfish man," he stated finally. "Very selfish. I tried to explain to him, Annie. I said we were busy. But he wouldn't listen."

Annie wasn't sure what to say. She didn't know if he was angry with her or not.

"He wants to stop our lessons. I told him I would teach you for nothing."

He pulled the wooden chair over and sat down. He seemed for a moment to regard her sternly, but then his gaze drifted and his expression became wistful.

"I had a selfish father too, Annie," he said, and paused as if lost in thought. He seemed undecided about something, but then he clasped his hands together and fixed her with a scowl. "I was born in Poland and we lived in Warsaw and my father, he was a big shot. He said, 'The Germans will never touch me.' And he would puff out his chest trying to make himself bigger. When all the other families left, he said we would stay. The Germans were nothing to him. We had men working for us, hundreds of men. They drove our trucks all over the country. We lived in a big house and all of us took music lessons. Piano, cello, violin. Then the Germans said the Jews were the worst problem on earth. It didn't bother him. Not one bit. Then they said the Jews were not even people. The men stopped driving our trucks and one day my father came home, his face bloody, two teeth missing. But still, he refused to leave. They put us in the ghetto and we had one room for eight of us and two other families. My father, the big shot." He shook his head. "Then they made us march. For days we marched through the snow. My sister died on the way and we had to leave her where she fell. We came to a crossing and there was a train and people were thankful just to get on the train. They would go anywhere the train took them. My father told us all to get on. He thought he was still in charge. 'Get on!' he said. 'You're a fool if you don't get on.' But I wouldn't get on. I fell down in the snow and pretended I was dead. A soldier kicked me with his boot, but I didn't make a sound. The train left and I ran and hid in a barn. I never saw my family again. For two years I lived like a criminal, stealing anything that I could use or eat. I stole a violin and after that I survived by playing music for food. When the war was over I was put in a camp and then they sent me here. One day an envelope came in the mail and in it was that photograph of my mother and father."

He stopped talking and as his eyes regained their clarity he looked at Annie as if awakening to her presence for the first time.

"I'm sorry, I don't know why I say these things. It's of no importance."

He took the violin and bow out of her hands.

"We will not have a lesson today, Annie. Your father made you cry and I'm afraid I'm not in a very good mood."

"I'm sorry," she said.

"No, Annie, it's not you who should be sorry. I should be sorry. Your father should be sorry. But you have no reason to be sorry."

He replaced the violin in its case for her and together they went down the hallway to the porch where he helped her with her coat. As she descended the front steps he said, "Goodbye, Annie."

She turned and briefly regarded his stooped figure in the doorway. She knew that she would not be coming back and when she thought of this the sadness tugged at her throat. "Goodbye, Mr. Stedman," she said.

She set out toward home and as she walked along she summoned her powers of make-believe, trying to see the snowflakes as angels again. Snow swirled down through the air, but today was much colder than the week before and the flakes were smaller and the wind took them and blew them away before she could get a good look at them. In a minute her cheeks were numb, and she stretched her mouth wide open to see if she could still feel her lips. She thought of Mr. Stedman walking through the snow with his family and it seemed to her that she would get on the train if her father was telling her to get on. But then it occurred to her that her parents were separated and that she might not be with her father when the train came. She tried not to think about this and instead lifted her head to see where she was. But just as her moist eyes brought the street into focus a strong gust of wind jerked the violin case upward and threatened to tear it out of her hand. She leaned forward and resisted the pull of the wind, keeping the violin firmly within her grasp. It had turned bitterly cold, colder than she'd ever imagined it could be, but with both arms wrapped around the violin she marched forward, through the frozen air that whipped at her, past row upon row of barren trees, past tall white houses and lawns encrusted by ice.

# ACKNOWLEDGEMENTS

The stories in this volume were written between fifteen and twenty-five years ago. When I set out to write the earliest of them, journal publication seemed like an impossibly lofty goal. But eventually I had the privilege of seeing my work in print, and that experience provided much needed encouragement and confirmed that what I was doing was worth the effort. I owe a deep debt of gratitude to the editors of the journals where some of these stories first saw the light of day.

Over months and, in some cases, years of revision and re-writing, Richard Cumyn, Karen Smythe, and Brian Bartlett provided valuable advice and suggestions, as well as friendship and moral support.

Thank you to Stephanie Sinclair of Transatlantic Agency for finding a home for a manuscript that spent too long out in the cold.

Kate Kennedy made numerous insightful recommendations and observations that helped to shape these fictions into their present form. I am fortunate and grateful that she was available to bring her talents to this project.

Thank you as well to Whitney Moran and the entire team at Nimbus/Vagrant for their enthusiastic commitment to Atlantic Canadian books and writers.

The writing of these stories was generously supported by the Canada Council for the Arts.

My wife, Collette, has been there since the beginning. Without her love and sustaining presence in my life, there is every chance this book would not exist.

Tina Usmiani

Ian Colford's short fiction has appeared in *Event*, *Grain*, *Riddle Fence*, *The Antigonish Review* and other literary publications. His previous books are *Evidence, The Crimes of Hector Tomás,* and *Perfect World*. His work has been shortlisted for the Thomas H. Raddall Atlantic Fiction Award, the Relit Awards, the Journey Prize and the Danuta Gleed Literary Award. He lives in Halifax.